PATIENCE

PATIENCE

Toby Litt

GALLEY BEGGAR PRESS

First published in 2019
by Galley Beggar Press Limited
37 Dover Street
Norwich NR2 3LG

Text design and typesetting by Tetragon, London
Printed and bound by CPI Group (UK) Ltd, Croydon, CRO 4YY

This novel was completed during a Hawthornden
Fellowship – as the author very gratefully acknowledges

A CIP record for this book is available from the British Library

ISBN paperback 9781910296998
ISBN limited edition 9781913111007

1979

Please be patient with me

I looked at the white wall and I looked at the white wall and I looked at the white wall and then I looked some more at the white wall and then instead I looked as things developed quite quite beyond my control at the white of the wall and then at the whiteness of the white of the wall and then only at the whiteness as if it could exist independently of the wall and I continued to look at the whiteness of the whiteness until I began to look into the whiteness and then through the whiteness to see if there was whiteness behind or beneath the whiteness and in this way I continued for anyone looking at me from outside to seem to continue to look at the white wall for quite a while longer than I'd already looked at the wall that I had discovered a long while ago was white beyond whiteness and that was the very same wall I had looked at and looked at and looked into and through many many long long times over the long years years that I couldn't help but look back on as seven white years years almost entirely white although sometimes too they were green.

Because you see depending on how I had been how I Elliott had behaved the previous day sometimes I was parked facing not the white wall but in a position where I was able to look down and out through the window that looked down on the courtyard this depending on whether or not I had been good good meaning calm and more specifically good meaning quiet and dry because the wall calmed me whereas the courtyard and its visions of great human and avian activity sometimes excited me beyond what the Sisters termed reasonable.

The bulk of the wall from white-tiled but dust-greyed ceiling downwards was the granular white of whitewash applied with a roller efficiently if not hastily by a workman named Ted. Within this however as in front of me thin parallel vertical lines appeared that showed the paint had not been applied directly onto the plaster of the wall but that the wall had firstly been prepared and only then had whitewash been applied and then reapplied on what I knew to be an annual basis November in fact as if an attempt were deliberately being made to brighten the ward up during its dullest pre-Christmas-decorations month.

I know for certain that this was not the case and the timing of the redecorating was entirely down to the availability or non-availability of the workmen who had many other demands upon their labour and time.

Ted who had rollered this particular wall the previous two years had a wife called Sheila and a daughter called Diane and a Ford Escort that really hated frosty mornings Ted said and Sheila liked to drink didn't she just and what's more she liked to drink bloody Babycham which didn't come bloody cheap.

Working alongside Ted painting the same wall for the first of these previous two years had been Lee who was seventeen but had a girlfriend and a motorbike and could roll cigarettes in a small rolling machine with one hand whilst painting with the other the absolute hero.

The year after that Ted had done the wall by himself and had whistled instead of talking because Lee was not there to talk to and Ted did not think of talking to me even though I was there and listening and remembering and making the sound that came as close to laughter as my laughter ever comes.

I haven't yet been able to identify any of the tunes that Ted whistled and it's a fair possibility that Ted was the original composer and arranger of all of them. They sounded more like the tunes Sister Mary Margaret played on the radio in the office on Radio 2 rather than those Sister Cécile played there on Radio 3 or Mrs Beatles the Cleaner played on her portable radio-cassette-player of her red and blue and golden-edged Beatles cassettes which she played every day and only deviated from to listen to the charts on wonderful Radio 1.

Whilst he was whistling the year he was on his own Ted had made quite a good job of covering the wall with evenly distributed white paint however several drops had spilled onto the skirting board over toward the area beneath the window overlooking the courtyard because Ted had been lifting the roller off the paint tray and up toward the wall not having dabbed it at either end as he usually did and a trail of drops had fallen sideways and down onto the lower part of the wall the slightly yellowed skirting and the light blue of the lino flooring.

At the moment this happened Ted had been distracted and caused to flinch by some wild distant screaming distracted and as Ted later said to Sister Britta a bit bloody discombobulated although he should by then have known it was only beautiful Lise being Lise being beautifully bathed by Sisters Cécile and Eliza and Lise being Lise always screamed in the bath because she enjoyed screaming because it was a relief and a break from crying which she often did a short distance behind me along the long corridor and an even shorter distance in front of her brother Kurt who made regular thumping noises.

The drops of paint that landed on the wall and skirting landed as ovoid shapes on a diagonal axis whereas those that hit the flooring were generally round and haloed by a stippling of smaller droplets.

I tried to alert Ted to the wet paint not where it should really be but he did not understand my sounds nor register my distress although I am sure that he would have been a little bit upset to see the paint had spilt as it had never spilt before.

When he became concerned and came over to see if I was all right I shut up because I didn't want to be wheeled away by one of the Sisters. I was too interested in watching the year-old white paint being covered over in vertical fuzzy-edged strips by the new bright white paint.

Last year's white had significant stains on it too many for me to detail here although a little later I will detail some of the stains that covered the area of wall I was left looking at the afternoon that Jim arrived.

Over the course of a year the paint on the wall had gone slightly grey and a little yellow and a smidgeon one of my favourite hoarded from hearing words just a smidgeon olive green. It had also become slightly less matte in texture especially at the height where childish shoulders touched. All of this was covered over by the neutral new start of the fresh coat of this November's whitewash and as on the afternoon I'm thinking about fondly it was three months and ten days on from that date of dripping misapplication the white wall was now in a quarter-way state with quarter the number of stains and quarter the greying and yellowing and greening that would have occurred to it come the coming November in the normal course of childish events and if the workmen were free as they usually were.

The most extravagant stain was a pink horizontal smear about four feet off the floor that had originally been blood from Micky's poor forehead which Sister Eliza with her trembling hands had wiped up afterwards but had not done a very thorough job of it and the stain traced the movement of her right hand left to right.

On that day however I had been parked looking out of the window into the courtyard and had only peripherally been able to see Micky run smack or rather a sound halfway between crack and clock into the wall and then see Sister Eliza tremblingly clean up with bucket and heavy grey cloth half an hour later muttering. Sister Eliza was the oldest and most bent-backed of the Sisters older even than Sister Muriel who was the most pink-faced. From seeing the results of her cleaning that wasn't completely cleaning the following morning when I was wall not window facing and from knowing her to be right-handed and impatient I was able to imagine the gesture Sister Eliza had made with the sodden grey cloth rapid left to right like a mostly flattened-out rainbow.

I have more than once seen a real rainbow.

The resulting smear that became a stain was only visible on a careful second or third glance but I was of course lucky enough to have more than plenty of those. The red as pink was thicker along or across the top of the arc of the rainbowing but still perceptible I would say three and a half inches below that.

I had sometimes sat gazing at the stain imagining the gesture repeated and coming eventually to see a mirror-image Sister Eliza trembling within the wall and moving her mirror-image grey cloth left to right again and again as if she were grimly but enthusiastically waving at me where I sat gazing.

In this way I liked to see or make up the history of each of the stains and marks that made the white wall so interesting to look at witnessing their formation back to front from inside the wall for example the deliberate dash of bloody Micky right towards me and shrieking about flying and hitting his forehead at a height of four feet off the floor slightly less than his total height and spilling blood forward from the already bleeding contusion.

After this Micky was fitted for a while with a crash helmet in blue with a white go-faster stripe down the middle front to back that subsequently took chips out of the white wall in my visual field right in the middle and to the bottom left close to the frame of the wooden gate where he even left behind a track of blue helmet blue.

My visual field changed you see according to which shoulder my heavy head was resting upon although this was something I did not myself get to choose.

When I was agitated into a startle by a non-routine scream or noise I was sometimes known to flip my head across directly from one shoulder to the other as if two people were playing catch with it two tiny strong men one on each end of my collarbone but this was something of which I was not usually capable in fact of which I am still usually incapable despite the unlocking of my muscles by Dr Masters and his wonder drug Lioresal because my tiny strong men aren't usually quite strong enough.

My two views of the world and of my visual field are left shoulder and right shoulder and I am happiest if I can spend an exactly equal time in both dispositions so as to keep a balanced view of reality and to improve if possible my spine or at least not to damage it further than it need be damaged.

But it was hard when in front of the window looking onto the courtyard not to wish to incline towards the side that gave me the greatest most amazing view.

I will come to this later there is too much to think and remember about it when I'm also trying to think about what I thought about the wall and specifically what I was thinking on that one particular afternoon.

I remember that my head that day was in its left inclination meaning that the horizon seemed to be tilted up on the left side but although I did spasm between exclusively lopsided visual fields I was still aware that there was a fixed horizon that was of course horizontal and that I seemed always to see as level even though my eyes were never except when halfway through a startle exactly level.

And I was not doing my special effects because the gradual and fast changes in how light and time were seen that day were enough to keep me going.

I have about one hundred and seventeen special effects but my top three favourites which I always like to think of are in at number three the jumpy blink and shift of left eye right eye left right left right to the tune of 'Everyone's a fruit and nutcase' and number two the octopuses of light from watery eyes and still holding strong at number one going cross-eyed completely which you absolutely could not get caught doing by the Sisters because they would quite likely jump to the panicked conclusion that you were hyperglycaemic or even going into full cardiac arrest.

I had seen two children poor Nancy and poor Valerie go into cardiac arrest and they did look a lot like I imagined I looked when I crossed my eyes and sucked in my cheeks.

Nancy died because she managed to swallow one of the orange buttons off the orange coat she had been given for her birthday. Nancy had about as much motor capacity and neck strength as I did. She was right in front of me and I saw and knew what she was up to but try as I might my sounds even my ultimate wailing sound were incapable of gaining the attention of any of the Sisters so you might say it was my fault because of my quietness that Nancy died and you might be right because perhaps I could have capsized my chair with a big enough tense and that would have made a big enough noise to bring someone running capable of CPR but who knows.

I think about it often.

Valerie just died just as some children just do.

She was eight and a half years old Nancy was eleven and two days.

I still missed them and their sounds as I missed the sounds of the departed but not dead Graham-Ng-Ng Chris-Sss-Sss Bentley-Glug-Glug and Kevin-YAAAH-!YAAAH! Sandie-Wee-Diddle-Diddle Helena-Mumble-Mumble Jilly-Eeee-Eeee and also Eeee-Eeee Thomasina and both Sallys the one with the grey hair and the one with the port wine stain on the left side of her face shaped liked a small hand. I still miss them now.

Nancy had been parked next to me for about two years that is when Sister Cécile was the one who parked us and usually to my right which gave Nancy a better view through the window into the courtyard although I don't think she really appreciated it as I don't think she appreciated life in all its manifold glory even a tree with some birds in it a square of concrete and an octagonal shape of pink and yellow paving stones and children less handicapped than ourselves playing games.

I can't remember when I first decided not to go entirely spare as Sister Mary Margaret would say entirely spare with frustration and boredom it must have been some years after I had gone partly spare with frustration and boredom mustn't it because I had been alive for years before I came to any accommodation with the visual blankness with which I was so often confronted not least ceilings and corners or in front of which I was so often neglectfully abandoned but this suggests that a person can go mad and then go not-mad as the result of a rational conscious decision and I don't believe anyone believes this because the already mad by definition are incapable of making rational decisions and so if it happened like this it may have been my maddest decision ever I mean to return to sanity when that sanity was frustration and boredom and the constant possibility of going mad in a far less pleasant way that might involve biting Sisters in the bottom or on the hand like Jeremy does which is worse the hand because it involves important bones.

No I was never aggressive which isn't to say I never banged my head because everyone there banged their head at one time or another we couldn't go out into the countryside and cut down a tree with an axe we had no other way of going wild and I believe that if you can't go wild you end up going mad because all people need to go wild by which I don't mean attack something and possibly kill and eat it I mean lose control in a way that gets the inside out like screaming does.

After the change in tension and attention brought about by Jim's arrival I was still to spend a reasonable amount of time facing the wall or the window but never again was I able to devote myself so completely to their perception. You could say Jim broke my concentration a concentration that had been accumulating for about a decade but he also refocussed my concentration that same concentration upon him.

On that particular wonderful afternoon of arrival I remember after seeing the whiteness within the whiteness of the wall the whiteness overall began to operate as a glare and I could see retinal images left behind by the glare for when one sees an unbroken field of any sort mind-animals of some variety begin to cross to stampede across that field.

I saw giraffes lions wildebeest and all the other creatures from the framed poster in the long corridor of Wild Animals of the African Savanna I saw them as cut-out outlines moving as if held up by a puppeteer on invisible strings.

Although I did not see as many pictures within the white of the wall as I did within the dark of inner-eyelid-after-lights-out-black I still saw plenty of aggressive faces of creatures snarling mostly snarling but sometimes roaring biting screeching and rending with their sharp white teeth.

They shifted around within themselves these creatures not from minute to minute but from moment to moment a left eye looking rightwards becoming a right eye looking directly towards me or a high nostril becoming an eyebrow whilst a dim chin-shadow became a mouth with a dark gullet ringed by white and sharp teeth.

Sometimes they changed scale and what had been a laughing-sarcastically chimpanzee became a circle of elephants gathered benignly around a waterhole or the dark heads of wildebeest fording a foaming river against the paper white background of Africa became the characteristic spots along a cheetah's magnificent spine.

Although they not infrequently contained scenes of copulation African nature documentaries were apart from performances of ballet which Sister Muriel loved the one kind of television programme the Sisters permitted us to watch on the bulbous grey screen rarely wiped and so usually dusty of the television with woody-looking grille over the circular speaker in the corner the television of the Refectory.

I caught and hoarded a lot of words from David Attenborough's nature documentaries including Life on Earth just as I did from Humphrey Carpenter and others on the radio in the Sisters' Office and Mrs Beatles' long and winding cassettes and most of all from the Sisters' lunchtime readings of dapple-dawn-drawn Gerard Manley Hopkins and blissful Julian of Norwich and often-changing Cardinal Newman and other approved Catholic silencers of noisy-chewing ever-chatting children but also I caught fear from the wordless wildness of animals that really existed beyond and south of the ward.

For many years I had nightmares of being abandoned outside on the paper-white ground of Africa and being as a result taken for carrion by the vultures who seemed to feature at some point in every documentary as Nature's refuse collectors fighting with the earthbound scavengers hyaenas over the ribby remains of a carcase.

I could not convince myself upon waking that in the wild on the grassy plains of Africa I would not be taken for already injured and therefore practically dead meat and would instead be recognized as a living fearsome creature.

It would not be an exaggeration to say that above my metal-sided cot of chipped white gloss in the middle of England vultures had circled in the eyelid-dark for three or four years.

At times in amongst the wall-animals I saw images from my Christmas and birthday cards the black and white dog of Schulz who is called Snoopy throwing a snowball or Snoopy who my mother must have known I would adore typing up a birthday message on his typewriter sitting on top of his dog kennel that must be very large inside and perhaps contain several floors below ground to be large enough to contain all the sports gear Snoopy possesses let alone all the clothes and costumes and his vs the Red Baron biplane.

Snoopy-in-the-wall was occasionally oppressed by the wildness not to say the lack of civilization meaning sense of humour meaning sense of irony of the creatures from the poster and the permitted nature documentaries. This is not to say or imply that among the other children more mobile and less fortunate than me that I felt in any way like Snoopy among the animals. I was quite content and happy with all of them except knife-loving Charlie and would not have wished any of them to grow up or be taken away except knife-loving Charlie.

I was more fortunate more lucky than most of the other children because I knew how to entertain myself and because I had found a way to find myself entertaining not by doing anything or getting anything new to occupy my attention but just by being able to sit and see how much was going on that was hilarious and tragic and ironic and painful within an activity that most of the children would have seen as inactivity.

This had not been a choice and so it is nothing for which I can take credit or of which I can be proud and it is only in the years since Jim and what happened with Jim that I have found myself able to stop wishing for arms that could lift hands that could grip legs that could step and toes that could tip.

Because I am now so full of experience and potential experience and because that experience is itself so full even thinking of what I used to think about my lack of experience is enough to think about for a week.

I am never bored.

The Sisters call these Spiritual Exercises and I respect their terminology although I no longer believe in their Trinity although I respect what each of its three aspects is meant to stand for particularly the Holy Spirit or Ghost who reminds me in many ways of Snoopy's kennel.

I have no particular virtue or claim to virtue and anything I might think theologically would have been outthought long ago by the thinkers who the Sisters chose to do their thinking for them such as the miraculous and inexhaustible Saint Augustine from whom we often heard at lunchtime but that is the big difference because although you can choose to get great thinkers to do your thinking for you you cannot in any way get great believers to do your believing for you neither your major nor minor believing because that is a private matter between you and the deity however much you might pray to the Virgin Mary for faith and I am one who has frequently beseeched the Virgin Mary for just about everything for which the Virgin Mary can be beseeched healing health friendship faith.

At this pre-Jim time though during morning prayers and Mass and evening prayers in the Chapel since I no longer believed I was often more likely to be looking at and into and through the candle on the left and then at the retinal images of the candle on the left although it was always dangerous to give the Sisters the impression that your eyes were in any way closed and that you might be sleeping. I was either looking at the candle or if they were in view looking at Lise's knees.

Saint Augustine and Julian of Norwich and Saint Thomas Aquinas and Pope John Paul II and all the other great theologians who fit inside the Holy Spirit infinite dog kennel of Snoopy none of them can help me believe there is a greater sight than sight itself nor a greater insight than that there is no greater sight than sight Amen.

Sometimes I felt I had prayed more often and more passionately than any of the other children in the ward although that was vanity I know that now but I did feel it especially for that time in the past when I was eight years old and had only been on the ward for one Christmas card and two birthday cards and was very much not reconciled to staying here or to my place in the world which was a place stationary and largely ignored.

Around me almost by the minute I had the example of sincere and extreme piety I had expostulations followed by prayers and prayers that ended in ejaculations I had eye-witnesses to the glory and greatness of God and so was it any wonder that I placed my trust where it is most worthy that trust be placed? There are those who feel capable in all their virtuosic vanity and catastrophic conceit as our alliterative Priest might have said of calling into question the behaviours and moment by moment decision making capacity of an infinite being and what's more an infinite deity but I was not one of those and so what the infinite deity wished for and wished upon me I too wished to wish infinitely but I could not bring myself to do so even though I saw Christ carrying his own passionate asymmetry and saw him nailed conclusively to his wooden immobility and saw him suffer the indignity of his public prosthesis and saw him corpse-like cripple-like receiving assistance in undressing and washing and lying down to rest.

I knew that the crucifixion was an infinite spasm a spasm that outdistanced mine by aeons oh father forgive them they know not what know not what father father know not what.

In his painted wooden body upon the wall above the altar of the Chapel off the end of the long corridor I could not mistake the crucifixion for anything other than spasm but I knew Jesus knew His suffering was taking place in the witnessing and loving presence of His mother and within the loving concern of His absent but witnessing father.

It was hard to escape this faith as a resource for those in need when it made up so much of everything that surrounded me and supported me and all of us there but constant affirmation of faith in complete certainty oh lord surely creates the possibility of the suspicion of the opposite i.e. that this beautiful God of theirs they seemed to know so well and whose blesséd attributes they were able to describe so fully and with such melancholy authority might not exist.

I don't know how I came to know I just know I eventually came to know the Sisters weren't telling the truth not that they were lying because they were bless them all saying the very thing they believed was truest but it wasn't true so they were not telling the truth because deluded as they were they were incapable of telling the truth just as incapable of telling the truth as I was of speaking aloud the word truth which would come out from me more like krukrukk.

We the children their wards on the ward were so constantly reassured by them that God loved us that to me at least it became suspicious for wasn't it clear that the most that could be extrapolated or deduced from our spastic and mongoloid and mental and other conditions was not divine love but divine indifference or rather non-divine non-existence? This would leave us all on our own meaning each of us must discover for ourselves or find ourselves unable to avoid our own deepest krukrukk.

But I really really needed God who more so? I did not want even the possibility of no God in fact I feared His loss as cataclysm above me and abyss below and so at a certain point of growing uncertainty aged nine and three quarter years I decided to test God by putting my trust in Him completely entirely.

If He did exist He could cause my mother to visit me not my mother and father and brothers and sisters but only my mother.

I made it so I was asking for less for easier for just for my mother to visit or at least to send me a letter. And I gave God one calendar year in which to accomplish this less-than-a-miracle.

And He failed.

Even then I put effort into many prayers of wish to understand why or why not for it did not seem in the circumstances such an outrageous request for a boy to make of his mother and not such a difficult proof for a God to offer His devoted servant.

Answer and I would have been His for life.

Failure came instead and I fell into an abyss of black total point-lessness mere hopelessness would have been too much to ask for.

I could see no reason for having a reason for continuing and if I had been given a coat with orange buttons and had known what I could do with them by trying and failing to swallow them I would have choked joyfully or if not joyfully then with something approaching infinite relief for I believe I truly despaired in the full awful sense of the word and I have never felt more entirely abandoned and worthless with the worst part of my life-situation being that it was entirely selfish and unless there was some miraculous change I would never be capable of helping another person especially child but maybe Sister.

Of course there was the chance I could give an opportune smile that might make one of the Sisters feel her early morning washing of my various yucky crevices had not been wasted but I could not spontaneously act all I could ever do was reciprocate i.e. give back something I had been given in order to be given the opportunity to give it back which is what always happened at Christmas.

It was a terrible feeling not only to be helpless but beyond that to be incapable of offering help so all I would ever do was take take take as Sister Mary Margaret shouted to Sister Cécile in the Sisters' Office one day when I was thirteen and one month and not in relation to me at all but in relation to Sister Cécile who didn't deserve it but suffered Sister Mary Margaret's spiritual jealousy at her easy faith You all you ever do is take take take that's all you ever do you selfish woman you!

I felt this selfishness of mine as completely unbearable and I felt a great yearning to be of use partly I think because all day I watched the Sisters helping others but quite often badly or misunderstandingly due to lack of considered attention to the particular needs of others which needs I knew but could not communicate for example replacing blankets on knees not Lise's knees that hands had laboriously taken contorted minutes to push off because legs were uncomfortably warm or wiping spit from chins that were trying to impress other eyes in a bubble-blowing World Ward Championship that had just after a week reached its final round and was now undermined and ended completely for the rest of that day because thick spit of world-class level is only available at certain hours such as in the fuggy minutes before supper and a good fountain of it takes whiles and whiles to build up because I had been bronze medal World Ward Champion myself once.

I watched Sisters helping without consciously thinking what it was or what it meant to help someone for example they pulled curtains open or pulled them closed or forgot to pull them closed so I once saw through a doorway into a dorm what was above the knees of Lise as Sister Muriel and Sister Eliza chatted about the Monsignor and what he had learned in Rome or on another occasion I watched Sister Cécile and Sister Muriel wipe Jeremy's baboon bottom but with their minds entirely elsewhere and not as their smiles told me on Heaven or Hell.

But to my knowledge at that time of my test of God I had never assisted anyone in any way whatsoever no not so much as an It's over there or a Stop it you'll hurt yourself.

I very much felt the atrocious selfishness of my mode of existence and what I wanted was to be able to exist as the Sisters did for others and most of all I powerfully wanted to be able to give a gift but the Sisters denied me the possibility of this for when I was assisted in making something in the Craft Room usually out of pasta shapes it was ugly and for me rather than genuinely for anybody else.

I did not want to paint with brush in mouth an abstract and have Sister Cécile say What a wonderfully expressive painting of a splurge of a splodge I wanted to draw an accurate and wonderfully useful map of a diseased part of the body that would offer a cure or of a dangerous war-torn country that would help the lost.

Within the white wall I often pictured the gifts I would have given all of them and without being in any way proud of my generosity I knew yes I was sure I knew the particular gifts that would delight them the most and in this small way I would have made a positive contribution to the difficult lives of those all around me rather than being a constant trial to their already strained patience and a drain on their limited emotional and spiritual resources with my peevishness and neediness and in this way I would lift them rather than drag them down as I am sure I usually did and so be a balloon not a burden a bird not a hedgehog a hug not a hit.

For Sister Britta a week of vigorous hill-walking in the Alps or the Norwegian fjords to relax her and refresh her and return her to us happier and less full of divine vengeance. I knew she would want this as I had seen upside-down hikers on an upside-down mountain in one of the magazines on her desk when I was left in there one day.

For Sister Cécile a mother-of-pearl inlaid hairbrush for the wondrous long pale blonde hair that I knew she hid beneath her headdress.

For Sister Eliza a pair of supercomfortable orthopaedic shoes to relieve her poor bunioned feet.

For Sister Mary Margaret a box of Milk Tray chocolates and for Sister Muriel some fine hand cream for her cracked fingers.

For Micky a very large trampoline in a safe soft place so that he would come as close to flying as a person was able without dying.

To Lise in her flump of flowery brown dress fabric a bright friend who could find some way of addressing her inexplicable sorrow which seemed to be focussed on the fact she had no person not even her brother Kurt capable of understanding her.

And other presents for all the other children on the ward each one the result of probably a whole day's thinking and for only one of them Jeremy would the gift be immediate death because he really did nothing else but suffer the most unbearable physical torment as if he were being permanently burned alive for there is something wrong with his nerves as if they all ended in pricking needles of flame and it is only exhaustion that stops him screaming all the time bless him and protect him from his own body wherever he is now.

Gifts were often what I thought of when I became distracted from the subject of what was in front of me in the space that I could see oval space from left to right and narrower top to bottom I planned givings and festivals of imaginary generosity during which I turned aside people's gratitude by letting them know I was even more profoundly grateful than they because in these hallucinations I was quite capable of speaking clearly.

Mostly though when in front of it as on this afternoon I observed the gradual changes of the light upon the white wall and these I found completely marvellous and compelling even when in the summer they were extremely slow.

Of course my favourite was low winter sunlight coming in for half an hour sideways through the leaves and branches of the wych elm in the courtyard and so creating an effect that allowed me to think of my favourite learned and hoarded word dapple to describe the wall or if not dapple then stipple was definitely my favourite word the wall would be patterned at this hour like wallpaper showing leaves but these light-made shadow-left leaves of late winter had beautiful when it was a little windy had beautiful epileptic fits.

It would be easy-cliché to say they were dancing the leaves of shade but I never felt they were because their movements were too simply back and forth and dancers flow or should flow like Swan Lake swans on television and I strongly feel daffodils don't flow they rock like we all sometimes rock but these shadow-leaves moved at best like the gentle ebbing of a fit that at one point seemed likely to prove dangerous if not fatal but that no-one needs to take seriously any more as the teeth are no longer in danger of shattering with compression and the child is smiling inwardly with sweet relief sweet and almost religious and so taken for religious calm.

I had seen the toes twitching as the last spasms lovelily left the shaken body of the child on the blue lino unlike my body's spasm which was taking place so lentissimo as to last a long lifetime.

Seeing the wych elm as shadow indirectly was perhaps even better than seeing the wych elm itself.

Once three birthday cards before Jim arrived I even saw the shadows of the two familiar crows upon the white wall and I knew it was them because I could hear their caw-caw routine to my right almost within my peripheral vision but I knew their behaviours so well that I am sure I would have recognized their shadowplay even if I had been as deaf as Torin was before he died.

One crow was trying to land on the other crow's head. I could not tell them apart because I believe they were twins and they took turns in being the one to wait upon the long branch and the one to try and become the other's crowfeather hat.

A lot of time time I spent making an effort not to hate them they tended to dominate the wych elm like two knife-threatening Charlies and keep away other more modest less aggressive creatures even solo seagulls their the crows' black shapes were easy to pick out even when full foliage was in operation in July but I would have preferred it if the superlative thrushes and magnificent greenfinches had been able to mass less harassedly and hurriedly.

Perhaps though I should have been grateful because the crow twins forced all the other birds away from the wych elm which stood almost exactly central in the courtyard as if it had been there first and the building built around it because the central presence of the angry crows meant that once or twice a year a bird or two would land right in front of me and my lucky amazement on the grey window ledge of the window that looks down.

I can see all their feathers still these visions and the transitions between green and black and yellow all sheeny and as if painted verily by God taking especial care with the tiniest details that might give visual satisfaction to an attentive and loving viewer.

In that time I would try not to fantasize about being a bird and flying away from the ward but watch what was really in front of me until Lise wailed molto forte like a Wagnerian soprano or Micky ran past or Lise's brother Kurt banged his head against the side of the filing cabinet and the bird or birds were skedaddled away into the air.

These etched birds whose colours seemed deeper and sheenier than any other colours I had ever seen apart from the moss to the left of the window sill that was sometimes cleared away but regrew in a year or two that green was green enough to rival the wing-green of a greenfinch and had a golden undertone that could enter combat with goldfinch yellow and not lose straight away.

They didn't mean to be scary to birds my companions on the long corridor they just were.

This was what they were up to the children of the ward this meaning their usual things behaviours on the afternoon in question around four fifty six while I was patiently appreciating all that could still be made even after all my seven years of the white of a white wall even not taking into consideration the stains and stories and marks and memories.

Yes from behind me I could hear Lise playing one of the with-herself clapping games she sometimes played when she wasn't fully floored and grief-stricken and when also she wasn't absent because up to her occasional mischief which usually involved hiding from the Sisters by making herself silent and invisible then waiting to be missed and searched for and discovered and delightfully punished. Lise liked to be punished now and again because it gave her a chance to impress with her repentence at which there was no-one better not even Sister Margaret. Over the years I had been around her Lise in her fabric of flowery brown had hidden herself under beds and mattresses behind the spare wheelchairs in the Chapel and once most gloriously for three and a half hours beyond the wooden gate and in the Sisters' Office and beneath the desk where Sister Britta's thick legs usually crossed themselves.

Beyond the wooden gate. It was my life's ambition to go beyond the wooden gate and past the Sister's Office and then to take the lift down out of the ward down to the ground floor and then be pushed through reception through the double doors and out into the green world beyond and up into a dream of a wheelie and all of this without a Sister with me to force me to come back.

Perhaps Lise one day would decide to find a place to hide that wasn't in the ward. But at this time on this afternoon it was mourning-Lise not mischievous-Lise who pitter-pattered away lightly beside her brother Kurt who was banging his head into the Kurt's-head-shaped dent in the grey filing cabinet in the long corridor making the noises which meant ships were about to land on the shore of his land ships that he and he alone could see when staring through the small round hole in the side the left-hand side of the dented filing cabinet. The noises were regular coming one every half minute but still full of panic and confusion although the ships arrived in Kurt's land almost every afternoon at about this time.

I understood this repetition to mean that while the men who swarmed out of the ships and who I imagined as violent and armed with sharp weapons performed terrible acts upon the land and upon the people of the land that however every night when we had all been put to bed and Kurt was no longer able to watch their terrible violence they climbed back into their ships and sailed out to sea again.

At least I assumed what Kurt was seeing was the sea because the word he shouted when he sighted them was not Boats! but Ships! and ships I understood although I had never seen one were usually bigger than boats and more likely to be able to cross something wider than a pond which I had seen or a lake which I hadn't.

Ships! Kurt always shouted in between thumps during the late afternoon around a quarter past five and then Men! he would soon shout shout in a way that let everyone on the long corridor know they were men to be afraid of not friendly men and finally he would begin

33

to shout Land! Land! always that word twice never once that I heard even a single time although both Ships! and Men! could sometimes be repeated close enough together to seem a double outcry.

For a few months after he first arrived and after he discovered the filing cabinet I had been in some doubt as to whether Land! in Land! Land! was intended by Kurt as a verb or a noun and I had imagined with great concern that he was witnessing terrible shipwrecks within the confines of the grey filing cabinet and was trapped outside because he was too big and so unable to get in and help the little drowning people inside as helpless as real witnesses to a real shipwreck standing on high cliffs above violent waves and sharp rocks watching real people drowning.

This helplessness was my explanation for the bang-bang-banging of his head into the same dented place that Kurt rhythmically reverted to around a quarter past five in between cries of first Ships! and then Men! and finally Land! Land!

I had been able to solve this mystery one night when we were all in bed and there was a full moon and Kurt was unusually agitated because he usually slept silently enough for me not to hear him do anything but fart although he used not to be in my dorm but in the dorm next to mine Dorm 2. On this night the Sisters came to calm him and in between gasps and sobs Kurt who seemed to have woken from a violent nightmare of the men being violent shouted Land! Land! I was very awake at this point in white light from the moon through the blinds and I somehow knew from the fact Kurt was uttering it out of the hearing of his people that he couldn't possibly mean Get safely ashore! Get safely ashore! but that he must mean O my poor land! O my poor land! or possibly O my poor little people who live in my land in my filing cabinet! because land stood for people.

And from that time onwards which was about three Christmas cards before the afternoon of Jim's arrival the noises and shouts had remained much the same but the filing cabinet had shifted a couple of feet towards the Chapel been moved back into place and then shifted another foot and a half and the dent had become softer and rounder and a much better fit for Kurt's head which in any case never seemed bruised.

I felt I knew exactly what Kurt meant when he shouted Land! Land! although I could not honestly say whether the violent men were Vikings or what they were.

On that afternoon I was where the Sisters usually Sister Cécile wheeled me and put on the brake. I was close to the white wall just as I have been thinking and remembering in slowly typed words.

And Jim arrived.

The lift doors opened on our floor and Sister Britta led someone with strong even footsteps not the fzz of wheelchair wheels up to and then through the wooden gate after lifting the latch and then took them the footsteps along the long corridor to a dorm Dorm 3 and said 'This will be your bed'.

Then she Sister Britta took the footsteps further to show them the Craft Room the Music Room the Refectory and the Boys' Bathroom.

As was the custom the first night the footsteps had supper on a tray in their dorm on their own and I would not learn to whom they belonged until breakfast the next morning.

I do not know what it was made me so excited that night for I had heard nothing unusual no but I had as he passed smelled him Jim and he smelled of sea-saltiness as if he had just come from the sea which I had never seen but had heard was salty and this salty smell was free and healthy and of outdoors not antiseptic which made me know he was special.

By the afternoon Jim arrived I had become very good at being patient so good that I expected to be able to live out the rest of my time on that ward and whichever ward followed it for it would of course be a ward with equanimity a lovely word if not contentment a cosy word just so long as Charlie or another knife-loving bully did not decide particularly to focus upon me as the object of his cruelty for no apparent reason. Each new day I was able to take as something midway between a gift and a burden for as the Sisters I am sure would take the opportunity to say every burden is a gift and every gift is a gift from God and a chance to avoid unnecessary symmetry and neatness of phrasing though they would not say or even think that but I would because I cared about such things as accuracy of verbal expression with a passion that became an ethic because I so often thought how exactly would I say this or that were I able to speak or write it using my word-hoard.

The question of whether if I could suddenly gain the ability for verbal self-expression I would choose to speak aloud clearly with fricatives as well as plosives or to write handwriting neatly is one that preoccupied me very much and I think I can now say I would choose for myself writing because even with as much time as I have had to think about what I would like to say and how exactly I would like to say it and even after the unlocking years later by Dr Masters and Lioresal his skeletal muscle relaxant which enabled me to move my lolling head and roll my null tongue it still speech still goes wrong even in my head so often that it must be an unsatisfactory medium of self-expression but as I back then would not have been choosing only for myself but for myself on the ward in which I lived I think I would say the ability to shout Stop or to tell one of the Sisters exactly what the cause of Lise's distress was this or that morning would be the correct and only humane choice.

Of course after all these years around me the Sisters knew that I had sounds that were the equivalent of Stop but to these they did not pay sufficient attention in the moment for them to be useful so the perpetual frustration was that although I could in theory convey Stop or No this was ignored and even if it hadn't been I could not explain why they should stop or what it was that was so wrong with the present state of affairs that I had found it necessary to cry out and so I was always afraid that if I overused my cease and desist sounds I was likely to become the boy who cried wff because wff along with hff was one of the sounds I found easiest to make.

For at least two years when I was younger and after I first heard the story of the boy who cried wolf and also a radio broadcast of Prokofiev's Peter and the Wolf I used to think about exactly what I would do were a real wolf somehow to enter the ward seen by no-one else but me which was unlikely as even when parked in front of the white wall and near the gate there tended to be another child within ten feet of me Lise and Kurt or at least within sight further along the long corridor which was a long straight corridor of blue floor tiles and off-white ceiling tiles fluorescent strip lights with seven doors off to the right and two wide windows off to the left then the framed poster of Wild Animals of the African Savanna then two more wide windows before the Chapel.

What I had concluded was that the best thing I could do would not be to risk enraging or alarming the wolf by crying wff! wff! but to attempt to buy the Sisters as much time as possible to come within sight recognize the eruption of a wolf in their safe space and to escort or carry the remaining children down the fire escape past Dorm 7 the Princesses' dorm into the courtyard and safety. The best thing I could do would be to draw the wolf's attention to me and to attempt to keep it there by whatever humming or wriggling was necessary and although I do not mean to sound heroic or martyrish if it was necessary even to allow the wolf to begin eating my feet or more likely my exposed hands then I would endure as long as I could for then I would finally be useful and maybe yes a bit heroic.

I used to have many dreams to this effect.

I remember the dream I had the night before Jim arrived I dreamed of falling down the stairs with my father behind me like a big shadow as if this had caused my paralysis rather than the hour of my birth being a real hour an hour long that towards the end involved minutes of strangled suffocation of which I have heard the medical details many times but I do not remember the dream I had the night of the day of the evening Jim arrived because I hardly slept for excitement so did not dream and woke in the morning exhausted but exhilarated and lay flat in my barred cot and listened to the radiators gurglingly tickingly filling with hot water always a deep joy as it not only meant I would not be cold for much longer but also because it was a rich series of unpredictable sounds a soundworld as they often said on Radio 3 most notably the first time when I was eight years old talking of Gustav Mahler the doomed composer who wrote music they told me about the death of his child before his child died and who showed extreme and painful tenderness not only for separation from his own flesh but for all human separations fleshly and spiritual and he did this through an ambitious music that was cut off when Sister Cécile went for a haircut and Sister Britta turned the radio off but I had heard enough of the first movement and a half of Symphony Number 6 to know what a soundworld was and to learn that I lived in one a great long one.

My favourite soundworld aspect apart from the radio on Radio 3 in the office was Sister Cécile in the Music Room playing waltzes down the echoey corridor when the light was low and supper smelling up and childish whooping was at a minimum because we were all tired after a day of being ourselves perhaps a little hysterical earlier on playing waltzes to calm us for then I could imagine I was near a ballroom where as Sister Muriel vivaciously described waltzes were first performed in Vienna and where people danced and fell in love with other people as flowing dancers first and as people second so even when there was no radio going swoop and ching and brr and la-la-lah I could tune in to the latest hits of the heating system from boiler upwards that in the morning really did become like the timpani section of the Berlin Philharmonic under their conductor Herbert von Karajan playing the kind of modern compositions that even Sister Cécile tended to turn off or turn down if she was not occupied elsewhere.

The soundworld I loved most was Christmas carols because they floated on the air like icing on marzipan that is pretending to be snow on a Christmas cake with the smiling snowman cake-decoration and the Santa's sleigh cake-decoration that came out every year although the Sisters were very careful with me because I could so easily choke and choke to death on a currant or a raisin just as if it were an orange button but the peace of O Little Town of Bethlehem travelled in a straight line parallel to the floor from the radio to my heart and I believed that at that precise moment my mother who must love carols because carols are the sound of a mother a mother like Mary's wall whiteness and plain love for her infant child born in Bethlehem or anywhere in the world amid woe and straw and kine and need to be redeemed she heard my mother heard as I heard and in our ears we met as if our ears were touching and her ear was tender against my ear and her cheek was motherly against my cheek like marzipan beneath icing like snow though warm and blushing with happiness to think of the faraway son having his best Christmas because of the three wise men card and Snoopy book and blue and white stripey jumper and together travelling along the long sounds of we see thee lie.

I wished her my mother a Merry Christmas through the still small voice of the carolling that hymns on high in the human heart and cannot but be felt wherever kitchens are full of roasting smells and brothers and sisters who can stand and walk in and out of rooms full of gratitude for their presents from their parents and appreciation of every bauble on the Christmas tree and every link in the paper chain with which they have festooned the ceiling from corner to corner marvellous word festooned above their diagonally crowned heads because they couldn't wait to crack the crackers and so become on this day a royal family with Princes and Princesses as well as King and Queen before the real Queen's speech that is warm but wise as she offers motherliness to everyone in the Commonwealth sometimes in front of her tree which is bigger than the trees of almost everyone else in the Commonwealth she sent a great message from me to my mother speaking of the importance of family at this special time of year or the especial importance of family at this time of year I can't remember which she said exactly but the Queen comes after the carols from King's College Chapel Cambridge and for an hour and a half the long corridor of the ward was a soundworld of choirboys with voices like snowing singing notes like icicles to listeners as cosy as fires in hearths with stockings hanging on either side just like the Christmas card from one birthday card and one missing birthday card before Jim arrived.

My poor mother when the Queen speaks of the especial importance of family must think of me with warmth and guilt and longing and Mahler sounds but we have already been together at Yuletide in O Little Town and in our ears of beautiful white cake.

The whiteness of the Christmas cake is a whiteness I often discovered in the whiteness of the white wall but the morning after Jim's arrival as excited as at Christmas I still had to go through my usual morning routine which went like this after pretending to wake and gurgle clank listening bang echo and warming and then being told to rise and shine by Sister Britta and light in through the lifting blinds sniff and sniff and tiny wince because you need changing young Mr Elliott and I knew I did because along with the radiators all my senses had been working and my smellworld was as stubbornly present as my soundworld.

On this morning I had not been able to wait because I was so excited at the prospect of a salty new child on the ward and a new source of interest a new instrument in the orchestra and a new sound in the soundworld.

Jim was special yes Jim was an answered prayer even though I had stopped praying except when I was pretending to pray during service and ended up really praying to make that easier and more believable and so I think I can forgive myself for thinking at this moment that morning as Sister Britta began to remove my pyjamas before changing me This day is going to be or This day stands a small chance of being a special day and I think I can be even more completely forgiven because I followed this by immediately thinking Patience Patience above all things It may not happen today Nothing may happen today and so patience always patience although the truth is because I had not slept I had been counselling myself patience most of the long night through.

Being changed is just that being changed changed as a being a thing in a profound way but on the surface level it is a humiliation and I am more than grateful for that and I realize that I would not be alive to be able to express internally or even feel gratitude if it were not for them a long line in time going backwards to my birth of them them after them after them Sister after Sister and beyond and neither would any of us be here not only on the ward but beyond in the world because each of us was nursed from birth each started as a helpless thing prey to any passing rat or fox or wolf and if we hadn't been picked up and carried we would be nothing but food for a crow or as I think a rat.

I was and remain grateful for the opportunity to exist to be grateful so thank you to the whole society of thems I will never meet and most of whom will never know that I exist. Thank you especially to those who put money into the collection plates that go round during Offertory but thank you also to the men and women who work in the coal-fired and nuclear power stations that keep on the lights and thank you to those who work making our water clean thank you to the farmers who grow our food and the drivers who drive it to us and the cooks who cook it for us and the dishwashers who wash up after us and the bin men who take away the food we do not eat in black bags and the men who work the machines that bury all the rubbish we make and who help Keep Britain Tidy.

Someone had to change me on this first Jim day as on every day sometimes several times but that did not mean I had no preference as to who that someone was although it could not be my favourite because my favourite had been Sister Clare from Liverpool.

Sister Clare will always be memorable for her bleached hair cherry-sweet-smelling breath and her habit of saying flippety flip flippety flip very quietly but completely audibly whilst changing you she had marvellous changing technique but had to leave after Patricia almost drowned in the bath whilst she Sister Clare was bathing her still distracted by a phone call she had just received and she let Patricia slip underwater though the actual pneumonia only took Patricia two and a half weeks later but Sister Clare disappeared the very morning she left Patricia safely with Sister Cécile while she went away only long enough to say as I heard her loudly say Thank you for letting me know I cannot speak right now into the telephone in the Sisters' Office and went behind me silently back to Patricia that was not the last we saw of her although she disappeared until the leaving party which was the last we saw of her when we sat around a candle-lit cake and watched her cry.

Patricia had been everybody's favourite child. She did not do anything in particular but it was the way she did not do anything that somehow endeared Patricia universally even knife-loving Charlie was nice to her Patricia did not smile her face was more of the sneery snarly snaggle-toothed variety but she seemed to be content behind that and to us on the ward contentment was of all human qualities the most revered and so many of us desired to sit beside Patricia to be within her calm and so feel calmer themselves myself included if only I had been able to move into her vicinity.

The terrible thing that I think was a real irony was that the phone call Sister Clare had tragically taken because Sister Cécile said it was so important was about the near-drowning of her own son Petey he Petey had been surfing off St Ives in Cornwall and had gone too near the rocks and wiped out which I later learned means fell off the surfboard and got concussion he only survived because another surfer called Marv from Ontario paddled Petey back to the beach on his own board so of course Sister Clare was distracted after she again took over bathing Patricia from Sister Cécile who was blameless but who walked away and that was when Patricia slipped down and inhaled a sip or two of bathwater and Sister Clare should never have left Patricia unsupported not even for a second even though she Patricia was shocking calm and content through it all and even unto death.

43

Flippety flip flippety Sister Clare used to say flippety all the way through changing you and she was top of the Top Five in reverse order counting down Not arf as Fluff Freeman used to say in announcing the Rock Show Charts on Mrs Beatles the Cleaner's portable radio-cassette player. Holding steady at number five was Sister Cécile who was so superfast number four Sister Mary Margaret of the warm hands and sometimes chocolatey breath and in at number three posh Sister Muriel with her surprising dancer's strength to flip you over as if you were some bread she was kneading like the others did in the Craft Room to make plaits number two it has to be admitted Sister Britta even when you were hating her for something else a quick change by Sister Britta made you realize how she had got where she had rough but perfect and as the senior Sister she always had access to talcum powder and never left you raw and still at number one three years after the cake crying the greatest of them all Sister Clare who had an impossible way of making it seem as if throughout the whole performance of you being changed you were miraculously levitating.

Some others the bottom three of the bottom caused something like actual bodily harm each time they came near I will not think to name them except to say because she like Sister Clare has now died that if Sister Penelope ever did your nappy it dug in like a blade.

Sister Penelope was eventually given a cake for hitting Micky across the face after she tried and failed to stop him climbing and he in response started poking her nipples as if they were the buttons of the lift and saying Call lift for the left one and Floor four for the right one Sister Penelope's nipples were the most prominent through the habit I have ever known in fact they were the ones through which we boys were all introduced to the concept of female nipples that did not belong to the Virgin Mary feeding the Infant Christ with which we were of course all long familiar.

We had not known before that summer of Sister Penelope that the flat brown coins of the girls being changed within our field of vision could sometimes grow like flowers into those raspberries that changed from moment to moment sometimes into angry blueberries placid strawberries and exhilarated loganberries Sister Penelope was very beautiful in other ways legs and hands and face and that might explain why she did not feel it necessary to work on her changing technique no-one was very good at telling such a beautiful brown-eyed woman off even Sister Cécile became embarrassed the one time I saw and could not go into specifics Just try to be a little more gentle she said after another child it was Princess Pretty my interpreter one of the three Princesses had been discovered with raspberry ripple-like rash only three hours after being smooth as.

The Sisters were constantly fighting rot our bodies wanted to turn fungus-y our bodies were like a bowl of week-old fruit not rotten or rotting but getting ready to rot. Just touch a banana in this state and it bruises for if you changed redheaded Glen badly one time two weeks of whimpering agony would follow.

This first morning I was lucky that Sister Britta holding steady at number two dealt with my number one and my number two with her usual talcum powdered efficiency in very short order and with the arriving help of Sister Cécile she had me dressed in grey trousers black socks floral shirt with poppers instead of buttons acceptable grey white bib and so dressed and ready to be wheeled along the long corridor and left and right and through to breakfast which I had been smelling up the lift-shaft for twenty minutes.

Others had toast spread with lime marmalade containing toenail shaped slivers of rind on top of margarine where the bread that made the toast was white or brown and either crisp or chewy depending upon how long it had spent or not spent in the toaster in the kitchen and how humid the kitchen was but toast was too much of a choking hazard for me in fact if you had designed a perfect choking hazard for me it would look very much and very much have the texture of toast with sticky sweet floppy objects on top.

My breakfast was Ready Brek with as much sugar and honey on it and in it as I with my wishful mind could persuade the Sisters to sprinkle or drizzle or just dunk in stir in but they were very careful however because they didn't want me to get fat but I loved the taste of anything sweet and I didn't get much sweetness the rest of the day in my food so when Sister Cécile poured I made the sound for More because the sound for More was any sound and the sound for Stop was to stop making a sound.

But I could not concentrate at all on my own breakfast because I wanted to know what breakfast the new boy Jim was capable of having because from what I had guessed from his powerful footsteps he was one of those bold adventurers capable even of Weetabix and butter or cornflakes without milk which food to some of us would be a bit like a bowlful of orange buttons however from where I had been wheeled up to my usual place at the near long table in through the double doors and round to the right at the end facing away from the door with the pink hippo place mat gift from four Christmases ago smiling up at me a little paler and with a tear down from the top of its left ear and with Sister Cécile at the head and to my right with Finn directly opposite me an empty seat to the left of him and with Micky's always-empty-at-breakfast seat to my left and I could not see anyone new and I knew if I saw anyone I hadn't seen before it would be him Jim although I did not just yet know his name or for certain that he was a him.

This his absence made me feel sad sadder than I should have done and not only because I had been looking forward to his presence for several of those awake-in-the-night hours but because I already felt as if I already knew sea-salty Jim and his appearance in the morning was part of my morning every morning and the fact he wasn't there turned it into a new thing a big event and I wanted Jim to be my friend already which was ridiculous I know when I come to think about it because I had never even seen him and then when my Ready Brek was down to its last teaspoonful after twenty minutes of spooning and wiping and milk running down the inside and outside of my throat then I did see Jim there he was at last but I did not see him directly only reflected in the glass of the picture on the wall opposite me behind Lise on the far long table the picture of people in a snowy landscape with tall dark trees around them and I only saw Jim's thin shape for half a second because the light was behind him silhouetting him as he was guided in by Sister Mary Margaret because he was blind blind from birth born I later learned with no eyeballs at all in his head.

Sister Mary Margaret brought him through the door of course through the door but behind me where I couldn't see but could hear her telling him where the near long table was and they had thought to place him on the near long table through the door and down to the left beside Sister Britta to make breakfast easy for him at first.

Children said Sister Britta looking at everyone I am certain with her brightest most holy blue eyes Children this is Jim.

Some of us said Hello and some of us including myself made our Hello noises and some of us carried on doing what we were doing Now she said you shouldn't take advantage of Jim because Jim is blind and Jim is also dumb but he is most definitely not deaf are you Jim? And Jim then clapped his hands twice a beautiful strong clap a hard and heroic sound.

Jim has got very good hearing Sister Britta said and he will hear if you say anything negative or mean-spirited so receive him in the spirit of the Lord. That is all. Get along now.

What would you like for breakfast I heard Sister Mary Margaret ask and then answer herself as if Jim had answered Toast and butter thank you very much Sister Mary Margaret and Fine she answered herself Fine and dandy she said then went off to get it just as my last spoonful of Ready Brek became a mouthful at the top of my mouth and went down the wrong way because I had been so focussed upon what was going on behind me rather than on keeping my head at the correct angle for efficient swallowing.

Luckily this time cough and a cough and a sip of milk took the little bit of off-white not-quite-sugary-enough paste down the right way not the airway and I lived to breathe another day but soon too soon was wheeled away by Sister Cécile fast too fast and not even past Jim who I imagined had both his hands on a piece of toast without lime marmalade but clockwise round towards the right hand edge of the room with my head on the wrong shoulder to get a simple sight of him.

I would have to wait.

Left turn and right turn and halfway along the long corridor my chair was stopped and Sister Cécile moved away with a sigh to deal with something happening in Dorm 5 and I was left with the full magnificent view straight down the long corridor towards on the right the four windows overlooking the courtyard then the white wall with the wooden gate in it and then hidden behind the wall the Sisters' Office and beyond that the rest of the corridor the forbidden corridor and the lift.

I had been down the forbidden corridor and out of the ward twenty five times since I came there I had been to pantomimes every year around Christmas card time and inbetween then there had been some trips to A&E some of which I hadn't been conscious for because I was halfheartedly dying and most of all twice we had been to the Arndale Centre to do something normal and go shopping.

On both occasions I wanted to buy a gift to be sent to my mother but had not been able to communicate this so ended up with a scarf for myself in white orange and purple for a football team Luton Town I did not support or anyway did not support before I got the scarf because once I got the scarf and it was tied onto the end of my cot I thought I had better start supporting them and also I got some hand cream which was a Heavenly balm for as long as it lasted on my mantelpiece with my birthday and Christmas cards which were up all year round because the Sisters knew what I would do if anyone ever tried to take them down which one year was the cause of an A&E trip for I could sometimes tip my chair backwards if I spasmed hard enough with all my body with feet hitting the floor and this is what I had done when a temporary replacement cleaning lady called Maxine standing in for Mrs Beatles and her blue and red cassettes took down my Christmas cards not my birthday cards and ripped them in half and put them in the wastepaper basket which was why nearly half my cards at this time the time of the start of Jim had a rip across the middle and Sellotape holding them together.

As I waited for another Sister to push me to my morning place the morning after Jim arrived I thought about what I had seen of him so far just a sliver of a vision that was a reflection of his silhouette I did not know what colour his hair was but I did not believe he was black-skinned like black Toby and I did not either expect his hair to be black what my glimpse had shown me was a thin head with sticky-out ears and that is still how I remember Jim even though eventually I was to get a better look at him and in fact get to know him physically by sight very well indeed but waiting there in my wheelchair I imagined him as thin altogether with a thin body fitting his thin head which did not turn out to be true.

I looked again towards the lift and for some reason thought as I often thought of what I had seen beyond the wooden gate a blue penis and a green gherkin I will get to soon and then I thought more explicitly of the blue of the most graphic act of sex I had ever witnessed which was in a public toilet in the Arndale Centre where I had to be taken after I puked deliberately so as to extend my stay in the fascinating shopping centre and see something new of it if only the toilets and see something new I certainly did because there on the disabled cubicle wall causing Sister Britta to tut and turn me away from it to where I could see it even better in the mirror there was a most elaborate blue biro drawing of what I later learned was a blow-job but at the time and much to my distress thought was a picture of a woman being forced to drink a man's wee because wee was how I interpreted the blue apostrophe shapes that jumped from the end of his very large blue penis towards the woman's face of course I could not expect Sister Britta to comment on it any more than the tut and the muttered Heavens preserve us that followed but that was enough to tell me that the blue drawing was of something wrong and quite possibly shameful and almost certainly sinful although it was not unlike a painting we had once been shown in a visiting Priest's slide-show of the Virgin Mary feeding the baby Jesus an arc of milk from her breast at a distance of six or seven feet.

The blue drawing was so elaborate I later realized it must have taken at least seven or eight drawing sessions to complete just the man being fellated who as I thought of him over the coming years of Radio 3 and occasional Bartók I began to think of as Bluebeard because he had a beard the standing man had a face full of blue biro hair highly detailed every follicle was there just as if the artist had been compelled to include them all in order for the picture to do its job which I suspect was not to be a self-portrait because that would just have been asking for trouble but a portrait of a lucky and happy and disgustingly ugly man he had several moles and perhaps the exact placement of them did mean that this was a portrait of some sort but whether it was intended to humiliate or glorify the subject I still cannot decide certainly any man would count himself lucky to have such a very large penis and here in the drawing of this was where the greatest amount of detail had been applied in the shading of the 3-D veins in the mushroom shape of the bit on the end whose name I still don't know in the beard of wispy wavy hair beneath it in the globular flight of the sperm toward the open waiting mouth of the beautiful woman wearing the Iron Maiden leather jacket and all of this I should emphasize again in blue biro against dirty whitewash surrounded by backwards swearwords replying to backwards swearwords.

As I saw it first time in astonishment and horrified wonder at all I was learning of the outside world and what people in it got up to I thought the kneeling woman seemed to be as delighted at drinking Bluebeard's wee as Bluebeard seemed to be at using a woman as a urinal for she was smiling with big lips apart and huge teeth and eyelashes all over the place and she was wearing make-up that made her cheekbones dark and her hair was curly and she wore leather trousers and biker boots details I only came to understand later after much thought just as it was not until after the rescue by young Brother Benedict and the unlocking by Dr Masters and his research team that I was able to ask the question by slowly typing it out letter by letter and was shown Iron Maiden on the television programme Top of the Pops and so learned they were a heavy metal rock band who I quite enjoyed.

I thought Iron Maiden the words I had been able to read on the back of her jacket was the name of the woman Miss Iron Maiden.

I never returned to that disabled toilet although I did the next year go back to the Arndale Centre but this time when I deliberately puked they took me to the toilets in the Burger King and so I never got to know how long this blue masterpiece lasted on the wall of the disabled toilet but it was enough for me that I had seen it once and over the following months I began to understand it as it began to appear in my dreams as an animated scene. But it was only a couple of years later listening to the old white wall painters those ones before Ted and Lee that I learned of the existence of the blow-job and connected it to what was going on on the wall in the drawing.

I was not supposed by the Sisters to be sexual a sexual being although my nocturnal emissions were later to become as glutinous and as frequent as any other adolescent male's but this was only in the year after Jim for at the time of his arrival my sexual feelings were mainly directed towards Lise's knees and Lise's hair that was long and brightly ginger and thick like the wool hair of Patricia's doll and most of all Lise's beautiful pale skin with the dappling of freckles and the speckling of significant and beloved beauty spots especially the two at an angle on the skin down the base of her neck where I imagined my hard head softly resting after a day of strain and shame as Lise happily told me about what it would be like to have a mother like neither of us had who visited you every other Thursday because I did not adore Lise for her sorrow it was not because she wept like the Virgin Mary for sinners that the line of her white neck was so important in my world it was because of the Lise she might have been if only she could have found utter consolation in a way not possible on this ward in this fallen world but if she had been taken home by her parents and loved as she deserved to be loved because all of us deserved that love.

O Lise O Lise my poor sad weeping girl with your drooping dresses and woolly tresses and your dropping white socks that always seemed too big and too thick for your slender ankles which were neither too slender and therefore scrawny like mine nor too muscular and therefore grotesque like Micky's from all his frantic walking and antic jumping instead you delicate Lise made the rest of the world seem a size or two too big and a bash or two too brutal and perhaps it's this that made you cry and made me wish that I could shrink the world to fit you and pacify it too so you would no longer have to say It's just not fair It's just not fair.

This is what I had learned over the four Christmas cards of looking at and trying to understand Lise through love and the love of looking at and listening to Lise for what went on with Lise's skin was always the same or a type of broadcast version of what was going on inside her in her soul but not the Sisters' religious Catholic soul of damnation and purgatory and glory options but instead the expression of what she Lise really was at that moment and that expression might be for example and often was a very red nose that was dry skinned and sore through sheer power of crying from tear ducts on either side and even though her hair was bright red her nose still became the most colourful thing about her but to me it was a rose of sadness that bloomed more beautifully when watered with the gush of greater anguish.

And for another example her knees which were comparable to other young knees on the ward although I would have known them even were the rest of Lise behind a pulled-across screen or curtain and I had known them as all that was visible of her from outside the confessional whenever she spent long minutes such was her guilt such was her contrition observing them with love I had learned that her knees whitened with her anger but as a self-made expert on whiteness and I suppose I should allow also an expert on Lise's knees I could be sure the whitening of her knees was different in tone depending on whether her anger was at one of the Sisters where it was pale bluey and murderous or at herself where it was greyish and suicidal or at everything at once when it was green and nauseous or at specific people such as her pink white mother or her golden white father.

The knees went before the eyes did although this was not of course in isolation because Lise's whole physical posture was a leap into her own mental future and if her toes touched while her knees were far apart I knew she would soon attempt something mischievous like hiding herself under something or more likely something flirtatious to do with one of the younger and more humorous Sisters whereas if her head went back and she seemed to be looking at the ceiling for a while then she would never be pacified until she had broken something and I was not unique in knowing this observing this because Sister Cécile on seeing Lise's head go back as if neck-broken was once wise enough to fetch three plastic drinking cups from the Infirmary behind the Sisters' Office for Lise to smash with her fist Sister Cécile knew that because once before when Lise had nothing to destroy she'd hit her right hand so hard against the wall that bones broke.

Sister Cécile was wise enough to know that if it wasn't plastic that was smashed by Lise it would be a window or a flower vase or possibly the side of someone's head if they happened to get in the way when Lise picked up and threw the flower vase although even as the flower vase was flying Lise would be appalled by this violent action and her knees would immediately start to go greyish because all Lise wanted to do was avoid destroying herself or a delicate person by destroying an object whose destruction would bring upon her the wrath and punishment she knew she deserved and if Lise could have achieved the same effect upon herself by singing a song or kissing somebody then I know she would have done that because it wasn't about the violence it was about putting a break in the time of the world by breaking something in the world by making it making the world like her making it into a thing that could not be used again by creating another useless thing that at least was how I came to understand those exciting moments during which I saw the smoothness and muscularity of her throat where the skin seemed to contain in it all at once all the colours that came out elsewhere in her body but most of all silver silver like raindrops on the outside of a misted-up window with the lights off inside but November sunlight outside.

All of this to me this life of watching Lise's body displaying Lise's mind was like the phrase used on the radio by a female composer to describe the work of Wolfgang Amadeus Mozart as inexpressibly tender or maybe she said because the volume was low and it was hard for me to hear maybe as containing an inexpressible tenderness as was in me for Lise for in me there was a Mozart soundworld of inexpressible tenderness for her while we were in the ward because most basically I was incapable of expressing anything towards her except in the sounds I made while facing in her direction and looking towards her with my eyes and listening to her as if my whole body were an ear but my sounds were not communications in the way Lise understood for Lise understood only powerful physical embrace and this was usually if rarely achieved by a Sister and Sister Cécile was very good at it at pacifying Lise at her most raging by wrapping a grey blanket tightly around her locking down her arms and allowing her to feel embraced almost head to toe then she could be happy but this was a secret thing the Sisters could not allow anyone from outside the ward to see see Lise's joy when they put her in a fabric confinement that I couldn't help but see as a woven version of my own paralysis although Lise was always lying down when metamorphosed into what I thought of as the Lise-worm.

More basically Lise's pale skin with its bruises and cuts and scratches and scabs was and scars too of course was the record of where the world had hit her where she'd forced the world of the ward upon herself and I watched them like goldfinch nests in the wych elm assembling and collapsing I watched them happen and darken and fade and whiten oh Lord Lise's constant minor wounds fifty five per cent I would estimate not self-inflicted O poor Lise my poor dear Lise.

As soon as I started to be pushed forwards again toward the wall or the window the day after Jim arrived wall or window I knew it was still Sister Cécile behind me doing the pushing I knew this before the person it was spoke which would have given it away immediately and I knew it firstly from how they pushed the chair and secondly I confirmed it from how they smelled because different Sisters pushed harder or steered more jerkily and different Sisters had signature scents when they were doing things for us buttoning our shirts or pulling down our socks for at this juncture the Sisters came very close to us and more importantly we came very close to the Sisters so much so that it sometimes felt as if the sides of our heads were designed to fit into the cups of their armpits and our nostrils to be sliced by the harsh seams of their habits and after a day of nursing any woman is going to smell of her natural smells for example by teatime Sister Mary Margaret smelled of a burnt fish pie with grey egg halves and small brown prawns by contrast sometimes Sister Cécile's right hand was smoky and bitter and sometimes it wasn't and then it smelled of ginger or sugar and I noted she was sometimes not careful enough and brownness developed between her index and middle fingers Sister Eliza was perfumed in the morning with the artificial scent of small sweet violets but by lights out she was peppery and in summer

Sister Britta began by smelling of shampoo and ended by smelling of puke even if no-one had puked on her and in winter Sister Britta smelled of a wet animal that I had just before Jim arrived learned was a Labrador dog she walked in the park for an old Catholic woman she knew so when I began moving in my wheelchair and smelled faint smoke to my right I knew it could not be anyone but naughty Sister Cécile steering me in her smooth and no-nonsense and twinkle-round-the-corners style.

I also knew that because of who she was and what she was like and because I had been a good quiet calm boy the day before that she was almost certain unless she had been ordered otherwise to park me at the window looking down into the courtyard where she knew I liked to be and so it was so it was and normally at least she parked me just in the perfect spot close to the fascinating silver radiator with its five dustballs beneath it for a view all the way down to the base of the wych elm where the faintly pink and yellow paving stones in an octagonal shape left a space of earth around the trunk and leaves sometimes gathered but this spot of vision was only perfect on a normal day because for today the day after Jim's arrival I would have given one at least of my Christmas cards to be facing 90 degrees to my right looking back up the long corridor towards where Jim would have to come into sight at some point during the day but I knew that if I made my distressed sounds Sister Cécile would well-meaningly interpret them as meaning something they didn't and would park my chair facing the white wall in order to try to give me the calm I seemed to her to be trying to say I wanted.

The view along the long corridor when I was left there a few minutes earlier by Sister Cécile had made me remember two things the blue Iron Maiden drawing and the green gherkin I will get to soon and now the glass of the window in front of me when I focussed on it

57

instead of the pinky and yellowish paving stones and the tree and the roof opposite and the sky made me again then remember the pickled gherkin but I was interrupted in these memories by the sound of the others the other children emerging into and across the end of and sending echoes down the long corridor and although most of the time most of my physical effort was put into putting less strain on my spine I could not help at this moment but head-to-toe stiffen in fresh hopes of hearing the new sounds of Jim joining in or not joining in.

With the slap of his flat feet Kurt made his way to his grey filing cabinet and began once again his hopeless morning vigil over his defenceless land but today there was no arrival of Lise to sit and weep nearby probably I thought because unless she was being mischievous and absenting herself it was her turn for catechism with Sister Britta or piano lesson with Sister Cécile no that day the long corridor seemed remarkably quiet without even the yeahs of Mrs Beatles' red and blue cassettes to distract me from the steady thump pause thump of Kurt's head that was doing its best to distract me from the courtyard whose usual excitement despite the presence of two sparrows I found it hard to get at.

So I distracted myself from my distraction by thinking as brightly as I could of the green gherkin which happened the day of one annual day trip when we had all gone to the nearest Arndale centre forty miles away not the year of the blue drawing but the year after.

It happened after what was meant to be the main excitement of the day i.e. being stared at by the able-bodied in a clothes shop C&A whilst choosing new shirts and trousers and doing as Sister Britta had brightly and sternly said Something nice and normal but fun and useful out in the fallen world.

Our coach had stopped for a few moments on the return journey at some traffic lights we were the nearest vehicle to them and so very close to the crossing where the pedestrians waited on the spangly wet pavement starred with dropped chewing gum among them a school-boy maybe thirteen years old freshly come out of the McDonald's restaurant we had just a minute before driven past he was eating with pleasure his face down in his burger when he looked up and saw me looking at him with I admit envy of many sorts in my heart and it's possible he may also have seen several others of us on that side of the bus for he reacted with a wince and by mouthing an obscenity that began with F and ended with a small gobbet of Big Mac being projected from his big-lipped mouth.

It was clear he was distressed by the sight of me and made angry by the way I looked and maybe made more angry by the way I looked at him for because the traffic lights were taking so long to change he had time to reach into his Big Mac and pull out from it a gherkin slice and just as the lights changed to green and the coach began to pull past them he was able to Frisbee the gherkin slice with a beautiful flick of his slim wrist toward me in fact at me all the way to where it stuck on the window right next to where my forehead was touching because I liked to listen to the engine through the glass and feel the vibrations of the road passing through and perhaps giving strength to my body.

Splat went the gherkin slice though none of the Sisters saw it and if the glass hadn't been there as the coach began to accelerate the slice would have hit me in the left eye landing on it like a new eyelid and so the left eye had its view of the schoolboy obscured but the right eye saw him smile at his own speed and accuracy.

And even though I knew he had not done what he had done as a way of communicating anything but anger and disgust I was delighted at his delight and smiled back at him which seemed to annoy him even more my smile because he made the V-sign with some expertise and repeated the F-word and I think he was thinking about chucking the whole rest of his Big Mac at me and then he was out of sight and I was left in some shock and exultation to refocus on the green gherkin slice that hadn't been there a few moments before and in a strange delay it was only now that my brain seemed really to process the exact sound it had made when it landed and the satisfying mini-thunk of this combined with the remarkable greenness and stickiness of it to leave me with an entirely positive impression for even though it was not meant as a gift it had become a gift because I had received it as a gift because I had never been lucky enough to be so close to a McDonald's gherkin although the other children had talked about them in legendary terms of delectation and disgust and lawks-a-lordy as Sister Muriel would have said here was one astonishingly like some sea creature from a Wildlife on One nature documentary filmed on the Great Barrier Reef.

I was to become very familiar with the gherkin slice partly during the one hour drive back to the ward but also because it was still there two months later although fairly dried up when we made our annual trip to the local pantomime it was not chance that had me sitting in the same wheelchair gap because the Sisters tended to put us in the places they always put us in so I was twice able to examine the translucent slimy green wonder with lighter-coloured circular pips and a lattice of crossover struts that was the growth structure of the schoolboy's gherkin slice and during this and the time that followed I often wondered whether he the schoolboy was originally intending to chuck it the gherkin away anyway perhaps on top of a bus shelter or whether he had wanted to eat it but was forced by his rage at my disgusting appearance to seize upon it as the most dispensable-with and quickly gettable-to thing he had available to throw at me.

He had thrown it at me me Elliott I was sure specifically with great accuracy and great meaning right at my left eye and I'm sure the word he was about to shout after the F-obscenity as the coach sped away was Spaz and if not that then Spazzer or Spastic.

Often I thought of the green gherkin slice the elegance of its not design but internal construction or growth and often I wondered exactly what it would taste like at the same time as I recalled the way exactly like a Frisbee like the white Frisbee the ground floor children played with down in the courtyard it had spun as it arced through the air so wonderfully accurately on its way towards the window of the coach the coach that from the boy's point of view was filled with disgusting spazzers whose lives weren't worth living and who might as well be dead.

And often I thought about the boy's face which before it went into a snarl had seemed to me a nice squishy doughy face with fat lips and heavy eyelids that bespoke a deep contentment with the Big Mac he was about to eat and with the life he was living that meant he was able to eat Big Macs on the way home from school to his parents' house as he must have been although I reasoned later that his mother was probably not at home because otherwise she would have been there preparing him a cooked tea and he wouldn't have to have stopped off for fast food on the way home lucky boy so lucky and bless him for it.

Then from behind me that first morning I heard sounds that I immediately understood which meant that another game of Sockball was about to begin I knew this because some of the boys were shouting to one another in a way that meant they were choosing teams because the cry was Choose me! Charlie Choose me not him! Charlie choose me! I could not hear the details because there were too many voices shouting at once perhaps six or seven and the soundworld of the long corridor made them echoey and squidged into one another but by the end of the shouting there were two teams and Gate S.C. were coming towards me and Chapel United were staying up the far end but was Jim included? I did not have to wait long to find out because the gate end team began to choose positions and there were only five of these goalie left-wing right-wing midfielder and striker.

Jim go goalie said knife-loving Charlie. Jim go goalie you go wing you go other wing me go striker you go midfielder no said the voice of Finn who I haven't needed to think about before a boy not mentally impaired but suffering from a terrible skin disease that made pyramids of hard flesh stick up all over him pyramids that were cancerous and were to kill him one year later but on this day he was healthy and wanted very much to play striker for Gate S.C. but Charlie never let anyone else be striker so not-yet-dead Finn had to give up when an echoey shout of Charlie pass began the game as Charlie kicked off and the five boys of Gate S.C. began their first attack on Chapel United.

The rules were simple and very like football although I'd never then seen football even though I supported Luton Town F.C. and knew about Liverpool F.C. that is the rules were that a goal was scored if the ball which was two or three socks tied together in a grey black bundle because we did not were not allowed of course not allowed a real football if the sockball crossed over a certain line in the floor this line in the lino being a sacred threshold for players of Sockball and me being approximately six feet behind it so not on the pitch itself which ran all the way along the long corridor to just before the door of the Chapel where another sacred lino line-join ran sideways across both of which goal lines I could feel snicker beneath my wheelchair's wheels whenever the Sisters wheeled me over them and sometimes crossing one way or another I even let myself think of myself as a sockball and cried out in my head as I crossed the line because this is what crossing the line meant Goal!

Jim was in goal because blind boys almost always went in goal.

There was no referee's kick-off whistle as there usually was as the game had already started with an attack from the Chapel United team who even when they turned round and played the other direction in the second half would not change names but would still be called Chapel United and still be playing against Gate S.C.

From where I had been left that day I could only listen and catch stray reflections in the glass of the window whose glass I was about four feet away from and so for a second time my vision of Jim was indirect and indistinct and also moving a lot because it was clear from Chapel United's first attack that Jim was playing the game seriously meaning like me he was listening listening hard listening to feet and the patterns they made when patter-patter or shuffle-shuffle turns to patt or shuff because only one foot is on the floor and there's a pause as one leg or another left or right is drawn back to make a kick and take a shot.

Usually I was a neutral I did not support one side or the other not because they were not Luton Town F.C. but because it wasn't worth it because the side with Charlie on almost always won whether that was Chapel United or Gate S.C. but with the new child Jim playing for Gate S.C. I wanted him to do well so as to start earning his place in the ward and so I found myself cheering them on on the inside while adding some sounds on the outside which I am sure Jim did not hear because he was so focussed on listening for the next attack.

The game started well with Jim saving two early shots and only letting in a third shot because it took a deflection off a winger and up at the other end where most of the first half action was taking place Charlie scored the first as he always did and Finn had one disallowed for a foul Be careful Be careful I heard Charlie telling everyone then everyone repeating it to one another as if they'd come up with it.

The Sisters usually let Sockball happen as long as it stayed in the long corridor where there could be injuries against Kurt's filing cabinet but the only thing that could really get damaged was the Wild Animals of the African Savanna poster and just perhaps one of the crucifixes high above the doorway of every dorm probably they allowed it because Sockball was a way for the boys to release their energy because we second floor children were for some reason never allowed out in the courtyard unlike the ground floor children who were often there in Spring Summer and Autumn with their balls or their Frisbee.

In terms of my future for me the most important thing that happened during the game which finished hurray 4–3 to Gate S.C. after a late save from Jim at the Chapel end was that toward the middle of the first half Chapel United's squared-headed striker Gavin scored their second goal and just as I had been hoping the sockball flew over the lino line and in my direction.

My big hope had been that the sockball would go under the radiator right in front of me with the six dustballs and I'd be able to get a close look at Jim but as a good second best the sockball slid beneath the back wheels of my chair although I did not know this at first I just heard the goal celebration and felt a slight fabricky bounce against the wheelchair's frame but as the sockball might have bounced anywhere this was followed by Watch out Watch out He's and I guessed loud-shouting Charlie meant Watch out for me and Jim was being warned off from running into me and from that I could tell so much most importantly I could tell he was determined to retrieve to fetch the sockball from the back of his own imaginary net having let the goal in.

Elliott's there Charlie shouted. He's in his spazz chair Charlie added and Jim must have listened because he did not just run straight into me as some goalkeeping blind boys have done in the past.

I could hear him approaching even though his footfalls were mezzo piano I could hear his breathing and on top of that when he got really close I began to smell him.

Smells as you've already seen were very important to me particularly the smells of children because they helped me to tell their future because from a child's smell I could usually tell how long they had left on the ward if they were sweet and light they would stay a long time and I usually smelled like this myself but if their smell started to become heavy and dark if the girls started to smell of iron and fishpaste or orange marmalade and drains then I knew they would soon be leaving us to go to a women-only ward and if the boy stopped smelling of lamb hotpot and started smelling of roast beef I knew they would not be with us for more than a few weeks more particularly in the summer when smell-changes are more obvious than in the winter when none of us sweated so much and the Sisters sometimes did not notice the change for an extra month but on a hot summer's day the ward sometimes started to smell like Sunday roast gravy poured on top of tuna fish pie and I knew that soon friends would be leaving.

I found strong body odour of all sorts a very comforting thing perhaps I associated it with long-gone memories of my father's presence and my father's protection or perhaps it was memories of the gorgeous Jamaican nurse Eunice from the hospital I was at before I came to the ward the nurse who was the first woman to look after me after my mother didn't look after me because she couldn't look after me because she just couldn't cope any more for a while.

Jim as he came close behind me smelled what did he smell of he smelled like salt and also like pepper so salty and peppery but beneath it something a little meaty like a sausage roll and from this I predicted correctly as it turned out that Jim was not in any immediate danger of being taken away up the road to the Christian Brothers but that his days like all our days were numbered and that the number of Jim's days was less than three hundred and sixty five.

While Jim was close enough for me to smell him I felt him as a muscular presence like a shadow made of meat with a definite centre of gravity right behind me listening to shouts from Charlie that said On the floor and Under the spazz chair Under the spazzer to which Jim did not reply in words but I felt I thought his shoulder nudge the chair to the left not because he was trying to move me but just because his strength was such that a touch could become a nudge and through him the cross-section of the rubber of the wheels of my wheelchair was just for a moment moved from being basically circular to being something like a lopsided ovoid and then I felt a knock on the hard underside of the seat where I sat as Jim's knuckles in reaching in and under also must have reached out and up knock just one knock like a Sister testing to see if another Sister she respected was in a room with a closed door knock not like a joke knock knock but knock Are you in there? Are you free in there? Jim had longish fingernails because I heard them slide across the floor and give little clicks as they passed in their searching over rough patches in the lino and I was overjoyed I was already trembling like the washing machine on its spin cycle in the Sisters' washroom behind the Office for I had not expected to be given so much to be so overwhelmed by so many things to think of and remember for even if Jim had been taken away right then off the ward and I had never smelled or heard or heard of him again even then he would have remained with me and for me as a brave possibility which came close but did not get the chance to make its full impact like a meteor not a meteorite.

It could not last this closeness and soon one of Jim's large hands found out where the sockball had skidded to but there was one moment more of absolute delight left to happen even though it was definitely not one I caused or was responsible for in any way.

Jim I discovered had been in institutions long enough to know what a wheelchair was and what different designs of them there were so when he was standing up sockball in left or right hand though Jim I later learned was right-handed so probably right when Jim came to stand up he reached out with his free hand and took hold of my chair's left handle to help pull himself more quickly and efficiently to his feet not for any effect it might have upon me because I am sure at that moment I only existed for him as a name and a counterbalance with a set mass because if he had tried a similar choreography with an empty wheelchair it would have tipped back and fallen over probably with him falling too but as it was he relied upon my mass being there and took hold of the handle to pull himself off the lino the very first time he grabbed it but because of the downward force he exerted and because I was not so massive as he had calculated when he got part way through pulling himself up the smaller grey front wheels of my chair were for a couple of instants lifted off the lino and I was doing a wheelie I was doing a wheelie and glimpsing my constant dream of doing a real wheelie that went on for miles.

For Jim I am sure there was just a moment's worry that he'd fall over and perhaps tip up and injure some poor spastic called Elliott in a wheelchair and probably get punished for it but this is going too far this is too like me trying to think my way into Jim for Jim I am sure there was only a moment of whoa or oops and then the physics balanced and the front wheels made contact once more with the lino and Jim was on his feet and away both salt and peppery back to the game but a half second before this as the front wheels reared unexpectedly astonishingly dreamily they shifted position from inwardly diagonally pointing like the inturned toes of some children

67

I have known like Bentley and Patricia to swing instead into position parallel to the back wheels ready to roar off into the future like Sir Donald Campbell breaking the Land Speed Record and I had glory and fire in my imagination of what we could achieve as a team with him as the engine and me as the driver and the chair as the racing car.

The dream wheelie came to an end as the front wheels touched back down but they did not do this all at once there was a little give in them because they contained tiny pistons so first they took the weight softly and then they settled down just a little it was a bit like a smaller version of when the lift from the ward has almost reached the ground floor but not quite and it does one last little drop but is jouncily caught by the lift cables that I once saw hanging down when it was being repaired by Tim Horton of Eversholt and Harry Barnes who had a missing left index finger a soft settle of wheels and Jim was away but I was airborne I was buried in solid happiness I was galloping galloping happily galloping.

Even with everything that happened afterwards of Jim-joy this for me was like Lise being wrapped rolled up in her tight grey blanket and still remains one of my highest moments of pure yippee.

I had experienced wheelies once or twice before for the ambulance men always wheelied me backwards up their ramp when they took me into the non-emergency ambulance when I was still conscious not choking and needed to go to the hospital but I didn't count that as a real wheelie a real wheelie had only happened with flippety flip young Sister Clare a few weeks before the cake when she was rushing me along and it wasn't for my delight although I remember I whooped and she noticed and said Like that do you?

Over all the years of my life I had dreamed meaning I had had intense hour-long dreams at night of going fast fully under my own control and when I was littler new to the ward and more my mother's sweet horse this dream speed was a gallop across an endless grassy plain a gallop across an endless white African Savanna populated by familiar poster-animals but once I grew up a bit it became a specially designed turbo wheelchair that I could control with just my right hand which all my secret exercises had made full of strength and exactitude whee-ee-eee toward the horizon with nothing to hit or harm but some markings on the ground to give me a real sense of speed and running antelopes and zebras to overtake for fun and then when I was going fast as could be I dreamed my way up into a perfectly controlled wheelie.

For at least the rest of the game which I tried to follow because I wanted Jim to win even though they changed ends and he was at the far end of the long corridor for the remaining game time and then perhaps half an hour afterwards I was too happy to be all that conscious of what was going on around me I was too happy to be rational a rational creature but when I became a little more sober I began to try to think about regaining inner balance and I said to myself I counselled Elliott that what had happened had been a great great moment but I must not be so greedy as to expect life to bring me many more such or perhaps any more such.

It was not that I hadn't known even as Jim was walking away from me that I I I was too excited and that this was a perilous thing for me because soon I wouldn't be excited any more but would just be back to being normally there with myself and what was in front of me with my head to the left and only be able to lift my right hand half an inch but apart from that I wouldn't be able to change anything and so I knew quite quickly I needed to watch myself meaning both watch me being whee-eee-eee and all excited but also watch that I didn't let landing back on all four wheels make me sad when there was no good reason to be sad nothing had changed except potentially everything.

I still needed patience lots of patience but now I needed it to wait for something not just to wait for the end of every something meaning death my death.

I knew even as I was galloping galloping happily galloping that it was better for a horse to slow itself and canter and then trot slowing down to walking pace than to be pulled up abruptly by a rope around the neck or injure its delicate hooves by putting a fetlock in a pothole accordingly I looked out of the window and down across the courtyard with a firm purpose to bring myself back to myself and my expectations back to something like what was likely to happen rather than the dreamworld of fantasies of speed and of perfect control that the Jim-morning had brought me.

I thought at first I wanted and needed something to happen to distract me specifically an eruption of the unforeseen and so volcanic beauty of the natural world meaning a bird a crow a robin or a sparrow even a sparrow to land on the window sill and give me a pure object of a long while's looking though really what I needed was the strength to contemplate the absence of those bone-shapes and feathers and that black eye facing me shinily and that other eye away from me quite as if seeing me and not seeing me were the same thing.

As I was a lucky boy and was so even before the arrival of Jim I was able instead of experiencing a beauty-eruption to remember with exactness one of the many previous eruptions of beauty that had been witnessed by me by or beside the window sill and to which some of the gradually rain-washed-away droppings of the birds bore brown or black and white streaky witness and from all of these seventy three volcanoes I narrowed it down to two because they were the most powerful in terms of lava a. the first arrival of the blue tit and b. the greenfinch that stayed so long.

I could not choose between them and so for a while I ended up with an agitated in-between bird that flickered from blue detailing to a myriad of greens from blue to greens and back before finally I calmed my surging heart to settle on the greenness of the greens of the greenfinch.

What can you think when out of the whole universe right in front of you small and light yet absolute and infinite in detail appears such a beauty of a bird that even a voice from behind you luckily not loud enough to scare it off Sister Clare saying Oh look a greenfinch and the name was a gift to me as much as the three and a half more minutes the green vision danced and fretted and eagered and preened in front of me I could not believe who could believe that I deserved so many feathers that overlapped in such a succinct way and that slid over one another in greens that were doorways to shy sly gardens of other greens that tree green had only hinted at.

It was not just that I had never seen anything quite so perfectly what it was no it was that I felt that by its being there I too was allowed fleetingly to participate in perfection because my eyes my gorgeous-seeing eyes were able to see the details in the details of the greenfinch at the same time as seeing the greenness of its greens and as much as it was outside on the window sill above the radiator so much more was it inside my eyes and so creating a perfect greenfinch forever in my head.

I was looking at it and looking at my looking at it and it was being looked at even if it did not understand it was being looked at this greenfinch in my head that had made an eternal window sill for itself alongside all the other window sills that now plainly lacked greenfinches but drew miraculous grandeur like Mahler's symphonies both from that lack and from the new possibility of the eruption of a doorway into infinite green detail.

But I watched it not just as a series of eternal light effects on my eyes but as a living thing that all on its own was its own own that was just as important to it as mine on the other side of the windowpane was important to me.

I was very aware of the windowpane separating us not only because the glass of it and the dirt layer of it made the vivid bird slightly less vivid but because it was winter whereas in summer the window would have been open at the top where the oblong-shaped mini-window within it was situated and that would have meant that I could have heard any singing the greenfinch was doing but as things were with the window not open I could only guess because the bird's little beak was shut and its throat wasn't puffing or huffing that it the bird was silent and that even had the mini-window been open the only bird I would have heard would have been another out-of-sight singing bird.

The greenfinch was such a complete statement of a visual theme and all its variations there in front of me its wings were so apposite in how they fitted back into its body and its feathers each of its feathers so unique in itself and yet such a necessary contribution to the flight structure that I wished to be able to join the Sisters in seeing it as God's handiwork but I knew it was something even more miraculous than that it was something that had greenly happened not because it was willed or wanted as an iridescent background to salvation purgation and damnation but was a purposeless purpose not in the beginning was the word but in the middle was the bird.

Before Jim the greenfinch was the greatest thing I had seen and I still had not really seen Jim.

After and through the memory of the greenfinch I began to see what had been around it when I saw it meaning the bricks sky and windows opposite and also at the centre the tree and because I saw the tree I knew I must be getting back to myself and away from the greens.

A few minutes more of sitting looking at the tree had calmed me down almost as much as they always did and I began consciously to explore the thought that although I was feeling what I was feeling about Jim the tree was still a tree and the tree was still feeling what it was feeling or not feeling what it was not feeling and although I probably could not affect it it could affect me by being an exemplum for me of a thing with roots that is given a place in the world either by landing or planting and that whatever happens to it the tree has to endure in that place and so as I often thought I thought then in comparison with the tree I was a really lucky mobile thing that got to travel all over even to the Arndale Centre where the tree would never get to be but I unlike the tree was only mobile from place to place in space because I didn't have the mobility of seasons of green leaves in March and brown leaves in October and no leaves or just a few in January maybe though this this arrival this him this Jim was my season my Spring.

I was good at this and I knew I was good at this for I had been doing it for years suppressing myself calming myself not over anything half as exciting as this as Jim as a wheelie but on past days when I had found myself raging at a painful change by Sister Penelope or the pain and unfairness of Charlie's fists the view of the courtyard was not as accommodating or placating or suitable as the white wall and its whiteness but when as now it started to look too much like a racetrack and I could feel the wheels of my wheelchair clattering over the gaps between paving stones I was able to close my eyes and let the red-purple-black or orange-green-red or blue-black-brown or whatever colours I saw there give me the comfort of not being specific but still around the edges of this on this day like a halo was the not-to-be denied glory of the possibility of a new friend.

It took me several hours of hard looking to bring myself down to something roughly like my usual state and even then the slightest corridor sound that might be attributed to Jim was enough to set me back half an hour.

I knew that for him the moment had ended probably even before the moment ended for he was a very present boy and in that he was a lucky boy but I also knew that sometimes the things or people that are most important for our future exist for us for a while in a quiet unnoticed way like a disease without symptoms like a small benign or malignant tumour that exists and is significantly there long before we become aware of it or aware quite how long already it has been a quiet growing presence in our life.

The sky before and after lunch did its best display and I saw rising up above the opposite window and flat roof of the building opposite a spectrum that went all the way from low down red-and-orange to high up star-pricked violet-and-blue and I was in a crepuscular how happy I was when I learned the word crepuscular from a comment by Humphrey Carpenter my favourite radio presenter describing a song by Schubert I was in a crepuscular light before the gong was banged and Sister Eliza came with her snuffling nose to wheel me in towards the supper soup I had been smelling for half an hour and had correctly identified as leek and potato a midwinter favourite.

After nine times half an hour of this effort I was a different retrieved person far less likely to see dreams of unlikely days in front of me when what was really there was the texture of the surface of soup into which after the spoon had dipped and lifted a spoon-shaped divot was left with creases up the sides and the colour was exactly that of a pale-green angora sweater that flu-filled Sister Eliza used to wear over her grey-blue habit when the heating was broken in fact I think she kept it on the premises in the Sisters' Office for that exact purpose because I am guessing she did not want to be seen in it anywhere else or by anyone else except undiscerning children oh the little vanities of nuns!

Jim was far off to my left as he had been far off to my left at breakfast but he was not silent as he had been at breakfast because other children Charlie Glen Roger Gavin were talking to him or rather talking at him and into him as they tended to do when they were curious and fixed upon something meaning somebody new for although Sister Britta had announced very clearly and directly that morning that Jim did not speak that didn't really mean anything to us because communication was so many other things and what was being tested out now was Jim's vocabulary in other words his nods sounds smiles frowns raspberries farts etcetera and I listened as eagerly as any of the children immediately around him at the far end of the near table trying to prompt him with questions tickles strokes and kicks.

He was alive vividly alive full of mischief and quite prepared I soon learned to stroke back when stroked and to kick back when kicked beneath the table and this mimicry was wonderful to me because it suggested Jim learned very fast and that he could perhaps be trained I mean encouraged to respond in certain ways to certain stimuli that weren't given to him by grown-ups.

From the way he was responding over supper I very much got the idea that Jim had been in situations like this many times meaning that he hadn't come to us direct from a loving family home where his every nuance was known instead Jim seemed quite used to being surrounded and pecked at by lots of birdlike children oh I knew then he was an institutional boy just like the institutional boy I had myself started to become all those nine Christmases ago and he had surely hadn't he also gone through a series of institutions and found a way his way to survive in each of them because if he had come straight from his mother and father's home would Jim not have been weeping on this evening and if he had not come from another place like this wouldn't he have been flinching and confused or fighting and angry and so raging at blindness and muteness and at their being taken advantage of?

Still I thought the others particularly Charlie who I knew was sitting opposite Jim perfect for kicking him under the table the others should be more gentle with him for they didn't know couldn't be sure he wasn't feeling entirely orphaned at this moment.

I had seen it many times the awful awful bewilderment of a new child at a supper that wasn't just a single table with known family faces around it but two long tables with odd strangers with jaws that jutted and teeth that showed in lopsided mouths and forks and spoons going into them at all angles these strangers who didn't look like mummy and daddy and whoever else brother and sister and I had seen new faces new features look at me look at me in particular and then collapse into a wet pile of eyes and nostrils and many-many mouths for when orphans cry they cry from extra mouths that appear just for the purpose of saying all at the same time in a chorus No no I want to go home Take me home I don't want to stay here This isn't my home You're not my family I don't know who you are I want to go home I don't like it here I don't like it! Ah the song ah the song I have sung so many times Take me home daddy please please I don't belong here and they look at me the new orphans or at Jeremy and they think to themselves of themselves I don't belong here where they tie naughty children up in knots like these horrors Let me out Let me out! Orphans newly-made cry in a way that is in my sadly far from limited experience quite quite different to other children because other mothered-fathered children cry toward the world as if the world might hear and act whereas orphans cry as if they were the world as if they were the world crying in the full knowledge that there is no-one and nothing to hear them but the moon which appears some months in the top left-hand corner of the courtyard window and of my winter vision nothing but the moon to offer comfort and that the moon is entirely comfortless and is known in fact as a white image of total comfortlessness just as orphans are and know themselves to be a pure image of total need of motherly fatherly comfort that is not coming never coming.

The figure who should bend down warmly to say to them words between curtains of hair that tickle their left cheek consolingly and flick across their right cheek correctively with curlicues of warm breath that may smell of wine or cheese or other adult foods but which rises over a tongue that figures motherly and can say words that enter the ear of a child as soft perfect shaped keys made of sleep-marshmallows like the others eat after Lent and up into this space where cheeks bow down and nostrils hearken the child who is not an orphan can cry their worst of want their want of what but worship?

Worship me mummy.

Every child is Jesus for a while but every orphan is a single piece from a jigsaw puzzle the rest of which is somewhere else and so wherever it is is itself entirely ruined and frustrating although jigsaw pieces with four sticky out bits fat nubs often look like they are in fact Jesus being crucified but the piece of the picture on that jigsaw piece may only be cloud-edge and sky or artificial blue and the orphan will spend useless hours of years of hours worrying over what complete painting or photograph they should form part of.

I have seen in front of the doors of the lift as they finally closed I have seen little Jesuses be turned by the gap becoming a dark slit and a number counting down from 3 to 0 turned straight into jigsaw pieces I have seen and then heard them start crying as sons and daughters and finish crying as orphans not seen it because I chose but just because I was left facing in the direction of that event that atrocity by the Sister who went through the gate and to the lift in the direction of that event that really no-one should witness.

Of course I would have turned away if I could for who would want to witness such a thing as I did for example with Kurt and Lise who I think as far as I know is still standing on the surface of the moon staring in a gaze at the long black downwards slit where the mother used to be and the 2 counting down to exactly zero via 1 which still I suppose gave her Lise hope because a number counting down can always count up but zero remaining zero for the rest of the month and then added to the zero of the next month then doubled and redoubled slower every time but still only ever adding up to zero that form of arithmetic is hopeless. Hope is electricity on the surface of the moon but an orphan's heart soon becomes a fat crucifixion. Jim at supper was not like this and I have thought of the parents too descending in the lift accompanied by the decreasing numbers and by Sister Britta with her light blue eyes and hooked nose and her grey-blue habit and white wimple who will almost certainly touch an arm and say Pray for strength but is still herself at that moment reducing a relationship of love to zero and afterwards watching them the orphaned parents walk out into the car park and drive off down the road past other people in other cars who don't know what the people in this ordinary car here just did to someone small who didn't deserve it.

Drive moonfaces drive in a circle and come back and take your child away home.

Sister Britta had been the one who was the zero for Kurt and Lise's father who came by himself because I heard Sister Eliza tell Sister Penelope he could not cope without the mother and I heard Sister Penelope reply It's a terrible thing.

I do not know what kind of car moonfaces drive but I know their walk. It is like death and I have seen that too.

When someone a child is dying their breath bounces off the ceiling off the ceiling back to them back to them until it doesn't like a black ball that is thrown against a wall and caught until it is dropped thrown ball-like thrown up and every moment of throw breath-throw is a spasm.

I have lain beside this when it was behind a curtain and when it was not behind a curtain and when I was not facing the other way and when I was facing the other way and sometimes I feel I have caught the ball in my mouth although it is always difficult to know which throw is the last throw sometimes I caught the ball and swallowed so now today I have five black balls in my stomach Keith Nancy Valerie Torin and Finn in that order of arrival and also of death and I knew laughing Jim would never be one of them that I was far more likely to end up in his stomach but I hoped he'd catch me in his hands not a lucky blind catch but a skilled sound-listening catch because when someone is dying their breath bounces off bone because the ceiling is a membrane built of bone a tympanum and I as best as I could have caught as best I could the catch of their death and mouthed up the end of their ball-game Keith Nancy Valerie Torin and Finn.

But Jim was a strong and laughing one eating soup from a Sister's spoon and already making laughter happen in an area of the Refectory where before at the far end of the long table when it wasn't a lunchtime reading of Gerard Manley Hopkins or Saint Augustine there had only been Charlie telling his friends Glen Roger Gavin when Sister Britta wasn't there how he was going to kill them with a knife when he got his knife which would be a sharper knife and a bigger knife than Jack the Ripper's knife or where before when Sister Britta was there there had only been scrapes of metal on plastic because that far end of the near table was not a place of Princesses with their plots and hallelujah hallelujah like the middle of the far table or a place like the middle of the near long table of cooing and whimpering with Sister Mary Margaret and Jeremy.

The sound of Jim's laughter was round like the plastic bowls and it did not fly away from itself like a broken thing but turned always back in to gurgle and restart as a giggle and thus I knew for certain Jim had known love and Jim would always know love Jim would.

This was the down drop of my mood this thinking of deaths and I was aware in the middle of it of being happy that Jim was making other people happier than they would otherwise have been even though I was also envious that they were on his end of the long table that was already his end of the table and so got the luck of him and jealous that he was starting to know who they were whereas for him I was only the mention of a name and a slight physical obstruction avoided during an already forgotten time.

In Chapel in the evening Jim was behind me because I was among the wheelchairs of the tense and floppy ones up at the front in front of the altar and slightly down and to the left of the crucified Christ from the crucified Christ's point of view although He was in His wall-plaster-statue-form shown looking up and to his left which had once suggested to me when I first arrived that that particular direction was where God was for definite until I learned from sermons that God was everywhere and that the crucified Christ might just as well have been looking at the holes in his feet or at Sister Britta's bowed head or at his muscular legs or at me because God was according to the Sisters always and equally lovingly present in all these things which for a while made me feel really powerful and then after a while made me feel extremely anxious because there was no getting away from Him and would never be any getting away with anything.

After this I began to reason that if God was indeed always equally everywhere that that meant everything that was done was done by God to God and so the only person or thing that should get in trouble for whatever bad happened or naughtiness that was done was God and that the only person or thing for God to get in trouble with was God and because God getting angry with God was such a big high thing so much more important than were the sins of seventeen odd-shaped children sleeping in their beds off a corridor in a ward I began at this time to feel safe and covered in the way the roof and windows make me feel covered and cosy during a downpouring thunderstorm because if it was a Heavenly fight then the lightning was the blow and the thunder was the bruise and God's blows were fearsome but his bruises healed very fast.

There was no thunderstorm after Chapel at the end of Jim's first day and I was soon in bed without having seen Jim or heard anything more of him except Sister Britta's unanswered good night to him by name because everyone in every dorm gets a good night by name Good night So-and-So and God bless and everyone replied Good night and thank you Jesus so their last word if they died in their sleep and if they had not naughtily whispered after lights out their final word was a word of gratitude to our Lord which would wing them safely up to Heaven.

But I did not sleep after counting my blessings which even if there isn't a God is a good thing to do and so the hours and days of waiting and patience began the hours and days of being patient enough to have the patience of a fisher a fisher of men a man-fisher a fisherman. That period began because it had to begin and there was no other way for it all to happen.

And my waiting began that night when I should have been doing something else i.e. sleeping because that second night in Dorm 1 full of emotions I later after much thought and word-hoarding came to call bleak excitement and exultant agony that night I found myself quite unable even to close my eyes for when I tried to close my eyes they were immediately filled with noisy imaginary Jims saying Hello and offering to push my wheelchair wherever I wanted my wheelchair to be pushed so in order to calm myself down I kept my eyes open and looked sideways through the metal bars of my cot toward the bars of the radiator these the two sets of downward lines overlapping in a very familiar but always extraordinary rhythm of thin and thick far and near and compared to the Mahler or Sibelius whiteness of the white wall this jink-jink-jink was Stravinsky or Steve Reich.

The blinds were closed but some light from outside came through the gaps between them and more dropped beneath onto the window sill and this light was a combination of the pale yellow light of the security lights in the car park and the pale blue of moonlight.

I was easily able to tell the moonlight's contribution apart because it was the only element that varied and how fast it changed told me how madly the wind was pushing the high clouds and thirty three times on glorious nights of transport one of the Sisters had forgotten to close the blinds and I had been able to behold the moon clouds moon clouds moon directly.

Along with me in my dorm Dorm 1 were Glen Roger and still-alive Finn their beds were closer to the door than mine and each had a different degree of noise-making capacity Glen slept silently Roger had a nostril that clicked and Finn with his pointy skin snored like I imagined a lion snoring if its snoring was anything like its roaring Finn also suffered from sleep apnoea and so any halting of his breathing was possibly also a halting of his living but I had long ago overcome my frustration at Finn's nose and its noisiness and usually transposed his snoring when it was loud into the creaking of an imaginary sailing ship crossing a wide sea and sometimes his breath was the sail moving in its wooden fastenings and sometimes it was the hammock of a fellow sailor creaking as it swung back and forth with the rocking of the sea waves as we journeyed onwards purposefully through the oceanic night and thus Finn's snoring had become for me an adventure story that often continued into dreams of exploring fantastic new lands as a horse or an able-bodied human being or as myself in my ordinary wheelchair pushed by someone extraordinary I had never been able to identify before but who I now knew might just possibly turn out to have all along been Jim just Jim not properly seen or known.

These Glen Roger and Finn were my companions on my night-time crossings of the completely strange sea of bedsheets and light effects and Radio 3 in the distance sometimes forte enough for me to hear and also occasional screams from other dorms from Jeremy usually for no-one in our dorm was a horror-artist not like Jeremy.

For most of this clear night the moonlight was constant and my watching that wasn't as it sometimes was a watching for moths was mainly a watching of the things my mind saw in what my eyes saw because there was nothing else to see and so I saw the patterns of a giraffe's neck cracking throughout the darkness of the ceiling and the ripple of a zebra running behind a radiator but sometimes at other times my vision was real enough to be a moth and a moth once or twice a month landed on my forehead or my nose-blur and I lay there keeping my head still and not blowing out through my mouth because there seemed nothing else to do I didn't want to hurt it or scare it or try to eat it with it being so close up I couldn't see the pattern on its underwings but I could see the outside light coloured a different way as if I were suddenly completely in a moth-made world of warm greys and golds that were silvers and silvers that were if I looked closely enough bravely bronze so that even when the moth had flown off I still saw the moonlight as mothlike or mothlight.

It was anyway mothlike the moonlight when the clouds made it flutter and the hours of discomfort became an infinity of sensual comforts because I felt lucky just to be able to see anything when I knew how many blind people there are in the world not to mention those who can see but fail to see just as the Sisters pity all those who might know Jesus' grace and love and yet fail to do so even though it's right there in front of them and all around them if only they would have the humility to open themselves to it and in their voices the Sisters I could always hear their sorrow and in their faces I could see their pride that at least all of us us children would not miss out on the wonder and the blessèd relief.

Jim's face was the new thing I saw that night even though I had never properly seen Jim's face and until the light began to change into great big soft balls that rolled around the ceiling possibly sockballs I was smiled upon and promises were made in a voice different from my mother's voice which usually spoke in the watches of the night for the wishes of the night especially when I had been placed in one position and it wasn't comfortable or was truly painful and no Sister came all night as they usually did to turn me onto my other side so that my vertebrae didn't climb or sag too much one way or the other because always in the moonlight I was very bone-conscious and therefore pain-conscious and remembered the skeleton hanging in the corner of the doctor's surgery when I was little and someone talking about the future of my body which was a future of perfect bones being pulled into unorthodox shapes by overenthusiastic muscles that was the word the doctor said she preferred instead of spastic overenthusiastic.

I thought when I was little that the hanging skeleton was from a patient who had died and that in order to become a real doctor you had to have in your office the skeleton of someone you had killed to remind you to try not to kill anyone else and in order to get that skeleton you probably wanted to kill a patient with pretty bones so of course I was terrified that because my bones were perfect I would be handed over to a medical student.

In my dream that night I became convinced that my skeleton and the once-or-twice-a-month moth and the moonlight were of the same substance and this I think must mean I did fall asleep for a while in a dream of airborne vertebrae and moonlight condensing into scapulae those most winglike bones and then towards dawn the huge buffets of soft light rolling around started to become smaller and smaller until they were the size of lolling heads then the sockball then the size of Sister Cécile's fingertips pretending to be raindrops in Incy Wincy Spider and finally the room was light enough at this time of year for me to know Sister Britta would soon be telling us to Rise and shine Rise and shine always twice for each dorm.

Although I could not rise and like Glen Roger and Finn get down on my knees for prayer I did shine because there was a possibility that that day would be the day I would establish meaningful contact with Jim but the excitement and delights of an expectant night were not to be dismissed just because an exceptional day might bring major joys and on the third day my mood was still very much one of continued wakefulness meaning sleeplessness rather than normal daytime being-awake for I remember I felt as if midday was just very bright moonlight and later at midnight I felt as if my eyesight was powered by the sun so I didn't lose or lack anything because nothing happened with Jim in fact I gained hours of useful thinking time.

I waited as nothing happened and then all of a sudden nothing happened again but if I am good at anything I am good at nothing meaning I am good at being where or on the fringes of where nothing is happening or anyway where nothing seems to be happening because something really is always happening even when it seems to most people who do more than me that what is happening is nothing and I am definitely excellent at living with achieving nothing no gift no assistance and so the third day after Jim arrived was less eventful than the day preceding because there were Craft Room activities and no game of Sockball and I was left facing the white wall by Sister Cécile.

In some ways I was glad to have a little time to think about all that had happened so far because my life was already a different life perhaps only slightly but perhaps I hoped as I sat and looked perhaps different in a big way. I sat and looked and listened out for Jim who I did not often hear but when I did seemed happy in the rhythms of his footfalls.

The light of the wall changed colour the shadows moved the gong banged there was lunch of mashed swede in front of me and then inside me with Jim far off to my left then again the wall but greyer.

I cannot deny I felt my disappointment arising in the evening during Mass when Jim was silently responding behind me not that he could do anything then beyond performing the ritual standing up and sitting down and kneeling I could not hear him getting anything wrong or being guided or corrected so probably he'd been a Catholic all along but I was sad that the day was closing before another event had taken place and then it was toothbrushing Good night and Thank you Jesus.

My time was different though during this time of the third day and night because it was now purposeful and this because it was time between one significant event and another significant event for I knew I would eventually see Jim's face and probably some time after that he would encounter me as something slightly more than an obstacle though slightly less than a person.

It was indeed on the fourth day that the first of these events the face-seeing took place which means I don't really have to think back for much longer to the third day although I did see two crows trying to kill one another or so I thought and several ground floor children out in the courtyard playing kiss chase before they were stopped by ground floor Sisters.

And it came to pass that on the morning of the fourth day there was another game of Sockball but in this one Jim was on the other side to Charlie Jim was on Chapel United and I was facing the window. The sockball did not come my way during the second half when Jim would have been in goal down the end near me because there was no second half and this was because of what happened during the first half up the echoey far end and which I heard badly and had to reconstruct later because what happened was Charlie thought he had scored a goal against Jim and Jim the goalie insisted he hadn't because he Jim had stopped the sockball with his chest and it had failed to cross the line in the lino which Jim could feel very well with his big bare feet but at this juncture Charlie became furious became Charlie as knife-Charlie i.e. as Charlie really is and not Charlie when he's being nice to children who have just arrived and Charlie screamed You're blind You're blind and I can see It was a goal I can see and you're blind and it was a goal! I knew no-one would side with Jim or risk disagreeing with Charlie in fact because of course they always let Charlie score the first goal so he would be more likely to be happy and non-violent for the rest of the game but being new Jim did not know even this basic thing and so Charlie began to scream and Jim it turned out was not the kind of boy to change his mind just because he was threatened and all through this I was wincing because like all the others I knew what it would mean long-term for Jim if he became someone who Charlie hated and who Charlie wanted to stab with his new knife when he got it but at the same time I knew that a Jim who was playing all the time with Charlie as he had been since the second day was a Jim who was less likely to become friends with me therefore I was rent in twain by opposing forces of what would be good for Jim and what would be good for me.

The others playing the game with Charlie and Jim including Gavin Finn and Roger wanted the goal to be awarded to Charlie so the game could continue as usual for they knew the real score of the game was really always the score minus the gift-goal to Charlie but Jim shook his head No and kept shaking his head I know this because Finn and Glen later acted it all out for one another.

Charlie then suggested a running race to decide if it was a goal or not and this sometimes happened if no-one could agree. The two who most disagreed ran from Chapel goal line to Lift goal line and the winner was right but of course Jim was blind and Charlie firstly didn't expect him to agree to the race and then secondly made him go on the side of the long corridor where Kurt and his filing cabinet were and even though the long corridor was easily wide enough Kurt's feet did stick out as an obstacle behind where his knees kneeled and after Finn said Ready Steady Go Charlie tried to win but Jim I heard afterwards was really fast and was really in the lead although no-one was foolish enough to cheer for him against Charlie so they just cheered generally and hoped Jim would work out it was really for him.

Yes everyone said Jim was in the lead running well but Charlie was close enough to run across behind him just as they were approaching Kurt and Jim went sprawling forwards as if he was flying and what I'd heard before from my position was Ready Steady Go and cheering and slapping of two pairs of bare feet on lino one pair faster than the other and I had been cheering for Jim but silently so I could hear all this better and then I heard one pair of footfalls stop although the cheering did not react quickly enough to stop too because by running across behind Jim Charlie tripped him and made him fall headfirst so that the next thing I heard after the two sets of footfalls became one was a huge thump of skull against hollow metal against grey filing cabinet against Kurt's land and I knew instantly from the exact sound of it that it hadn't been Kurt's head but Jim's and it hadn't been in a cosy dent but had been edgy. Oh God.

Thump followed by silence followed by Charlie finishing the race and cheering himself right behind me but no-one cheering with him because they were looking at fallen tripped up Jim and wondering if he was dead just as I was wondering and fearing with deep terror because he might have a weak skull because his fallen body was completely still as one of the boys and later Finn said it was Finn alone and Gavin said it was Gavin and Finn together they or he ran to fetch a Sister from the Craft Room but Sister Cécile had already run past me to my left after coming through the wooden gate like a grey-blue shadow full of concern because although she had been in the Sisters' Office and not watching she could still hear and tell when sounds were emergency.

And now was when the fourth day become important because Jim had cut his forehead very badly and blood was already flowing out faster than it had even from Micky's wall-banging head.

Finn or Finn and Gavin together brought Sister Eliza sniffing along from the Craft Room and together Sisters Cécile and Eliza began to carry Jim who was fully unconscious straight towards the day bed in the Infirmary behind the Sisters' Office.

They would pass directly behind me and as they approached I could terrifiedly hear or imagine I heard the tickling tap of blood drops on the lino and when they went behind me I saw in confirmation first over my right shoulder then over my left Jim's face with eyes closed and a half helmet of blood reflected quite clearly against the darker parts of the glass where the branches of the wych elm and the red brick wall opposite made the window a better mirror and I saw Jim's beautiful defeated noble cheated face as if he were a Christian slave an enemy of Darius who Darius had ordered be thrown into the lion's den and who had not escaped through virtue and God's grace as did Daniel because he was found blameless before Him but who had died bloodied although innocent. But was he dead?

After this many things happened all at once and very fast firstly with phone calls and the other Sisters running towards and then away from the Office while many of the children gathered to look down at the blood on the floor not that they hadn't seen blood before but they always found it exciting either in its brightness or in the story it told of recent violence.

Charlie was grabbed by the arm and hurried away by Sister Mary Margaret to the Infirmary where I didn't hear but knew he would be forced to apologize to Jim and around and behind me some of the unsupervised children started to become excited by the blood and the three Princesses Beauty Lovely and Pretty began to touch their fingers to the floor and to apply the blood as lipstick because they were always after anything that could make them look even more beautiful and princess-like meanwhile Charlie in the Infirmary started to wail and say he was sorry which meant I thought that Jim was looking like he'd been killed and two men arrived in the lift and came through the wooden gate only one of whom I had seen before that being Ludvik the Caretaker and they went straight up to the blood and then returned back to the Sisters' Office so I knew they were related to one of the phone calls.

Finn and Gavin were now fighting and of course I was still facing the window when chocolate-smelling Sister Mary Margaret led Charlie behind me towards the Chapel of true contrition with his upper arm squashed by her tight right fist the Chapel where Charlie would be required to pray for Jim's recovery. I'm sorry I'm sorry he said as he walked past me and then past Kurt whose land at this hour was not yet completely blood-drenched.

Sister Mary Margaret must have sighted the blood on the Princesses' lips because I heard her tut and say Filthy little harlots then tell Charlie to stay put right where he was and then ran as I've never seen her run back to the Sisters' Office from which a furious Sister Britta came with Ludvik the Caretaker and he looked again at the blood on the floor and she looked at the spinning children play-fighting children crying laughing standing staring children but especially right behind me with their beautiful round pink faces at the Princesses and thrice her hand was raised and thrice it came down in wrath and fury at which the glee of the Princesses did turn to grief.

I was lucky to escape chastisement because while they had been applying more lipstick a few moments earlier I had made my sounds of Over here and wiggled a little and had pouted my lips meaning Me too me too and Princess Pretty and Princess Lovely had just touched my bottom lip with their flat-ended forefingers to start putting it on so even if he died I had at least received the taste of Jim's blood but my back was to Sister Britta when she arrived and smote the harlots and I had licked off and swallowed the little blood the two Princesses had applied before she Sister Britta or anyone else had a chance to see it.

Charlie was cuffed around the head by Sister Britta who took him over from Sister Mary Margaret and pulled him toward the Chapel in which I knew he would be expected to spend the rest of the day on his knees contemplating the fires of Hell meaning the punishment awaiting all sinners for he was a black-hearted sinner I heard these words some of Sister Britta's favourites when she was in the mood to terrify and Sister Cécile came out of the Sisters' Office to fetch away the three Princesses who couldn't go in the Chapel she found because Charlie the sinner was already in there with Sister Britta and God's wrath both so she took them to the Girl's Bathroom first then a few minutes later to their dorm Dorm 7 far up the long corridor and then left past the toilets meanwhile the ambulance still had not arrived but Ludvik the Caretaker had fetched a mop and bucket and begun to wash the floor but I knew from the splashes that hit me that the water was cold not scalding like the steamy lakes of Hell and some of the children lost interest now the blood was disappearing although they were glad it had been a special day and they could get away with small sins because Charlie's and the Princesses' were so egregious egregious being one of Sister Britta's fury words along with heinous appalling atrocious and mortal all of which I felt applied to the evil that was Charlie who I even then began to work to try to forgive.

By the time the ambulance and then the ambulance men arrived Kurt and me and Lise were the only ones left in the long corridor because Sister Mary Margaret had come back and called everyone away into the Music Room and Kurt's head was reassuringly thumping in its normal soft slow way whilst Lise made wailing noises as if together they were performing one of Schubert's songs and I was glad the beautiful Lise was there with her knees as I imagined white but tinged lime green beneath purple because she with her mystical sense of injustice always made me feel safer and closer to concern and care that was mother-like even if that concern and that care unfortunately weren't specifically for me but more for Lise herself and for the world in general.

Jim was taken away on a stretcher I later confirmed although that was what I heard two sets of booted feet beyond the wooden gate accompanied by Sister Eliza's sniffle and fpp fpp.

Lise stood up and walked along the corridor until she was right behind me to watch him go watch him through the tall wooden bars of the wooden gate and as she was right behind me I could see only the side of her face with the golden red ponytail behind it but I did see the ponytail swish from side to side with a shake of Lise's head rather than shoot straight up as it would have done if her face had dropped into her hands and I took this head shaking as a good sign because it was not despair like the ponytail upshooting that along with black knees would have been Lise's reaction to Jim's body being obviously dead so Jim as he was taken away was Jim still alive.

I rejoiced.

Jim was still alive and Lise at this moment I could tell by her ponytail was disappointed in the world and ashamed of it rather than horrified by it and despairing at us all having to live in such a fallen and constantly falling universe thump.

And then Sister Cécile who was the most musical Sister with the best touch on the piano began to play a hymn and I knew the non-corridor children were being encouraged meaning forced to join in with her singing to calm them down so that God's peace would once more come upon them and reign over the ward for she chose Let all mortal flesh keep silence which was and is one of my favourites for the tune as well as the words after this she went straight into O Deus ego amo te because we children were always reassured by the Latin that is by the words being in a language most of us did not understood although I had made a little progress and Lise quieted to listen and Kurt thumped only once per minute in mourning for his people and so peace overwhelmed the ward and I was left to consider blood both what it was and what it meant not Christ's redeeming blood with which I was more familiar than with almost anything else that existed or didn't exist but with Jim's blood a little taste of some of which was now inside me becoming my blood too.

At that time I did not know what blood was made of or what it did except redeem the sins of the world and before this incident I had just thought of blood as a simple substance like red paint and that if you mixed one lot of red paint with another lot of red paint like Ted and Lee mixed white paint with white paint all you got was more red paint but I felt then with growing certainty that I was and would become a different better stronger braver boy with some of Jim's blood working in my body for because it came from him how could it fail to make me more like him? I was a little worried his blood might make me go blind or make my eyesight a little less good and because my eyesight was the best thing about me physically if not ultimately this was not a small terror but over the following hours and the next day I tested them my eyes by trying to see the far-off things I could normally see through the window i.e. edges of clouds and eyes of birds and I was reassured they were just as good my eyes as they had been before the blood meanwhile I overheard some of the others on this the fifth day passing alarming rumours although no-one not during supper no-one said Jim was dead but some said his brain had been mashed and if he ever came back he would not be with us but up on the third floor with the old and dying and others said that one of his eyeballs had popped forwards out of its deep socket and by a miracle of Jesus and of Charlie it was now seeing perfectly but only when it was out on its icky string and when they popped it back in his head Jim went totally blind again and yet others said Jim's personality had changed completely and he was a raging Apocalyptic beast who was coming back to take revenge on his mortal enemy Charlie.

Charlie was no trouble to anyone. All the time Jim was gone he did whatever the Sisters asked and even if they didn't ask volunteered to do extra plate clearing yes Charlie was gentle with the Princesses didn't tell Lise to shut up and stop crying and absolutely refused to have anything to do with the long corridor instead he was seen quietly entering the Chapel by himself and of his own volition but whatever he did or didn't do when the Sisters were around we all knew for certain he hadn't changed because after lights out in his dorm Dorm 2 he loudly boasted to Micky and I suppose Kurt though Kurt wasn't listening that even without a knife he Charlie was a killer who had tricked Jim into killing himself and he insisted he'd won the sprint and therefore the Sockball match.

Although I knew never to believe Charlie and never to trust rumours I was still in a trance of suspense for all of the morning of the sixth day because every hour that passed without Jim returning seemed to confirm that Jim's skull had really been Humpty Dumpty smashed and that we would never and I would never see him back on the ward again and during this time I was parked looking out of the window because I think the Sisters wanted to show they were being gentle and loving with all of us and so I watched seven birds land on the tree and fly off again and I watched raindrops make the window wet and then dry off leaving shapes on the glass where the humps and trails of water had been and although I feared Jim would never return I hoped and trusted and believed with meek and faithful certitude that he would resurrect.

And he did.

I had trained myself not to get excited when I heard the shonk of electricity as someone on a different floor pressed the lift call button and the motors started and the cables went tense and began to raise or drop the compartment because there had been too many times when the doors opened and the person who came through the wooden gate was just Ludvik the Caretaker with a lightbulb or Mrs Beatles the Cleaner with biscuits or the Priest with the word of God but even so I could not stop myself feeling that the times when I could hear the lift motor running and the times when it lay dead silent were different kinds of time for even a lightbulb or pack of digestives or slide-show was an event and meant something but not an event like this time when the doors opened and shortly before supper I heard the fillip of wheelchair wheels crossing the ridgy gap between lift compartment and ward floor and then Sister Britta who had been gone two hours spoke to say Welcome back and though she didn't say Jim's name I knew it must be him because no-one else had gone away to come back to be welcomed.

Why was he in a wheelchair? He was no use to me as an engine if he was in a wheelchair. Anybody could be pushed around in a wheelchair even a dead person but not many could push a boy around in a wheelchair.

These my first thoughts were horrible and selfish and I am still to this day years and years later ashamed of them.

Poor Jim I should have thought and very soon I did think exactly that Poor Jim I don't want you to have to be like me. Charlie didn't really paralyze you did he? You aren't useless are you?

All I could hear behind me as she wheeled him through the wooden gate and then along the start of the long corridor was Sister Britta explaining where they were and I was disappointed to hear her say And here's Kurt and his filing cabinet as if she was using the conjunction And because she had already said Here is Elliott at his window but she only chose to mention Kurt I think because she felt it was necessary for Jim to know where Kurt was so he didn't run into the filing cabinet again whereas I was a thing that moved around so shouldn't be included on the tour as sometimes priests and parents were shown around the ward And here is our beautiful Chapel etcetera but I felt immediately sad that Sister Britta had not said my name to Jim to give him another chance to take it in and associate it with this area of the ward.

If only I had been a fast runner or wheeler I could have gone ahead of Jim in his wheelchair to announce his return to everyone loudly and proudly during callisthenics with Sisters Cécile and Eliza in the Music Room instead all I could do was listen out for and then hear the sudden happy hubbub of sounds and hellos when Sister Britta said loudly I am glad to say that with God's grace Jim has returned to us A little battered and bruised so do be gentle with him please especially you Princesses Beauty Lovely and Pretty You can nurse him but gently all right girls gently.

I was not there to witness Charlie's face's reaction to Jim's return and I did not hear anyone talk about it later so I had to imagine it as a mixture of relief and fear and if I was being generous to him guilt also and disappointment but probably mostly fear fear of two kinds fear of what he'd done to Jim and fear of what Jim might do to him and although I did not overhear a description of the sort I needed of what exactly Charlie's face did and what colour it went when Jim was wheeled in this was mainly because what everyone was talking about was the big fight that would one day soon happen between Charlie and Jim either because Jim would want revenge on Charlie or because Charlie would want to make sure Jim knew that he knife-loving Charlie was the main pain-giver of anyone on the ward.

Sometimes in winter with the radiators too hot to touch and something in the kitchen like spaghetti cooking and sending warm steamy smells up the lift-shaft and a big piece of news and gossip like Jim's return and the Sisters getting flustered because there was mania zapping around that wasn't about Christ or Christmas Eve like on a full-moon-night sometimes when many many things were happening at once and the night outside was dark and the light inside seemed more yellow and flickery than usual then I really felt there was nowhere I would prefer to be in the whole world than the ward not even at home with my mother wherever her home was now either Canada or America because what everyone on the ward was sharing in that atmosphere of electricity and steam was so intense and special and so much to do with every single one of us even the rigid and floppy and silent ones even Jeremy even I knew to do with me.

I went to sleep the night of Jim's return the sixth feeling extraordinarily safe deep in the belly of the ship far out at sea rocking on the in-and-out up-and-down tide of Finn's snores and in the morning when Sister Britta told me to Rise and shine I felt I would make my most extra special effort to do just that in anticipation of whatever might or might not happen that day the seventh or might or might not be true in general about God's wishes for all of his creation or there being no God to wish anything about anything and after prayers I enjoyed the soft feeling of my clothes being put on by Sister Britta's hard horny hands even the woolly scrape of the jumper collar down over my nose that left my nose feeling hot and after Mass I tasted every mouthful of my especially sugary because Lent was starting soon Ready Brek but what followed this happy shining start was a quiet seventh day still at the window a day of no obvious events and no Jim.

Jim was recovering in bed because even though he was well enough to leave hospital he was not well enough to play Sockball or run or even walk around not for seven days which is what I waited as February approached March and we lived in the last of Ordinary Time as Christmas and the holy birth fell behind us and Easter and the redeeming death came into distant view beyond the prayers for Christian Unity.

It was enough to me or almost enough that Jim was alive and nearby where I might see him again in fact very soon because a working week and a weekend's wait in comparison to my years of hours on the ward were hardly more than a blink of a moment for in the past I had suffered i.e. a month of expecting my Christmas card which one year had arrived as early as December the fifteenth but another later year did not come until December twenty-ninth and why was I waiting because I knew it would eventually come the card because it always came in the end unlike my birthday cards and because I knew it would tell me so much about how my family was and who my family was although after the sixth name apart from my mother's signed Mummy and my father's signed Daddy there had not been a new birth for three Christmases and I did not expect the joy of any more than two younger and four older siblings.

Jim had changed time for me or changed my approach to time ever since he arrived for he had filled it with events events more significant than any since the day I was given into care by my parents apart perhaps from the deaths of Nancy and Valerie and so by making me expect important things to happen prestissimo one after the other he had made me feel the quiet in-between time as a slow wound that instead of healing did the opposite by opening and suppurating until it was no longer just a wound but a baby pink lesion with orange details like Tchaikovsky's Serenade for Strings a pink orange wound at the thought of the sight of which I became seasick.

When I saw when I had seen the volcanic greenfinch I knew immediately it lived in a different time to me and that for it for it for it every twitchy moment was in fact a stretchy minute and this intimation was confirmed by an interlude talk on Radio 3 halfway through the glorious recital of some piano works by Olivier Messiaen that interpreted the exquisite songs of birds for up until that point I had assumed that every animal on earth either on the window sill or in the tree and or on the Wild Animals of the African Savanna poster lived in exactly the same kind of trogging along time but now I had evidence because Jim's events had turned my time from stretchy to twitchy and it was taking a lot of hard looking for me to keep myself from exploding or more likely imploding and hyperventilating with birdlike impatience.

I was for those seven days of waiting for Jim however much I tried not to be a relentlessly restless cluster of iridescent chromatic notes seen through a crepuscular gateway and amounting thematically to a twitchy twitchy imperfect greenfinch of a horse of a boy in a wheelchair looking looking looking into calming whiteness whenever I could encourage Sister Cécile to leave me with the view that other Sisters treated as punishment for overexcitement but for four of those days I was by the radiator at the window and singing inside my throat God Save the Queen hoping that one of the passing others would hear me and go and fetch Princess Beauty or Princess Lovely or Princess Pretty as this was my way of asking for them because sometimes but very rarely they were able to interpret my sounds and eye movements and do things for me like wipe my nose or scratch my neck.

After seven days Jim was allowed out of his bed in Dorm 3 and on Sunday morning after Mass I heard him at breakfast surrounded by laughter and when later I was in front of the window overlooking the courtyard I became aware of his slow approach along the wall behind my back and far to my right in my peripheral vision beyond and behind Lise's empty floor space although this is exaggerating because I sensed Jim through sounds related to Jim before I saw him in the shape belonging to him because other boys namely later-to-die Finn and Gavin of the extraordinarily square head were trying to persuade someone to play Sockball and from the way they spoke to whoever it was I knew it could be no-one but Jim he didn't agree to join in but kept coming down the long corridor towards me and then disappearing for a while into dorms all along the right hand wall when he came to them.

I now know from what happened two hours or so later exactly what he Jim was doing.

Jim had been tricked once by Charlie and had run straight into Kurt's grey filing cabinet because he had not expected it to be where it was because filing cabinets are not usually left out on corridors and even though Jim must have heard Kurt's thumps he did not in the excitement and anger of the race for victory against Charlie remember exactly where it was so now in this quiet late morning time on his return to being out and about on the ward Jim was making absolutely sure he would not be tricked or injured again by making absolutely certain he knew where everything was every door and which way it swung open every bed or cot and whose it was and every chair and where it usually stood every object that could be known and what could be discovered about it from touch and probably smell.

And although Jim did not know it yet those objects would have to include my wheelchair and of course me in it because he was advancing along the long corridor and although on the opposite side away from the windows was coming towards where my back was facing and he would I knew because he had to eventually he would make his way to the end of the long corridor where the wooden gate stood and beside it the white wall that for no real reason was built out across the long corridor no reason except perhaps to prevent easy escape to the lift and to give me something at which to look when

I was not sufficiently calm yes I was sure Jim would eventually find the wooden gate and find or be told that he was not allowed to open it by pushing down the high wooden latch and then continuing on his meticulous exploration he would turn 90 degrees and be within a very few feet of where I sat apparently looking out over the radiator and the window sill through the windowpane but really looking with all my senses at nothing but him.

Oh joy and cause for rejoicing that I was that day so close to the radiator that there was not a big enough gap between it and my tense and wonky feet on their metal support pads for Jim to squeeze through without making contact with something and so just as I had hoped ever since he arrived on the ward thirteen days before I would at that moment become his blessèd obstacle and he in some way would have to deal with to encounter me to acknowledge me yippee-ee-ee I was ready for this I had sounds ready not only grunts that sounded as much like his name Jim as I could make them but clicks whistles and hums that I was thinking of hum-singing for example the theme music to the television programme Match of the Day which Sister Mary Margaret who was a secret supporter of Queen's Park Rangers F.C. sometimes had on in the Refectory when she was alone of a Saturday evening during the football season eating chocolates the naughty wee thing.

My mind was galloping galloping happily galloping ahead to the moment when Jim's right hand or the side of his right leg would first touch my chair or part of my body. I could have started making sounds just as Kurt was making thumps or Lise would have been making sobs if she had not been somewhere else but my tactic was not to make a noise until Jim touched my chair or my body because then he would know the sounds were a reaction to nothing but him and were not just sounds somebody always made and although there was a risk I would surprise or maybe even scare him I was willing to take that risk and so although I really quite badly wanted to whoop I held myself my ribcage and throat quiet and listened to the slide of his approaching feet going into Dorm 3 Dorm 2 and right behind me Dorm 1 my dorm when as I could have anticipated because I had been smelling the mince and potatoes from the kitchen in the basement below all was interrupted by the banging of the lunch gong and Jim had to walk back up the long corridor towards the Refectory along with everybody else hungry or not for food or not.

Sister Cécile came from the Sisters' Office and wheeled me efficiently in and I was patient at listening to the day-to-day ecclesiastical trials of Cardinal Newman and being fed small safe mouthfuls until everyone else had finished and I knew Jim was gone back to the long corridor. Sister Cécile wanted me to finish the four last mouthfuls but I was afraid Jim would have carried on exploring past the place where he would have met me as a blessèd obstacle so I tried to convince kind Sister Cécile that I wasn't hungry any more by closing my eyes and mouth just as I always did but I had been losing weight recently and strength too throughout the time of waiting for Jim and she was determined I would finish every last mouthful of the four so in a panic I swallowed as fast as I could too fast and of course started to choke but was rescued by just the right swill of water at just the right angle phew then Sister Cécile fed me a banana that I now think of as the eternal banana of doom because it seemed to last an eternity and to doom me to loneliness and Jim however slowly he had explored must be at least next to Kurt.

Finally finally in a terrible state truly reduced to a wretch of a boy of a horse Sister Cécile wiped my mouth clean with my faded yellow bib and gave me a final sip of water from the beaker then put it back on the pink hippo wiped my mouth again took the beaker the bowl and the spoon to the metal trolley against the wall beside the door came back removed my bib took it to the laundry basket put her hands on the handles released the brake and began to wheel me backwards the wreck of a horse out of the Refectory then stopped and began pushing me forwards round to the right as if we were going into the Craft Room but no another 90 degree right turn was made to bring us to the very end of the long corridor and it was only now I realized that even if Jim had explored his way past Kurt I would for the very first time as I was wheeled along towards him get a full glorious view of him Jim yippee-ee-ee yippee-ee-ee.

I did I saw him I did immediately see him and he was at the very far end of the long corridor and not halfway back up on the right hand side beside the windows Jim was as we wheeled snickety over the Chapel end goal line and past the Chapel doors on my right and Dorms 5 4 3 on my left Jim was miraculously still only at the wooden gate but with his back to me but not yet even having reached the sticking-out white wall hallelujah no other word.

On the other side of the wooden gate and talking to Jim in a patient voice through between the bars was Sister Britta and at first when I saw this I could only imagine what she was saying to him but as I came within hearing distance this began to mix with what she was truly saying to him which was No Jim I'm sorry We have a rule and it is a rule that I'm afraid we can't break or bend for any child not even a child as special as you Not even a blind child at which I heard Jim growl and shake the wooden gate and put his hand up to flip the wooden latch that released it above his head height and well above where I could ever hope to reach but Sister Britta's yellow hand was already there pressing down and thus although the wooden gate was never locked Sister Britta was teaching Jim that it was forever closed to him unless opened by a Sister.

If we wanted a Sister from the Sisters' Office we had to stand there and press the bell-button which I could have pressed if my chair had been positioned exactly and someone had held my hand out straight positioned to the right of the wooden gate and press and wait for a Sister to come in her own good time unless it was an emergency when we could should scream we should scream.

Whilst he was in my approaching-him sight but with his back to me I took in that Jim had a white bandage on the right side of his head and was wearing a green jumper the colour of pea and ham soup without the pink bits and orange corduroy trousers the colour of the orange corduroy trousers Torin used to wear before he died and which I later realized must be the same orange corduroy trousers passed on because they were distinctively darker towards the belt area and faded away the closer they got to the feet and Jim's feet as I noticed from twenty feet away were noticeably big and he wore no shoes or socks and his hands too were just the large and useful tools I had imagined not like my twisted tree roots at all but his long hair over the collar of his check shirt because I was now close enough two dorm doors away to make out the check pattern on the cuffs but his long hair outside the bandage was the colour of my hair light brown mouse brown no difference at all between us so we could have been brothers.

Sister Britta held on to the high wooden latch and explained again to angry Jim the rule about children even children as special as him not opening the wooden gate in fact children not even being allowed to touch the wooden gate without a Sister's explicit permission.

You know what explicit means don't you Jim? It means spoken out loud clearly by a Sister or a Priest. Now I know you're a good boy and you understand what I've said So take away your hand now and we can all be getting along with our day.

Jim Jim I wanted to cry out You don't know what you're doing Get back from the wooden gate or you'll suffer the terrible consequences but of course I couldn't say anything he'd understand I couldn't give him the gift of knowledge and I was still keeping all my sounds in as Sister Cécile quite as if nothing was going on wheeled me perfectly back to exactly where I'd been before lunch in front of the radiator close enough to feel its heat but not so close that I'd be scalded by it and Jim's face had half turned at the last moment so I saw his thin cheek but he had not turned to face me and hear me better though he must have heard wheels snickety over lino lines Jim was starting to turn or pretend to turn away from Sister Britta and in that last glimpse I saw his eyelashes I saw his eyelashes flinch.

Sadly but also excitedly I felt I knew what was coming next as Sister Cécile's footsteps walked away towards the Music Room because I had seen it many times in others and recognized the false ritardando movement away that stands as prelude to the allegro molto furioso of exactly what Jim did next which was grab the vertical wooden bars of the gate and start pulling and pushing at them not just as if to pull or push them open but truly in a solid attempt to destroy them at which Sister Britta who also must have spotted the ritardando and been expecting the furioso called for assistance from the Sisters' Office Sister Eliza she cried calmly Sister Mary Margaret she added even more calmly and both were there a few seconds of wood-slamming later. Of course the wooden gate when it opened opened outwards towards the lift and so when Jim heard the catch click and felt the three Sisters pulling against him he put all his strength into pulling to keep the wooden gate shut.

Three Sisters now while still pulling back called echoey down the long corridor for Sister Cécile who took several moments longer than expected to come back from wherever she'd just gone meanwhile I was impressed so much that I was astounded by Jim's strength at keeping the wooden gate shut and even more I was impressed and amazed at his ignoring what Sister Britta was saying about how he would be risking eternal damnation if he didn't Let go right this instant but Jim didn't and like Samson with long hair in Judges 16 he kept his strength against force and I could tell it would take cunning to beat him.

Please don't hurt Sister Cécile I thought when the footsteps eventually returned and her image passed across the window right to left but although Jim was strong in pulling he was not able to resist her tickling of him under the armpits and all it needed was this small weakening of his hold for the three Sisters to take their chance and pull back the wooden gate and then be through it and upon poor frantic Jim who I could hear wailing in frustration because I believe all he wanted to do was blindly explore what was beyond the wooden gate.

He hadn't wanted to escape the ward. Not I believe until that moment.

Four Sisters in grey-blue carried Jim away from the wooden gate and back up the long corridor away from me towards the Chapel and I felt the injustice of Jim being punished just as Charlie had been punished but for something for a sin completely opposite to Charlie's sin which was one of deceit and violence whereas Jim's sin was one of curiosity and self-protection because if he didn't know what was on the other side of the wooden gate he didn't really know where he was and if he didn't know that how could he be safe here as the white bandage over half his brown head vividly testified but the Sisters were absolute in imposing their rules and so yet again I had to look out of the window and console myself with the hope that the Jim I had started to learn to know was stubborn and consistent surely surely he would return to continue his exploration of the walls and rooms of the ward just as soon as his penance was done.

Because he was new and was being given a chance Jim's penance was the day of his sin plus one whole day therefore one and a half days.

And so after a waiting day of morning-window and afternoon-wall on the fourteenth on the fifteenth after rising and shining and praying and Massing and Ready Brek eating and being wheeled I was back in the exact same place waiting waiting for Jim to come down the long corridor just as he did indeed do and put his hands on the wooden bars of the wooden gate just as he did indeed again do watched by Sister Britta and Sister Cécile whose footfalls I had heard.

Jim put his hands on the bars and held them there a long while but did not try to destroy them then took his hands off and shuffled to the right towards me I heard the sideways slide of his bare feet on lino beneath the close-up breathing of Sisters Britta and Cécile who did not speak but who I was sure I could hear exchange a look about Jim of the We'll have to keep an eye on this one variety.

Jim was now only six or seven feet away from me and in those last few moments I waited in gratitude because the Sisters were walking away Sister Britta to the Sisters' Office and Sister Cécile back up the long corridor and unless there was another unforeseen interruption of some sort a choking or a fire alarm Jim would soon encounter me.

I wished for there not to be another interruption and my wish was granted.

I waited.

Jim came closer.

I kept silent.

Jim came closer still came into the far left of my peripheral vision green on top and blue below same jumper as before different trousers but the main part of what I saw was still the wych elm with traces of my face in its upper branches because I was at a slight angle to the radiator which seemed unusually hot that day but perhaps only because I was noticing it because I did not want Jim to be shocked by the heat of it although surely he like me he would feel its warmth at a distance in fact would already be feeling its warmth through the faded blue corduroy of his right leg.

Kurt gave a thump which reminded me we were not alone. I wished Lise could be there to see what was about to happen because I knew one day she would recognize its significance for me and for Jim and for all of us but she was absent perhaps mischievously perhaps not.

Jim's saltiness and his pepperiness and his meatiness were now there very close up and to my left and I could see his clean fingernails moving across the white surface of the white wall over the whiteness of it and when I really turned my eyes I could see up into his chin and the darks of his nostrils and the underside of the fringe of his already familiar brown hair.

My left hand was in its usual split-fingered place on the left arm-rest covered in black plastic with the texture of leather and so just exactly as I had blessedly hoped the first contact between Jim and me was when his ribby orange leg touched my left little finger at which moment just as I had planned I made my closest-to-Jim's-name sound but I had kept so still and silent had I been up until that moment that Jim hadn't suspected I was there and I suppose I must have made the sound too suddenly or loudly and really I should have started with a hum because the combination of flesh touch and Hnyhmm gave Jim such a shock that he twisted to the right and with his right hand at the perfect height smashed me right in the nose with his thick knuckles a punch almost as hard as one of Charlie's playful punches when what Charlie wanted to do wasn't really to punch you just to remind you that he could punch you whenever he felt like it because you couldn't move your arms to defend yourself.

I knew right away my nose would bleed because it often did and still does but I also knew my nose was not broken as it had been twice by Charlie and has been since once by a forward fall into a wall and once by Brother Patrick God forgive him.

Jim let out a sound that was the first sound he made to me and it did not say Sorry because he was a little slow catching up with himself and I might still for all he knew have been a chair so it was a sound that said from him to him What? meaning What are you? or perhaps just What's this? But even with his flying-sideways-in-shock hand Jim could tell the difference in feel between hard surface of furniture or filing cabinet and nose crunch and his next sound as his hand retreated and the realization got through to him was a grunt of fear that he had done something very like what he had done which is hurt someone smaller and weaker in an obvious way that would get him punished again.

His retreating hand went back to his chest I saw it make a fist above his heart and then it returned it flew out with his other hand but with soft extended fingers to try and find out whose nose or soft bit he had made go crunch and it was in this way that his hands alighted on my head and began to feel yes hair on a dome and ears yes to either side nose with wetness beneath it mouth and wet chin and then shoulders arms and shape of thin arms especially forked fingers on arms of chair then wheels and then Jim stepped back and smiled.

I have always admired the unembarrassed way blind people do things particularly the way they use their fingers to explore the faces of people they do not know it makes me very much wish I could do it too and makes me think there is something about being shy like I was and still am that depends upon seeing other people seeing you and if you've never seen this you never became shy in the same way instead you are bold and heroic with your touching of things even when there is a possibility they will hurt you or you will hurt them just as was the case now because when Jim's fingers came back and carried on exploring they picked up speed and spread a few smudges of the blood that was already flowing from my nose.

I could feel a fingerprint on my neck and suspected more were on my cheek and hand. Jim I think felt it too because he lifted his pinkened fingers to his face then sniffed them then licked them.

His blood was in me and my blood was in him yippee-ee-ee his blood was in me and mine was in him by accident yes it was true but it had happened and whatever else happened this could never be made to unhappen whatever the Sisters did.

After tasting it and knowing what it was Jim's hands came quickly back to my face to check gently roughly how much blood there was and of course in doing that made it worse by picking up more sticky flow and touching more places but at that moment despite whatever punishment or misunderstanding might and would take place I desired more blood to flood out of me flood out of my nose and mouth and ears onto the floor and then rise up around us covering coating cloaking us in a shield of armour that could keep out the Sisters and all other people and make of us a special sealed thing away from time and hurt and sin and death in other words a covenant protected by the blood and protected through the blood.

Jim did not speak words but of course Jim spoke otherwise and knew how to say I'm sorry simply and clearly by galloping down my arm with fluttering fingers until he came to my hand and grabbing my left and nearest hand with firm fingers and all of this from first touch to handgrab can only have taken five or ten seconds but for once I had no sense of time.

He found and held my left hand with fingers cupping my fingers and other hand cupping petalling both our hands but I was too bewildered and joyous to be able to take in which hand was which or even whose hand was whose.

Jim held my hand. And I squeezed a little to hold Jim's hand back I squeezed the way I did to shape clay into useless and ugly half-bowls with fingers I knew were limp like a girl's fingers they squeezed but did not challenge or combat his grasp as the hands of an angry bleeding boy in a wheelchair would have done and I had the thought and fear that Jim would think I was a girl probably one of the feeble ones who I did not encounter very often because they were usually in the Music Room girls like Grace Maria and Shirley draped in chairs wearing braces to keep their spines from disintegrating under the weight of their heavy heads and I was able to have this thought because the hand-holding went on and on perhaps because Jim thought he was comforting a girl he'd hurt so I squeezed as hard as I could to tell him I was a boy.

Jim pulled the top cupping hand back but I kept the other tight and even pulled him down a little and was able to look right up close into his face for the first time hallelujah chorus and see the sunken sockets where his eyes were not and the sharp angles of his forehead cheekbones nose and chin Jim's face was a strong injured face the face of a boy who wanted to go beyond the wooden gate without asking just as I wanted to go through and out and into the green the face of a boy with my perceptive blood already flooding inside him he kneeled down and put his other hand on and then under my right hand at which I made a sort of honk of joy he was bringing his face to me perhaps because he thought I was blind he was bringing it up close so I could feel it as he had felt mine but my hands couldn't lift that far not even when he tried to bring one up so he brought his head even further down towards me and put it face up under my right hand and I think anyone would say that even if he was still thinking

I might be a girl this was when Jim became my peppery and salty and meaty friend.

It was all curves and angles his face like a dozen spoons in a pillow-case the nose had a bump in the middle that felt like the dice the Sisters got me to throw or drop for Snakes and Ladders the cheekbones stood out as if they were doing the looking instead of the eyes which went in and in at the sockets and which I was afraid to touch in case I pushed too far and hurt Jim's brain.

Quite a few hairs were growing beneath the nose and the lips were not tight in a smile or grimace but relaxed as he let me explore more treating me kindly treating me blindly just as the blind treat others and just as the blind expect they too shall be treated.

It could not last of course it could not last it was too perfect to last and if my life could have ended at any moment even with all the moments that followed even the most precious moment of green and grey galloping vision on the greatest day I would have been happy for it to have been this one and would now looking back choose this moment because even though it did eventually end it did still last in our world in our time for a good while and so because it did once happen it will always in some good part of the past which is still definite because it once was it will still be happening and so Jim is forever offering his face and I am forever accepting it and the window reflects it all back at me looking at it against the darker branches and windows and bricks and Sister Britta the interrupter is still behind the wall that sticks out and she is still yet to see what she thinks she sees which is Jim's violence and sin written across my face in blood. But that blood was irrelevant blood because much more important blood was adding to blood in two places because his blood was in me and my blood was in him his blood was mine and my blood was his!

After a while though Sister Britta did come through the wooden gate and saw blood and misunderstood it and thus Jim was again dragged to the Chapel with now a reputation not only for being a difficult child but for being a violent child and being a difficult and violent child was only one off being an ungodly child and so two off being a Devil's child we had had a few of those before Charlie who even if you didn't believe in the Devil was a Devil's child but none of the others had been as bad perhaps because as I'm sure the Sisters thought the Devil knew he had to send a worse one than he'd sent before so as to test the Sisters' faith even more than he'd tested it already with Conor and Heavens preserve us Jemima.

I was left in ecstasy to await what I knew would come my way and which did come my way which was a big ginger-smelling rush of Sister Cécile and unearned unmerited sympathy and a rapid whizz not quite a wheelie up the long snickety corridor and round the corner to the left to the Boy's Bathroom to be stripped and have my face washed with cold water and scrubbed with a rough towel followed by a new shirt slightly damp on my chest a burning sensation on my upper lip and then to the Refectory for a spoonful of lavender-infused honey so as to make up for cruelty that was nothing but amity and for suffering that was grace.

I could not explain this even to Sister Cécile who knew my sounds better than any other grown-up almost as well as my interpreter Princess Pretty. I could communicate with lento sounds that I was calm and hmm sounds that I was grateful for the gift of honey but I had no sounds exact enough to point out injustice or to tell Sister Cécile to tell Sister Britta that Jim was a good and kind but strong and sometimes a little clumsy boy deserving not of their anger and punishment but of their love and praise.

What I was left with in the time after the first really meaningful communication with Jim was that I found myself living within a horn concerto of emotions like a Mozart confection including happiness love glee regret joy embarrassment and any sudden combination of these so not only joy for love but embarrassment for glee and also combinations of even greater complexity such as happiness for regret for embarrassment and joy for embarrassment for regret and of course it took me years to begin to understand and to name the giddy-up syncopations and melodies that were only going on inside me but seemed all around me as if I were the radio in the Sisters' Office and Sister Cécile was playing Radio 3 on me so loud I made everything around me vibrate and I too vibrated with everything vibrating.

The wych elm too had explored Jim's face with every single one of its tender-ended twigs on its supple branches on its firm trunk on its deep roots in its good earth and the air beneath the wings of the sparrows as they angled to land and tangled their take-offs was edged more sharply during these after-moments because they had known the exact contours of Jim's cheekbones just as well as if they had fluttered over them repeatedly as they entered a nest that was a skull Jim's skull with eyeholes for entranceways to a speckled soft bowl full of delicate grass stems woven and lined with down from the chicks they had once been.

Even as time kept going onwards I was all of me back in my hands in my fingers back in the important forever time of Jim's head on my lap and tiny minute things of detail I had not felt back then such as the tickle of nostril hair against fingertip or the roughness of a bitten lip-crease beneath thumb all these recent facts were magnified and glorified during the empty moments of fermata of life I was being given to let them bestow themselves loopingly upon me sparrow-like going from time into time through time around time under time in such a tangle of motions that the facts could not help but form knots knots so complex in their forwards and backwards as to keep my fingers busy for years with the motions of loving untangling.

And all that afternoon back in front of the white wall I knew Jim was on his knees praying for me and praying to receive my forgiveness which of course I had already granted him for all future trespasses against me or sins deadly and mortal that he might one day commit within the world or the ward or the world of the ward or the world because I was temporarily temporally feeling like I feel Jesus should feel which is full of forgiveness which is not preparing to come in mighty wrathful judgement upon all mankind but knowing and understanding and forgiving in advance His whole creation because it is His responsibility just as He and the Holy Spirit are the responsible creations of His Father and yet are no younger or less essential than Him and so must have been created at the same moment and by the same cause which is nothing but the Trinity that is One and so why is not creation itself forgiveness? Creation must be forgiveness or else God is not God but Jehovah Jesus is not Jesus but the Thief and the Holy Spirit is not Holy but Hollow and is not a Spirit but a Sprite full of Spite and full of Holes and thus was I angry that afternoon at the Sisters and especially Sister Britta for making a guiltless boy pray to a guilty God or a God who did not exist making him pray for forgiveness for a sin that never existed except in the guilty head of a Sister.

Jim should be with me and be free and see with his hands see me freely and help with his hands help me wheelie and free me with his hands so we were free he and me bloody he and me lovely he and me eternally he and me.

I fainted.

I must have fainted as I do sometimes when nobody is around and something gets me so angry or excited that I hyperventilate and my brain deprived of oxygen decides to shut down in order to save me from getting even more excited and oxygen-deprived.

I woke up slumped hunched forwards but not so slumped that I couldn't breathe because then I wouldn't have woken up at all so I suppose the important thing to think is that I did wake up and the sky was darker and I was calmer and the air was full of supper which was to be sausages with mashed potato and onion gravy and after a few seconds of telling my nose to smell inside this spicy and starchy scent for the sweetness answer I was able to tell that pudding would be Spotted Dick with custard all being cooked in the basement below and sending smells up the lift-shaft to tell me what delicious food we would have to eat that evening probably all except Jim whose punishment would I was sure mean no supper.

If the boys in his dorm liked him as much as I hoped they liked him they would stick a sausage in their pocket and risk the grease stain and smell in chapel to keep him from hunger just as Jesus fed the five thousand Jim would like the sausage as much as the five thousand would have preferred the sausage to bread and fishes. Jim looked like a boy who would like a sausage and his face felt like the face of a hungry boy who needed every sausage he could get.

We ate after the gong was banged and Sister Cécile made sure I cleared and cleaned my plate and then my bowl after which Chapel and then the usual routine of teeth-brushing being changed and pyjamas but all of it infused with my awareness that I was a much more important person in the world because I had a friend who knew what shape my face was and knew where I had been sitting that day and so might if that was what he wanted find me again go back to that place again to find me there especially as he had been wrongly punished for an interaction with me and that meant any interaction with me would be at least a private excitement and probably a public defiance of the Sisters most of all Sister Britta and I knew as I lay in hardly any moonlight after Jim's punisher had said Goodnight and God bless to Glen Roger Finn and I and we had replied me grunting quieter and more grudging than usual to try to communicate to Sister Britta that I was not thankful to her or to God because I had not been hurt deliberately by Jim as I so often had been by Devil's Children and I knew as I lay in hardly any moonlight that even if he was at that exact moment not specifically thinking of me Jim would almost certainly be thinking about the events of the day in which a major part had been played by his soft-nosed and easily bleedy new friend.

For the first night in days I slept fully and well all the way through until Rise and shine which solid chunk of slumber made me feel the power of Jim's blood working in me to bring strength to my spine and to fortify my mind against the little difficulties of being me in my body and equally of my body having to put up with sometimes not grateful or patient enough me.

I think of myself with pity on that day the sixteenth after Jim's arrival Ash Wednesday not because of anything to do with my body or mind or any combination of the two but because what can the day after the greatest day so far of someone's anyone's life be but a great disappointment? And after the horn concerto where everything in the air shone brassy and time itself was burnished into a loping major key I was back to something like the plink and plonk of Princess Pretty's piano practice every note being equal to its prequel and sequel like a work of twelve-tone Viennese serialism as far as I understand it plink plonk accompanying me through my prayers my change dressing Mass Ready Brek and snickety-wheel-along to the horse's usual stall the wall because bolting my meal and being bloodied yesterday had made even Sister Cécile feel I needed more than anything today to be calmed although I was desperate to be left in exactly the same place as Jim had found me.

He did not come he did not return because as I guessed he was not sufficiently contrite and so a day in Chapel a day in which to pray himself away from violence and towards peace was required of him of Jim and I waited and suffered through a game of Sockball started by knife-loving Charlie which I knew Charlie knew Jim could hear but take no part in and Charlie's team Gate S.C. won 5–0 against Micky's Chapel United which it would not have done if Jim had been free to play in goal against them and every goal celebration by Charlie hurt me because I knew it would be hurting Jim in the Chapel just as his knees would be hurting him if they the Sisters Sister Britta had made him stay on them since breakfast which he had not eaten.

When I think of the morning that followed this morning meaning the seventeenth morning I don't see it as an individual but as a twin like Tim and Tom on my first ward had been twins a twin morning to the morning of the sixteenth day because I woke having slept a blood sleep and was routinely washed clothed redeemed fed and wheeled where I waited and Kurt thumped and Lise snuffled and Sockball happened and Charlie's team won 5–0 but thereafter everything was different for Jim was allowed out not cowed by contrition but determined to pursue a course of discovery and if necessary disobedience and I knew this because he was getting closer and closer to the wooden gate as he came along the long corridor and I heard the high tremulous voice of Sister Eliza who had obviously been told to watch him by Sister Britta I heard Sister Eliza's beautiful flutey but flu-ridden voice warning Jim by name not to touch the wooden gate Because she said you know what happens when you touch the wooden gate.

Jim kept walking I heard his big bare feet on the lino and his footfalls fell neither accelerando nor ritenuto nor rallentando but continued onwards in strict time and when he was a few feet away from me I was able to confirm by sound that he was walking along the middle of the long corridor not following the right hand wall in order to touch a shoulder or finger on them blind Jim was instead showing that he could walk without help of any sort in a strong straight line straight towards the wooden gate and thus behind me he went and I saw his faint reflection pass in the glass but he kept going and I think now he must have been counting his steps or listening like a bat because as Sister Eliza trotted down the long corridor towards him to stop him touching the wooden gate Jim kept walking and walking until he suddenly stopped and Sister Eliza flitted behind me all atremble shouting thickly Jim No but when she got beside him she said immediately Oh because as I began to guess Jim had worked out the exact length of the long corridor and had walked until his feet were less than an inch from the wooden gate and then he had stopped.

Oh said Sister Eliza and sniffed and I still to this day like to imagine Jim standing there so close to the wooden gate that his nose as I later heard many times from almost everyone who could speak was stuck out between two of the vertical bars but not touching never touching because if it had Sister Eliza would have had no choice but to call Sister Britta and tell on Jim but instead she said with a shake Oh and then said not without admiration Well how on earth did you do that?

Jim was standing miraculously right in front of the wooden gate miraculously from Sister Eliza's point of view but I felt it wasn't a miracle just a demonstration of how extraordinary my friend Jim was as a human being and even more extraordinary but in a different way was what he did next which was nothing except stand there as still on his feet as I was sitting in my listening chair.

Jim stood and began waiting at the wooden gate for the moment someone one of the Sisters or Mrs Beatles the Cleaner or Ludvik the Caretaker or the Priest needed to come through yes he waited I waited he waited but Sister Eliza did not wait because she knew what Sister Britta would want her to do and she was afraid of Sister Britta and what Sister Britta would think and say and possibly do if she Sister Eliza didn't do that thing which was tell Jim to Come away from the wooden gate.

So Sister Eliza blew her nose and breathed in and told Jim Come away from the wooden gate but he did not move so she told him again in exactly the same I am calm I am not angry voice but Jim stood still right where he was so Sister Eliza whispered Jim my child I understand what you are trying to say but this is not going to help your cause All that will happen is that you will find yourself in deep deep waters.

Sister Eliza did not want to or need to mention Sister Britta by name because everyone in the ward even newcomers knew that if there were any deep deep waters they were Sister Britta but I don't think going by subsequent events the thought or fear of Sister Britta would have had any power over Jim because Jim was fighting the injustice of not being able to explore the ward and world between the wooden gate and the lift and although she was its chief enforcer Sister Britta was only an apostle of that injustice.

Sister Eliza whispered something quieter to Jim so quiet that I only caught the word Chapel but that was enough for me to know what punishment she was referring to and by this time my body was vibrating with the nerves in my body singing zinging with excitement like the notes on a piano at the end of a climactic chromatic crescendo resonating seemingly everlasting what was the brave and foolish boy doing? Even Kurt's thumping had stopped so I knew Kurt was paying attention to the ward and not his land and this silence meant one or two others came out of their dorms and made noises I could hear behind me and to my right noises of curiosity that meant Sister Eliza knew she had to act quickly or she would soon have a crowd on her hands.

Jim please come away now she said loudly enough to be heard in the Sisters' Office or I will have to inform the other Sisters and she added You are a fire hazard where you are standing presently although I did not hear her correctly the first time because her nose was bunged up with cold and I thought she'd said You are a fine hazard.

Sister Eliza's volume would have been enough in itself but coupled with her tone was bound to bring Sister Britta immediately from the Office and what happened was what anyone could have known would happen Jim was asked to move Jim didn't move Jim was told to move Jim didn't move Jim was given one final chance now watched by I estimate nine curious others including Kurt Finn Gavin one final chance before Sister Britta called for Sister Cécile and Sister Mary Margaret and then Jim was escorted back to the Chapel and everyone was told Go back to what you were doing by Sister Eliza and Kurt did and I did and we apparently all did but I was thinking and I knew others were thinking of the wooden gates in a new way as if before they had been room temperature and were now hotter than the hottest radiator.

Finn and Gavin walked up to look at where Jim had been standing and perhaps also to look again at the wooden gate almost as if it was covered in blood and they were told by Sister Eliza who was taking a minute to catch her trembly coldy breath Go away you silly boys Don't come near here and that only confirmed to me looking at two pigeons on the roof of the building opposite one upright pigeon being chased by another pigeon with a big puffed-out chest these words Don't come near here only confirmed to me that Jim by his action had made a Here out of a nowhere and what a different and dangerous place that Here now was.

The following day the eighteenth was not routine for me even as I was taken through my usual routine because I felt absolutely certain Jim would return to the new Here and my only doubt was that his prayers in the Chapel for the strength to obey or the will to submit his will or however Sister Britta would put it to him that the prayers would last another full day but what Jim had done was not as sinful as violently bloodying my nose so he was let out on the eighteenth day immediately after an extra set of prayers after breakfast which meanwhile gave Sister Cécile some time to wheel me back to the white wall which I was happy about very happy because the white wall was closer to the Here than was the window and that would put me closer to Jim in blood brothership with him when as he would and as he did he came back he gloriously returned.

Others knew because others were already looking out of Dorms 2 3 and I think if I heard correctly 4 when he Jim began his walk down the middle of the long corridor followed by the footsteps of Sister Britta. What I had not seen so had to imagine was her releasing him a few moments earlier from extra prayers in the Chapel and him getting up from his knees and walking out through the doors and turning to her dismay hard right and beginning his soon-to-be legendary second walk to the wooden gate and back to the Here accompanied by giggles and coos from those watching and also from inside me an immense crescendo of pride and anguish pride that he was so firm and anguish at what his firmness would cost him. I hoped he had had a good large breakfast because he would not be eating for the rest of the day if he carried on as he was which he would.

Sister Britta took the part of Sister Eliza and the other Sisters were closer to hand but the scene was the same scene same words same result just like a rehearsal of the Nativity Play on the raised platform in the Chapel when one Virgin Mary one year has been replaced by another Virgin Mary the next year but wears the same costume and says the same words in reply to the same words just like when Princess Pretty took over from Princess Lovely who took over from Princess Beauty while I remained the donkey because Sister Britta said I was without a shadow of a doubt the best donkey that they had ever had and in fact that I got better at being the donkey every year which I think I probably did because donkeys are steadfast and I was becoming more steadfast.

Jim walked past already-silent Kurt and then behind also-silent me leaving him only a few footsteps before he reached the Here at which point the scene started and after thrice being asked first nicely then just asked and then asked for the last time Jim was grabbed by the upper arms by Sister Britta and also by Sister Cécile and marched again along the long corridor to the Chapel to the wonderment of all the others whose morning routines now had a new feature the fun of Jim getting himself in big trouble by being as Sister Britta's scattered words fell like the seed in the Parable of the Sower A very disobedient boy A really terribly disobedient boy A really terribly disobedient and black- and then she became too quiet to hear but I knew that the next words would have been-hearted boy.

After this I sat for a long time imagining the other things Sister Britta would be saying to Jim in the Chapel and how Jim would be made to feel that he was at that moment Heaven's greatest concern and that his sinful behaviour was putting more at risk than just his own immortal soul because by being bad he was making the whole world a more evil place. I knew this would be Sister Britta's argument and she would ask Jim or any other sinful child And do you want that? And she was always very good at making you think that not only did Jesus die for your sins but that he specifically died all those years ago at a place called Golgotha because a disobedient boy walked up to a wooden gate and stood there after having been warned not to by a kindly and patient nun who not only had the best interests of the whole world at heart but also those of the ward and the boy himself.

Her favourite tactic which Jim might not know yet but he soon would was to ask you And what if Jesus were in this room right now? What if Jesus were standing right over there looking at you with his eyes full of love and sorrow and pity? Then whatever you said if you could speak or however you nodded if you could only nod she would say Because Jesus is in this room right now looking at you with his sorrowful eyes and his heart full of pity and love He's right here and he's in your heart too He's in your heart like you are in this room.

Sister Britta would then tell Jim to speak whatever was in his heart aloud to Jesus in whatever sounds he was capable of making because Jesus wanted to hear it spoken aloud even though he already knew the darkest secrets of Jim's heart because that was the miracle of confession that if Jim spoke his sins aloud in a way that was truly penitent even though he had thought thoughts of sin and done deeds of sin then he Jim would be forgiven for the sin because he had spoken. Deeds was one of Sister Britta's Top Ten words.

I am sure that what Sister Britta really wanted in her life was to be a priest and to take confession and that getting us to speak to Jesus as if He was in the room at the same time that she was in the room was her way of being like a priest and so getting to hear from the children who could speak the things that a priest would hear in the confessional which stood over on the right hand wall but when like me and like Jim a child couldn't speak but only make sounds then Sister Britta would start to speak their replies for them and get them to make a sign usually by nodding their head in my case by moving my head in a slight nod make a sign to show that what she had just said was exactly what they would have said but eventually this duet between Sister Britta as the priest and Sister Britta as the penitent would end and Sister Britta would leave the sinful child you undoubtedly were alone in the Chapel with Jesus with the task of convincing Him that you were firm in resolving to mend your evil ways and when the doors closed with a bang behind Sister Britta and I was alone in the big boomy Snoopy's kennel space of the Chapel I always really did feel however I felt about God as if I were trapped in there with Jesus and not just the plaster one crucified up on the wall and that I had no escape but confessing that I was truly contrite for deliberately and repeatedly spitting my food out of my mouth because I was so upset for the silly reason that my Christmas card hadn't arrived before Christmas and forgive me Jesus please forgive me.

How Jim would endure I did not know but when I heard the Chapel doors shut and heard Sister Britta walk towards me and saw her pass behind me and click open the high latch of the wooden gate and sigh as she went into the Sisters' Office I felt that I too was with Jim left alone with Jesus in the Chapel and I imagined I was saying to him Jim what I would have said if I could have spoken aloud which was that Jesus would not have been the one telling children Thou shalt not pass through this wooden gate He would have been the one saying If you bar this wooden gate to the least of my children you bar this gate to me Matthew 25 verse 40.

But once I had said this to Jim I would have also said Don't try to beat the Sisters at anything because the Sisters cannot be beaten and especially most of all Sister Britta because you may charm Sister Cécile and you may trick Sister Muriel and you may appeal to Sister Mary

Margaret's sense of pity and you may defy Sister Eliza but if there is something Sister Britta wants you to do you will end up doing it and even more if there is something Sister Britta doesn't want you to do you will live a life of hunger and suffering and boredom and isolation until you stop doing or trying to do that something and right then for him Jim that something was standing where he'd made the Here.

I know now that Jim would not have argued but he also would not have taken my advice instead by his behaviour and example he would have started to show me that as well as being charmed tricked filled with pity and occasionally defied the Sisters even Sister Britta could be beaten and that he was going to beat them over the wooden gate he was going to beat them over the Here his here which spot was very close to where I was through the rest of that eighteenth morning and afternoon with a break for lunch of delicious baked beans mashed up with Cardinal Newman and tea-time orange squash and I felt it like a second radiator the Here but this one radiating not air-swirls of heat but waves of righteousness because it had been a while since one of us had been so simple and clear in saying the Sisters were wrong usually we were forced to be sneaky and sly if we wanted to fight against or correct them rather than out in the plain light where no-one could protect us by distracting them with illness or pretend choking.

Here is where a hero would become a hero by refusing to be any-where but Here where he knew he had every right to be and so what happened towards the end of the next day the nineteenth was some-thing I do not exactly regret but is still something I am ashamed of my part in but before then came the rest of the eighteenth day starting with an afternoon of quiet during which I watched the light on the white wall change to evening light and then the things within my field of vision become bowls and spoons then mirrors and toothbrushes then a ceiling with fluorescent light on it then a ceiling with faintly reflected streetlight on it then dreams of woody confusion and stern voices and Jeremy screaming and then hours after midnight all those things in reverse order except the bowls and spoons coming before the mirrors and toothbrushes and the light on the wall was morning light everything bringing me back to where I had been beside the Here but now it was on the nineteenth day.

I expected Jim's penance this time to be longer than it had been the first time he touched the wooden gate but shorter than for making my face bloody so more than a day but less than two days but it turned out to be a day for although Jim did not join us for lunch of fish pie with Cardinal Newman vegetables he did through the generosity and forgiveness of the Sisters meaning Sister Britta he did find himself released from the Chapel after tea-time meaning half past four on the nineteenth day at which time and for which event many of the others started to gather in witness of Jim for Jim once outside the Chapel doors turned hard right and began his third and already legendary walk straight down the middle of the long corridor towards the wooden gate and poor me I was already in anguish I was again a wreck of a boy of a horse not for what had happened already but for what would happen if Jim reached the Here and stood there and kept doing that day after day week after week just as Kurt thumped Lise wept and moaned or as Micky ran into walls.

I was itchy all over with intolerable itchy feelings of anger resistance fear and tenderness and I knew even before I did it that I wouldn't be able to stop myself from trying to stop Jim from doing what he was so nobly and foolishly doing.

Thump went Kurt but everyone else was silent in their witnessing of Jim's walk down the first half of the long corridor. Kurt didn't thump again because he sensed what was happening outside his land and so the silence for the second half was even thicker and more gooey and for me more full of pricks of conscience over what I knew I shouldn't do and prickles of fear for I knew I was going to go from prop onstage like chair or table seen by everyone but noticed by no-one to actor speaking important lines looked at and listened to by all the audience by Sisters as well as children. When Jim reached Kurt I could no longer restrain myself Jim was getting too close to a life of nothing but defiance and punishment and I had to help him I had to save him I had to teach him there was another way perhaps not such a noble and just way of martyrdom and example but a way that would give him greater purpose.

Hnyhmm I said I dropped gift-like into the silence of thick and prickly goo feeling my word his name come out of me just at the moment he was passing closest by me feeling it fly out and get stuck even though it had changed the silence to something else something more flowy and had changed me from prop to actor even though all I was capable of was repeating for every listener the sound that had shocked him Jim into accidentally punching me and so I did I repeated it a second and a third time on this the afternoon of the nineteenth day at half past four because I knew that Jesus was waiting in the Chapel for Jim the useful made-up moral Jesus of Sister Britta with his sorrowful eyes and his knowing heart punishing you with disappointment judging you with kind dismay and I wanted to save Jim from Jesus I wanted to save Jim from the punishment of being left alone in the Chapel with whatever Jesus he did or didn't imagine to be there alone with him but most of all I wanted to save Jim from himself because he was being too noble and too much of a martyr and really really above all too much like Jesus if only the Sisters could see it thrice they denied Him and thrice He forgave them.

A fourth Hynnhm would not have made any difference so I did not say it and in the following moments the pricked silence became gooier and gooier though absolutely transparent because through pure clear air that still smelled slightly of carrots and cabbage from the lunch Jim had not eaten everybody watched Jim and I suppose watched me and watched the meaningful gap in between us and in between us and the Here with eyes of clarity and concern and glee because for lots of them this was the best fun since waiting for the fight between Charlie and Jim which still needed to happen after whatever happened now and I didn't not know what was going to happen now I really had no idea for either I meant something to Jim or I meant nothing.

I meant nothing it seemed and Hyhhnm meant nothing and I could not save him because Jim did not deviate not one bit he kept walking at exactly the same pace his big feet making soft slapping sounds as they followed their straight line their steady course straight towards punishment and already footfalls of various varieties were speeding along the long corridor to catch and grab him Jim away and I do not like to think it makes me itch all inside my head to think of the way the next few minutes were such a repeat such an exact repeat of what had happened on the seventeenth and eighteenth days except it was made completely different for me because what was done was done despite my intervening my making the Jim-name-sound despite my actor's love.

After Jim was back in the Chapel my life was instantly a bad life and although I was glad that in the place I had been left I could look towards the memory of the whiteness of the white wall and think about what it had meant for me in the past and also try thinking about what it might still in future mean yet even more did I despair and even more despair of my despair as if it were not only every effect ever but every cause ever and throughout this bleak blank intermezzo I know I lived and suffered years between each rallentando thump of Kurt and it felt at times as if it was only Kurt's thumps that kept time going at all and perhaps because of this for the first time in several years I felt what it must feel for Kurt to wait all day and then watch the invaders come and destroy his beautiful land and kill his wonderful people and yet for everybody else on the ward not really to care unless perhaps some of what made Lise cry was sadness for her brother. Poor Kurt.

Lise was not there to start with but after the excitement which even in the thick of my years of despair I still knew had been exciting to everyone even the Sisters after everyone returned to the Craft Room the Dorms or their usual places Lise did come and flop into a heap on the floor and cry for herself and I decided to cry a little too for Kurt and a little for me if I could borrow some of her crying to add to my own to add to the wreck of a boy of a horse weeping in shame shame and yet more shame for I had done the wrong weak thing and I had been rejected just as I would always be rejected and Jim had done the strong right thing by rejecting me just as I should always be rejected by those who were strong and righteous.

I could not see them but I tried to speed up time by picturing on top of the whiteness of the white wall Lise's knees and the colours they would be at that exact moment I thought that they would be grey beneath white but grey that was partly green or blue and in fact seemed to pulse between blue and green either that or her knees were pink and shiny but with small veins of pale violet but however I imagined them the colours and their combination made me feel nauseous not because they were Lise's imagined knee-tones but because they were a projection onto whiteness of my shameful feelings and however they came out they were essentially wrong and guilty and I wished more than anything else that I could be roughly wheeled back through time like Sister Penelope had sometimes wheeled me doing spine-damage back to the moment when Jim passed Kurt for then I could shut myself up and let what should have happened between Jim and the Sisters especially Sister Britta go right ahead and happen rather than undermine it with needless compassion for if no-one had made a noise not even Kurt then Jim would have looked like he was acting for all of us because our silence would have shown our approval.

That afternoon the nineteenth lasted longer than the whole rest of my life and I suffered like the Israelites in the wilderness for forty years surviving on manna as I survived that evening on Irish stew which I would have choked myself on if Sister Cécile had let me have a chunk of juicy meat or a cube of potato but all I got to fill my stomach ready for the emptying I knew would soon come was the rich brown gravy that usually smelled so delicious and that Jim in the Chapel would be smelling even in the righteousness of his martyrdom as so many Catholic martyrs had been haunted and taunted by the smell of Irish Stew as Sister Mary Margaret often told us.

I puked brownly just outside the Refectory door brownly on the way to have my teeth brushed as that seemed more efficient than puking once my teeth were brushed and my pyjamas were on and even though I was puking to express self-disgust and disgust at the Sisters' treatment of Jim I was still personally considerate of Sister Cécile who now began cleaning me up she wiped and washed as I was surrounded by the smells of peppermint and spearmint which I couldn't be bothered to tell apart although I usually could and did and the sight of Charlie flicking water from his cherry red toothbrush at not-yet-dead Finn whenever the Boy's Bathroom was empty of Sisters and I wished Charlie could humiliate me instead of Finn for no-one deserved it more.

The nights that at the time I most wanted to pass quickly were of course the slowest and the nights I most wanted to forget afterwards are those I can now remember in such absolute detail with such precision of moment-after-moment agony that it is as if they had happened to me the exact same way one hundred times so that I would become demented with boredom at their unchanging never improving details like listening to a terrible performance of a great symphony on a tinny radio over and over again until it becomes hard to believe the wrong tempi aren't what the composer wrote and the wrong notes aren't full of greater meaning than the right ones.

On the nineteenth night still-alive Finn's snoring was soundtrack to a voyage nowhere but out into my own skeleton with a left-behind mouth and mind full of acid as again and again I thought about how much I wanted my painful bones to dissolve like aspirin in a glass of water to keep their shape at first but to become puffy and then fluffy and weakened until they weren't pill-femurs and pill-vertebrae any more just organized underwater dust skeleton-shaped and waiting for the slightest twirling twizzling current to spin them off into spirals of transparency and plinks of nothing much.

At least I was hungry as Jim was hungry in Dorm 3 even if someone probably Micky had stolen him a bread roll because by suffering as Jim suffered I was offering mute solidarity and by my increasing hunger at three and then four in the morning I was at least able to tell that time was passing though I suppose the worsening ache of the muscles on either side of my spine would also have told me this but in a way that separated me from blood-friend Jim because his body was no problem to him a fact I had been able to tell the first moment I heard his strong footsteps walking in alongside Sister Britta Jim would never until he was much older be kept awake just by the pain of simply being himself with no Radio 3 after closedown to distract him from the pain of simply being himself because tonight it was not Sister Cécile but Sister Mary Margaret and her muttered prayers and clicking rosary and the resolute click of her kettle not for tea but for hot chocolate and for the pink hot water bottle with the green knitted cover with the shamrock on she carried with her on her rounds and had more than once placed by my head as breathing fierce fumes she turned me from one side to the other at which time I smelled its smell of rubber and boiled water and Ireland.

On the twentieth day and for most of the morning and afternoon of the twenty-first day I did not see Jim and I could not hear him although I did once or twice hear Sister Britta speaking to and of him and after that I could hear the awful silence of Jesus' sorrowful gaze as it saw everything inside Jim which was not cornflakes or oxtail soup and brown bread or roast chicken and roast potatoes and peas and carrots or stewed apple without sugar which were the meals of the twentieth day and which did not go inside Jim and nor did the cornflakes or mince and tatties of the twenty-first day but he was escorted in that evening for semolina usually my favourite when served with lemon curd but we were now in Lent.

I did not see him but imagined him looking pale and angry as he was brought in after the roast peppers and rice my least favourite meal even when puréed were finished by all and sundry pale and angry he must have looked but not I hoped defeated or entirely submissive to Jesus or to Sister Britta.

And thus on the morning of the twenty-second day Jim was at breakfast being asked by the others because Sister Britta's chair was empty What are you going to do you loony? Are you going to touch it this time? It being the wooden gate and them thinking he just wanted to touch it and I could see and feel Sister Cécile close beside me with my beaker in her gentle hand Sister Cécile listening and getting ready to report back to Sister Britta who had absented herself almost certainly for the purpose of getting Jim to relax and behave more freely nodding or shaking his head so she Sister Britta would find out indirectly whether she needed to swoop and pick him up in her talons and carry him away to the front row of pews in the Chapel or whether he could safely be left to the obedient disobedience of Sockball though how she knew he would know she wasn't there somewhere I didn't know and inside me I felt the vastness of Jim's bravery and nobility because as far as I could tell he gave no answer nod or shake beyond making all those around him except Charlie that is Glen Roger Gavin laugh like they hadn't laughed since he'd begun his round of defiance penitence defiance penitence.

Everybody got their answer at half past four that afternoon after a session in the Craft Room in which both I and Jim took part which was pot throwing. Sister Cécile knew I loved the feel of clay and the smell of clay and that I enjoyed dropping blobs onto paper on the floor so she brought me in for that and afterwards there was tea-time and then with my mouth still tasting of orange squash I was wheeled by her to the window which surprised me as I was fully expecting another dose of whiteness to keep me calm amid all the anger and fluster of Jim's repeated defiance which as I sat in place with the wheels of my wheelchair hardly settled I began to hear or think I could hear starting to be repeated his defiance with accompanying giggles and coos as Jim's big feet came straight down the middle of the long corridor followed by Sister Britta's angry clacking heels and Sister Mary Margaret's squeaky scurry and Sister Cécile's high tippy-tapping and Sister Eliza's mysterious quiet fpp fpp of stickiness so was there anyone important in the ward who wasn't watching this fourth and final time Jim made the walk? Only Sister Muriel missing out as she usually did.

I got the sense even the sparrows in the air outside were paying bird-like attention peeking sidelong or even cocking their heads in the direction of Jim's direction and this silly idea helped strengthen me against letting out the wail of pain fortissimo pain I was feeling at the thought of all the punishment Jim was prepared to accept in his quest to fight for justice which this time would be more mortifying than kneeling and praying and would surely involve the sainted metal ruler across the palm or the sainted cane across the buttocks.

I was not going to humiliate myself again by humiliating Jim by making him seem ignoble so ignoble as to pass by and reject a whimpering sufferer just as the Priest and the Levite passed by on the other side the man who fell into the hands of bandits going on his way down from Jerusalem to Jericho.

Although I did not recognize the full significance and magnificence and mischief and wit of it at the time the time that was half past four which meant that the events that were about to happen were taking place exactly one day to the second after the events of the day before the seventeenth day and if I could have seen a clock the hands would have been in exactly the same place and the shadow of the wych elm on the yellowy and pinkish paving stones which shadow I could have seen if the sun had been out would have rotated only a little further round the tree trunk and so everything to make Jim's point all the clearer was as much the same as Jim could make it to the day before when just as he did now Kurt stopped thumping and for the fourth time Jim passed by him on his way so it seemed to everyone watching on his way to the wooden gate.

I have subsequently thought a great deal about what I would have felt if he Jim had gone ahead with an exact repetition rather than carried through the wonderful other thing he did. I have spent many happy hours comparing the two different sets of emotion and I have concluded that whilst if Jim had done what I expected Jim to do I would have felt pride awe glee and pity as well as love that when he didn't do this but instead did the other wonderful thing I felt these exact emotions but later and beneath a flash of my first and foremost emotions which were surprise delight awe and love even more love than I'd thought possible because instead of continuing to walk defiantly to the wooden gate Jim just at the moment he was closest by me the moment that exactly twenty-four hours earlier I'd cried out Hyhmmnh Jim stopped and in the window I saw his reflection cock its bag of spoons head just as if he'd heard something that had given him pause after which I saw the head incomprehensibly turn towards me as it was not supposed to do as it could not do if Jim were continuing on to the Here and instead of continuing Jim broke his walk and broke also time and space and nobly came to me as if to the aid of the man who fell into the hands of bandits.

In that instant Jim transformed me as I'd transformed myself the day before by my Hyhhmmh-into-the-silence goo from a prop nobody saw into a prickly actor everybody saw but not a donkey no a fine proud horse galloping galloping happily galloping across a wide flat space towards vaster faster possibilities and more glorious escapes and escapades.

Some people laughed at the joke of it even though it took me several years I think to recognize the true deep wit of breaking time the way Jim just had in pretending he was hearing no truly hearing a cry of anguish that had been let out exactly one day before and responding instantly to that cry in that place nearby the Here as giving him a reason but a self-chosen reason of emergency to turn away from the straight line to the wooden gate and to attend to his blood-brother who no-one but he Elliott knew was his blood-brother.

Even the Sisters made sounds that I could hear among the high chortles and tinkling mirth for they too were relieved Jim had turned aside from the ruler and the cane even if he did not know that was

what he was doing Sister Britta gave a dry yack like a mezzo soprano's cough Sister Eliza tittered pizzicato then sniffed Sister Cécile
spluttered I heard her splutter then she liquidly peeled out coloratura
laughs and Sister Mary Margaret gave a single contralto whoop of
surprise from the County of Cork and then said Bless him after which
a lot of Bless hims rained down upon Jim and were then followed by
Glory to Gods from all the Sisters because it was necessary for them
to attribute Jim's turning aside not to Jim alone but to Jim and Jesus
which saviour had it seemed to the Sisters been so instrumentally
miraculously persuasive to Jim when left alone with him for all those
hours in the Chapel.

What Jim did first on reaching me was find his way to my head by
finding first with his fingers the back of my head for although he had
shown he could walk the length of the long corridor and stop within
an inch of the wooden gate I was not exactly to the inch where I had
been on the fifteenth day the day he accidentally punched me in the
face and bloodied my nose.

I was I estimate four inches closer to Kurt so Jim first reached into
the air at the point where my head had been when my mouth facing
away from him had cried out for him to stop and do something like
what he was doing now which was be distracted from the wooden
gate and the Here by compassion for his weak friend through whose
mouse-brown hair he was a moment later running his exploring
fingers.

Jim was not directly congratulated by Sister Britta and the other
Sisters but he was admired for a while from a distance so audibly
that I am sure he heard cannot have missed the lioness growl of
Sister Britta's satisfaction the tssks of Sister Eliza's approval the hum
of pleasure from Sister Cécile and Sister Mary Margaret's encore of
Bless him Bless him.

Another childish will broken they must have thought another soul brought a little closer to obedience to God's will and yet as the praise continued and Jim's hands moved down onto the sides of my skull I began to feel him go tense and grip me every time one of the Sisters made a louder than usual noise.

Without really thinking about it I began to hum to him Jim not a loud hum of a tone of a tune that others might hear with their ears but a buzz through the bones ribs to neck to skull up through all my bones to his finger-bones that was meant to give fuzzy reassurance that I was there and I cared and that for the moment that was all that mattered because he was not on the Here or being hauled to the Chapel or in the Chapel with Sister Britta and Jesus or just alone with Jesus he had instead chosen respite from punishment and wanted I thought to know he wasn't a coward for doing so so I hummed to him bones to bones that what he had done was right and when he too began to reply by making his hands on the sides of my skull shake a tiny tremolo shake I knew he got it got what I meant by what I did.

Hmm.

All of this was through a thick mist of embarrassment because I knew even when the Sisters departed shooing away the children and Kurt's thump began again that we Jim and I were the subject the few particular tender notes upon which all that day's fugues of improvisations and variations of gossip and game would be based and despite my Hynnhm and going from prop to actor actually being a subject was something I had avoided so successfully that I usually thought of myself as a plain-view-hidden object like the prop that was Kurt's grey filing cabinet and though I knew everyone knew my name and knew me as fed by Sister Cécile and being near Kurt and Lise when parked and as a Donkey at Nativity with birthday and Christmas cards that must never be touched or else he may die from exploding with anger and you'll get the blame just like that replacement cleaning lady Maxine who ripped them in two did. I knew I was known in exactly these limited ways for I had deliberately and carefully not done anything in at least two birthday cards to change what I was and meant for everyone else especially not to let the Sisters know of my word-hoarding and secret in-head-writing so causing Jim to be near me was world-changing for me as well as ward-changing for the long corridor.

And so indeed it turned out to be but not immediately and not without interruption because as soon as the Sisters had gone their ways Sisters Britta and Mary Margaret to the Sisters' Office and Sisters Cécile and Eliza to the Craft Room where Sister Muriel had missed everything and would need to be caught up because as soon as they were all gone Charlie was upon us jealous Charlie jealous of me and because of this and because Jim was no longer being punished Charlie wanted Jim to rejoin the Sockball game and as I suspected do something in the game to give Charlie a reason for starting the fight that everybody knew was coming and everybody also expected Jim to start because he must be angry if not furious with Charlie for tricking him into running into Kurt's filing cabinet and breaking open his Jim's head and yes Jim was angry and I could feel his fury in his hands when Charlie came up to us and spoke to him saying Sockball Come on You can choose ends and all of this to find a way to trick Jim into being in trouble and in Chapel again so Charlie could rule over us.

To my great disappointment Jim said Yes by letting go of me and going away from me and joining in the game which meant starting up the other end as goalkeeper for Chapel United no sooner were we together than we were apart and I had not even been able to put the first part of my plan into action because Charlie's words Come on had come just as Sister Mary Margaret was going through the wooden gate so Jim didn't hear the cluck of the sound of its high latch dropping and couldn't hear the beautiful copy of this sound I made with my throat and tongue and mouth just a moment afterwards because Charlie was then loudly saying You can choose and Jim had chosen and he had chosen to leave me although he must surely have known that I would be sad if only because he probably thought all boys who couldn't join in with Sockball because they were tense or floppy or mad were sad but it was for other reasons that I was sad.

Yet I was only sad for a few minutes because I rejoiced in Jim's freedom and in the ingenious genius way he had broken time and space and then mended them again to make his escape from Jesus and so let him play Sockball against Charlie I thought let him play because one day soon they must fight and the sooner they fight the sooner Jim will return to me yes I thought let them play on the afternoon of the twenty-second day and the morning of the twenty-third day but not more than that not play every day forever not leaving me in anguish after what seemed likely to become Jim's routine morning visit to check I was in one of my two places a quick ruffle of the hair once he knew I was there and off he went to play and when on the twenty-second and the mornings of the twenty-third and twenty-fourth days he was on the side that lost to Charlie's side with Charlie scoring first I began to despair that nothing had really changed in the long corridor and that Charlie and Jim might never fight because Jim would be too understanding of him and of the weakness of Charlie's strength.

I watched the leaves grow greener on the slowly growing tree a tiny bit every day and two new blackbirds arrived and began building a nest and both of these signs of Spring brought me my usual hope.

I did not hope for a fight for war but I did trust because of Charlie's sinful nature that war would come for a Devil's child can only play nicely for so long and on the twenty-fifth day it happened.

It happened when the Sockball was kicked by Charlie on the Gate S.C. team into the gap between Kurt's filing cabinet and the wall behind it and Charlie ordered Jim to fetch it Charlie did not do this out of laziness but because he like everyone knew Kurt would take any touching of his filing cabinet as an attack on his land by new forces Charlie did it to show Jim his power but Jim wanted to show Charlie that he didn't respect Charlie's power and that he knew where the filing cabinet was and also that he had learned the rule of not touching Kurt's land so he went towards Kurt and stood between him and Charlie and from what I heard Finn say later Jim nobly shook his head and stood with his arms crossed and a few seconds later I heard the familiar thick smack of a Charlie punch for it did not seem to matter whose face he was punching Charlie's punches always sounded the same.

In response my body went even more tense than usual as I felt Jim's saltiness pepperiness meatiness being put to the test either a victory or a defeat might bring him back to me but an interruption by a Sister would only delay the fight until later so I was glad no-one immediately began the chant of Fight! Fight! This only usually happened when Charlie was winning and we wanted to call the Sisters even Sister Muriel to pull him off and stop a worse duffing up stop the thick punches when the person being punched was on the floor because usually there were lots of punches quick punches that sounded like a quieter version of Micky's head hitting a wall but this time on the twenty-fifth day in this fight I only heard one Charliesque punch the next thing I heard was big bare feet slapping behind me as Jim charged Charlie like a rhino as Finn re-enacted it later in our dorm

Jim put his head down and charged straight through Charlie's belly but took the rest of Charlie with him he powerfully rhino-charged him on and on I saw their reflection pass behind me in a whizz of angry muscle and then they both hit the wooden gate which made a horrible splitting sound that I knew meant broken.

And but for the fluster of arriving feet and the dismay of the Sisters especially Sister Britta and the slap and rattle of departing feet and the loud closing of the Chapel doors that was all we were to know of Jim and Charlie for the rest of the twenty-fifth and then all of the twenty-sixth day for they were not allowed either to eat with us or to sleep in the same dorms as us lest the contamination of their ungodly sinfulness should foul and pollute us and lest they be granted remission from even one instant of their shared mortification and penance and for Mass too they were removed from our sight.

I thought about moss to distract me from a combined disappointment and hope that was very like the first movement of Schubert's String Quintet in C Opus 163 i.e. Schubert's usual disappointed hope but also his hopeful disappointment because after Jim was free again whenever that turned out to be surely surely he would return to me from the simple world of Sockball and boy fun and shouting and final scores of victory to Charlie's team and so in the meantime I wondered how a piece of almost greenfinch-green moss with gorgeous golden flecks bright as a Sister's torch at the end of a long dark corridor how moss could grow on a window ledge without any earth for its roots if moss has roots and I suppose I was using the moss as a way of both thinking about and not thinking about myself although legs are not roots and a wheelchair is only occasionally when it is doing wheelies a golden-flecked thing and if the ward was a window-ledge I could only grow and develop as a person and a soul by falling off it even if I was picked up and put back afterwards as did happen and as proved true.

What happened first was what I had thought would happen after more time passed than I thought would pass during which Ludvik the Caretaker carefully and entertainingly for me repaired the wooden gate namely Jim and Charlie were released halfway through the morning of the twenty-seventh day Sunday when I had thought if not for Mass they would be out in time for breakfast perhaps the Sisters did not want them to make a big dramatic entrance in the Refectory and cause giggling and perhaps choking along with pointing and even cheering so it was not until after the second Mass and after everyone was done with breakfast that they emerged onto the long corridor side by side released through the Chapel doors and Jim turned right towards me and Charlie I learned afterwards turned left towards the Craft Room which Charlie probably thought was the winner's end of the ward because it had more stuff to do and he and Jim had been told by Sister Britta to keep far apart for the next few days and No Sockball for a week so Charlie got paints and clay and Jim got Kurt Lise a renewed wooden gate and me yippee.

I had a plan by then after days to think about it as well as thinking about moss and as soon as Jim reached me and reached out to find my head in front of the radiator I began to hum my bone-hum but also to listen out for what I needed which in fact came almost straight away for Sister Britta finished in the Chapel with the Priest and I could see in my imagination her crossing herself and then starting to walk with him down the long corridor towards us which was when I started to hear their hard heavy footfalls and so began to get my throat and mouth ready because when they had passed us with the single word Good Sister Britta lifted the high latch on the wooden gate by pressing down on the left side of it and after she had swung open the wooden gate outwards and said Father and passed through I waited I waited until the high latch fell absolutely predictably back in place with its familiar cluck and right away I made my vocal imitation of it I went Cluck too letting Jim hear just how exactly I could mimic it Cluck and Jim just as I'd spent days hoping and planning he would Jim gave a gritty laugh because this moment confirmed we were now in communication not only by touches and bone-hums but by sounds that meant definite different things and I had started with the most important of them the one we were together against.

Cluck I did it again expecting Jim to copy me with a mouth sound rather than laughter but he didn't instead he made a sound with his hands behind my left ear that was more like a clup than a clap and when I saw it a few days later I realized that he was doing this by bringing his hands together in a usual clap the sort I absolutely couldn't do but he was cupping them his hands before they reached one another so that they had between them a sockball-sized pocket of air which didn't sound exactly like Cluck or like the wooden resonance of the high latch falling back in place surrounded by walls and lino but did clup sound different enough from clap for me to know it was his sound for wooden gate and thus did we begin to speak to one another in a language that was entirely of our devising.

Jim was very pleased with Cluck and I could tell he was waiting for another Sister to go through the wooden gate so that we could repeat the trick but meanwhile I took the opportunity of a more regular sound to teach Jim our second word Thump from Kurt's thump. This I made with my voice low in my chest and my tongue high in my mouth just after Kurt went thump.

Jim laughed again so delighted was he and in all the days of my life I have never met anyone so delightfully delighted but for some reason Jim found Thump harder to imitate than cluck and I had already done my Thump three more times before Jim replied by patting his hard tummy up under his jumper with a cupped hand and in this manner Thump not I thought a very useful word was accomplished.

After these first two successes we immediately became a bit stuck because no more ward-sounds come our way to imitate and though I tried whistling to teach Jim Bird he only hissed back out of politeness and I could tell he had no real idea what I meant because although we could hear faint birdsong through the windowpane and I could repeat it I don't think birds were something Jim could picture clearly certainly not as clearly as he could Thump and Cluck.

It was a quiet morning and for an hour no-one came through the wooden gate and not even Lise's weeping was there for another sound to make a word from but when Sister Muriel went through liftwards Cluck was confirmed and when she came back it was reconfirmed but she took Jim away I never discovered where and he did not return after lunch or before bedtime and so I had no more significant contact with Jim on that day but in a way I was glad because my deep emotions were ready for an epic voyage on Finn's snoring oceans the vast sea was where I very much wanted to be because I needed to find my way into the heart of a night sea storm and then weep in my cot with relief gratitude relief that Jim was not lying in bed in disgrace hungry and facing another day in the Chapel but even more so weep with gratitude that I had finally found the person I needed meaning the person who needed me.

It seemed so natural and so perfectly set up for whenever Jim was next standing behind me surely it would happen after Cluck and Thump and me trying to bird-whistle surely he would rest his hands on the handles of my wheelchair of course he would hands go to handles because that's what hands are for and if the brake of my wheelchair were off Jim would feel when he leaned his weight against me the wheels move and I would be nudged straight ahead into the radiator with one of my big toes bending back as it was sticking out from the footplate and then the footplate itself would hit the radiator with the metallic tonk that when Sister Cécile did it by accident resonated through my whole body and sometimes for some reason gave me an instant headache yes if the brake of my wheelchair were off then Jim would move me.

More than this Jim would have understood with his hands on the handles that he could move me and then that he could steer me and after that we would have been off on our way over the wide flat surface of my imagination toward the never-to-be-reached horizon of my hopes but meanwhile together we would accomplish the wheelies of my dreams.

I was racing forwards fast seeing nothing but a sky that didn't seem to be moving except very slowly with blue and white over and against itself but I could feel my pure horse-like speed.

By the time morning made burly balls of light roll around the ceiling of our dorm I knew what I had to do that day although I knew I very well might not accomplish it that day or the next and so I began before breakfast during prayers by significantly humming the National Anthem at Finn so that Finn heard and understood which he did because although I did not use this very often only in emergencies everyone knew the National Anthem meant the Royal Family and that the Royal Family was Princess Beauty and Princess Lovely and Princess Pretty who liked to help the common folk with their kindness and their magic so Finn knew I wanted the Princesses and when he with his spike-surrounded gaze looked at my eyes to understand more I turned them to look sideways to the right meaning out through the door and by implication down the long corridor.

I thought I could rely on Finn but something must have happened to distract him and make him forget because after Mass and breakfast once Sister Cécile had left me in front of the window and put on the brake of my wheelchair as I knew she would despite me making noises to say No once I was in position close to Kurt Finn did not bring the Princesses and he did not even come all by himself but Jim did come and after we had repeated Thump and then Clunk even though no sister was going through the wooden gate and then I tried with a new word Wheelchair because it was important and Jim as I had hoped was standing right behind me with his hands on the handles Vroo I said Vroo and at the same time I wriggled my bottom from side to side to make the wheelchair shake and Jim answered using the strength of his hands to shake me in my wheelchair and so for the moment Vroo meant Shake which was wrong but at least another word.

I had thought that all the teaching would be in one direction me-to-Jim but Jim had things he wanted me to learn and the first of these he acted out again and again by whacking his right hand against the side of his head and falling to the floor and not moving all of which I understood to be a re-enactment of him running into the filing cabinet but I could not tell if he wanted me to understand Filing Cabinet or Fall or Head or Charlie or possibly the whole thing.

It was very frustrating for a while but an enjoyable kind of frustrating and Princess Pretty who might have been able to interpret was not there with us so we had to cope by ourselves and eventually when I made a sound of pain like Ow Jim quickly jumped up and hugged me.

I had been wrong because I had been thinking he was naming something like Gate or Filing Cabinet but all along he had just wanted me to show him that I understood that his running into the filing cabinet had been really painful but also very funny.

In other words I was trying to teach Jim a basic vocabulary and he was already wanting to have a conversation with jokes.

After Ow Jim was happy and I was happy but as he fell down and picked himself up fell down and picked himself up he began to sweat and among the saltiness and pepperiness I could smell more and more meatiness and also when his hands came close to my face I was able to see small brown hairs on the tops of them and I had already felt there were a few hairs beneath Jim's nose so I knew we did not have many months perhaps three because he was a big boy and he was every day becoming a bigger boy and closer to being too big to be a boy.

Also if he kept fighting with Charlie Sister Britta might decide to move one of them up the road to the Brothers and although I was sure she would be blissfully thankful to see the back of knife-Charlie as would we all still Charlie wasn't as meaty on the nose as Jim was and if they were looking for an excuse the Sisters to move one of them up the road to the Brothers then it was likely Jim would go before Charlie so I had to hope Charlie's armpit hair grew faster and his sheets in the morning were stickier and smelled more of freshly baked bread and he fought back more manfully all of which I had witnessed many times as boys in Dorm 2 reached the point they could no longer be restrained either from impurity with themselves or violence towards others or both and sometimes both at the same time restrained by the sainted efforts of five nuns even with the occasional help of Mrs Beatles the Cleaner and Ludvik the Caretaker.

Lise arrived mid-morning to see her brother Kurt and to collapse on the lino in her usual beautiful heap of soft damp flower-patterned fabric and unassuageable black-kneed grief like an incarnation of Tchaikovsky's Symphony No. 6 in B Minor The Pathetique which gave me the chance to try enlisting her help by humming the National Anthem and hoping she would hear and understand and go and fetch the Princesses as she had done a few times before but today her trag-edy the mysterious tragedy of herself was so deeply felt by her that she either did not hear or could not understand or had not enough psychic strength to go and fetch the happy Princesses or even to lift herself from the lino once she'd sobbingly collapsed.

After it became clear Lise would not go Jim and I were at least able to discover our word for her which from me was an obvious sob but from Jim was a very clever dragging of his big bare right foot across the lino so it made a sad squeak and so delighted was I with this that I not only made my laughing sound trying to make sure it was distinguished from my choking sound to make sure Sister Britta didn't rush out to save me I not only laughed but also did my difficult best to bring my hands together and clap. Jim did not of course see the effort I was making to bring my hands together he just felt the wheelchair shaking shaking on the lino and thought I meant Vroo.

Ha ha I said as clearly as I could letting the yack yack sound come from my belly straight up to the roof of my mouth but Jim for some reason misunderstood this as me asking him to rock me and my wheel-chair from side to side quite violently and I had no sound for No to stop him although I tried the closest I could come Uh-oh Uh-oh.

Luckily no Sister heard and came but I realized I had to be extremely careful to do nothing that might get Jim banned from visiting me so I began bone-humming and Jim understood this to mean Calm Down which was a relief because even if I did not have No and Stop I still had Calm Down.

All of this learning was a bit like being tickled at least a bit like how I experience tickling that is it was funny terrifying paralyzing giddy and because I liked the person who was tickling me funny and giddy overtopped terrifying and paralyzing so it was like being tickled by

Princess Pretty who was a demon of a tickler rather than by Charlie who was just a demon.

However tickling of any sort can only go on for a certain while before it becomes painful before it becomes an agony like the agonies of Hell but the agonies of Hell are not terminated as this was by Sister Mary Margaret coming out into the long corridor and banging the lunch gong.

It was tomato soup with potatoes and Cardinal Newman in it which Sister Cécile mashed for me so they turned the colour of the soup from reddy-orange to orangey-white and because the gong had ended the tickling just as the soup had ended the hunger so I was ready for an afternoon of learning-talk with Jim but this did not happen because as I later heard from Finn the dreaded basket-weaving happened instead although this was the only time Jim took part because he got so bored he began to roar in frustration and Sister Cécile as if she knew I would need a way to calm my disappointment left me facing the whiteness of the white wall into which I found I was not able to travel half so far as before Jim's arrival on the ward and I regretted this because it had been my deepest greatest comfort along with the birds and the moss and the wych elm and the beautiful proximity of Lise.

Jim was bringing me new things things that were closer up and more fleshy funnier and more purposeful but he was taking me away from and so taking away from me the gorgeous details of the world that I had once upon a time seen as the gorgeous details of the Creation left there by God the Father for the edification of His wayward and sinful children but which I before Jim had been trying to see as simply and as purely but as deeply and as truly as I could so for example when I looked at the white of the wall or when I looked at the pink scar on Sister Cécile's slender wrist I tried to see them as they really were by looking at them until I forgot it was me looking at them and forgot there were other things around them so it was a bit like looking at the scar or the pink as if they were gods that had created themselves and nothing else as background in the universe not even me not even Jim.

This had been easier with the white than with the scar or its pink because the scar belonged to Sister Cécile in a way that the white didn't belong to the wall and also the white stayed still a lot longer than the scar ever did but that was the challenge of really deeply looking at something in either a gaze or a glimpse you needed to capture it profoundly in your head and then entirely shut your eyes to the rest of the ward and the world and its sound dance and word-jangle and potato smell so that you could contemplate it in itself the way the Priest sometimes said in his sermons about God and his greatness being the origin and end of all things the alpha and the omega also the causeless cause but Jim had interrupted this way of seeing and was forcing me to deal with everything that was happening to do with him all at the same time.

It was exciting but also made me panicky because there was far too much going on and it was changing too fast for me to keep up with when all I wanted to do was be adequate to the moment and live it vividly at the same time as realizing it was always overflowing and escaping in waves of complexity and confusion that might be Jim's two hands touching my two shoulders whilst the breath from Jim's nostrils with a twirl of curlicues like Princess Lovely's curly hair entered the gap between my shirt collar and the nape of my neck at the same time as I was trying to calibrate how much more meaty he was compared with the day before and simultaneously disentangling this from the head-swirling deliciousness of scent of salt and pepper and friendship that seemed to sing along to the silence that wasn't silence after Jim had finished bone-humming or had laughed after saying Thump with his hands.

I made my panic worse by trying to remark and remember each moment distinctly because I knew that one day all I would have was the memory of Jim and not Jim himself present in my peripheral vision making all my other senses go zing and now that time has indeed come and Jim is not present and has not been present for many years what I remember and want to record in long-hoarded words and word orders is not only the delicious presence of him Jim but also the delicious panic of that time during which I often told myself Calm down and take it all in but there was always too much world to take in because there was always more gorgeous detail than I had time or senses for and every caterpillar-of-a-When immediately became a butterfly-of-a-What and flew off into the flock of a thousand interplexing Whats whose air-dance of now being like this and now being like that was too delicate for anybody to remember but a god.

Of course at the time despite my word-hoard I didn't think it this way with these sentences in this order because often I was just a mute panic and a fantastic feeler-of-feelings. Even so it turns out didn't do a bad job of remembering this or that butterfly of present-moment Jim with his warmth and goodwill towards all men but particularly it seemed towards me.

And though I do have more language now thanks to the unlocking by Dr Masters and the books I am able to hear and the questions I am able to ask people I still know that even were I time-travelled as I am now back inside myself as I was during the Jim-time I would remember it no better because at the same time as watching air-dances of Whats I would be putting together words I wanted to remember in a particular order with a particular resplendence of rhythm and crumple of sounds and so the world would become lost to me trying to get it right in words rather than simply being the world of deliciously panicked now now galloping now giddily giddily galloping.

And now that this time in the rethinking of thinking has become a bit woozy I can afford to think for a while about the twenty-eighth to the thirty-fourth days not in all their detail but about a period an intermezzo of Jim and I getting stuck after our first breakthroughs and failing to come up with much new shared language because we had begun by depending on external sounds to prompt us into copying and so learning and this meant that in a quiet world of a quiet ward we were left for a long time waiting and although I tried again with pyramid-skinned Finn every morning during prayers humming the National Anthem he was in some sort of a huff with me perhaps because I had a new friend in Jim and so he wouldn't fetch the Princesses to help interpret for me.

I was afraid of the return of Charlie and the return of Sockball and the inevitable loss of Jim to other boys and their sporty preoccupations that would waste our time and bring him closer to a meatiness that even Sister Eliza could not but notice so I persisted in trying to get Jim to explore the wheelchair with his hands in the hope that he would accidentally get to the brake and release it. The brake was just a lever down and to the right of my right hand and with its shiny black plastic knob it could only be pushed one way until it clicked and released which was what other wheelchair users with shoulders and arms and hands less tense than mine were expected to do but which was completely beyond my powers before the unlocking by Dr Masters who so believed in the capacities of those thought spastic imbecile that he did whatever he could to help free their perfect skeletons from the bonds of spasm and overenthusiasm.

Something needed to change or at least to happen and on the thirty-fourth day a Sunday the woozy time stopped because something did happen on a dull white morning shortly after the second Mass and it happened on the usual long corridor with the usual fab four in their usual places and it was a realization and a revelation to both of us at the same time halfway through a bone-hum when I had run out of hymn tunes to hum that I hadn't hummed before and so knowing that it might confuse Jim but also hoping it might make him laugh I changed from Veni Creator Spiritus to Happy Birthday to You which of course he knew better than he knew anything else musical and as soon as I began it he joined me in it to you Happy Birthday to you Happy etcetera until the end when we both started again because we'd had the same idea at the same time with the hum of the two-note opening tune to Happy and then having made the idea of that first word we both stopped and left silence because we were we were both not Birthday to You but we were both Ha-ppy and we laughed harder than we had ever done before and harder than we were ever to laugh again except for one time because we had a new wonderful way to make words and Happy hummed Jim and Happy I hummed back and then his Happy and my Happy overlapped in a partsong of pure harmonic understanding between us that from then on where we stopped in a song was what we meant wordwise.

Kurt was confused and stopped thumping I think because he thought we were humming Happy Birthday to him and Lise gave a wail I could hear when I peeped out through the curtains of our laughter and she started weeping even harder but I could not stop celebrating and mourn aloud along with her as I had done so many times before because Jim was humming Happy Birthday to You and stopping right on the note that meant You and squeezing my head in his hands and when he eventually paused I sent the same meaning back to him by bone-humming Happy Birthday until I too reached

You then nudging my head back into his hard tummy so he knew my You meant him.

After the impasse and intermezzo of the six days waiting for sounds this was total joy and we began to communicate far more freely as long as we could think of a song or a hymn that contained the word we needed so Happy Birthday after it had given us Happy and You and To and Dear was not much more use and neither were the hymns which soon gave us God and Jesus which were words without a great deal of practical use for a blind boy and a spastic boy on a long corridor ending in a wooden gate with a high latch although if Jim had worked out the meaning of some Latin as I had by that time then they would have been full of vocabulary Meum Teum as well as Deum.

Again we were stuck and again we waited and went back over what we'd already taught one another delightfully and frustratingly until Jim casually so casually started to hum Let It Be just after Sister Mary Margaret had walked past Cluck on her squeaky way to the Refectory of course what Jim wanted to show me was that he knew from the shoe-sound who this was and what he wanted to teach me was the Mary part of Mother Mary so we could refer to at least one of the Sisters by name but this was the miraculous breakthrough and eternal thanks go to Mrs Beatles for her incessant playing of her red and blue cassettes on her radio-cassette-player for we both now knew most of the lyrics to most of the songs on those four long and winding sides and within an hour we also had I and Me and We and Speaking and Words and Comes To Me for Come To Me which was to prove very useful and then when this was exhausted for the next song I tried I Wanna Hold Your Hand which Jim with a joyous laugh let me do immediately but then he pulled his hand free to clap along with the clap-claps clap-claps in the song a song which I instantly realized was wonderful because it had the supremely important function of getting Jim to Hold My Hand but which didn't have much more scope for language apart from Tell and I Wanna.

The lunch gong stopped us but during that afternoon we had a fairly uninterrupted run through a whole new world of words that I can still remember and which all came from the first verse or chorus of the songs we tried next because otherwise it would have got very confusing and I remember we got Day Alone Fool Sitting Nobody and Town Born Man Told and also Submarine which at first didn't seem to be very useful and in fact was a word for a thing I could form only a vague picture of something under the sea with men in it and nuclear weapons but which after Jim ran up and back down the long corridor loudly humming Submarine Submarine I understood was how he thought about where we were the ward which for him was under the sea.

That night the thirty-fourth following a memorable supper of leeks in white sauce and stewed prunes without custard I smiled widely as my teeth were brushed and went to bed with a head full of possibilities but also frustrations the biggest of which was that there wasn't a single Beatles song that contained the word Wheelchair in fact the closest I could find was Armchair nor could I think of any song from the red and blue cassettes that said Brake in the first or any verse and by the time I fell asleep I was sad but I must have dreamed something helpful because I woke up thinking Beep Beep and Beep Beep and then Yeah!

By nine o'clock on the thirty-fifth day we were back in position in Jim's submarine beside the radiator and Jim had obviously been dreaming or thinking too because he started the morning with Hello from Hello Goodbye and then he made me laugh by also singing Hello Thump as he turned towards Kurt and after that Hello Goodbye turned out to be a lot more useful than I Wanna Hold Your Hand because it gave us Yes No and even more usefully for the future Stop and Go Go Go which brought me exactly to the subject I wanted to open up with Jim and not in the ghastly literal way that putting together the word Wheelchair would have required.

As before I started bone-humming a new tune and I don't know if I've ever been as relieved as when Jim immediately joined in on the first verse and when we got to the chorus I reached the line about Baby You Can Drive My Car and stopped after Car then wiggled my bum as much as I could to make my wheelchair move. But Jim kept humming and when he reached the end of the next line he gave my wheelchair a little shake back to me in fact he give it a tiny lift off the ground which was thrilling but made me think he'd got Be A Star rather than Car in his head so I started again at the beginning of the song and stopped again and wiggled again at Car but Jim again kept going and again gave the front wheels a tiny horse-like buck in the air.

I waited until Jim's hands were back on the handles then just hummed the line ending in Car and gave the most definite shake of the wheelchair I could but also made my Car sound which was a sound I wasn't too bad at because it was quite close to choking in fact too close because I felt Jim go stiff and listen to see if I was really choking. Happy I hummed Happy so he knew I was fine and because we were onto that I hummed I Feel Fine the guitar introduction to which was quite exhausting and by this time Lise had arrived and flopped down on the lino and begun crying so Jim didn't respond with another verse of I Feel Fine but tried to start another song but time after time found it too funny to keep going.

Jim fell flopped onto the floor and rolled around and slapped his bare feet for a couple of minutes and then with snorts and guffaws stood up and took hold of the handles and hummed the four opening notes of She Loves You Yeah before falling to hilarious bits again on the lino She Loves You meaning Lise Loves Elliott and although it was a joke it immediately caused me heartache because I had for so long hoped it might be true and I hoped at that moment Lise might understand and confirm or deny but I also feared she would be scared or offended and go away forever.

Lise it seemed was too deep in her weeping to understand anything but flower-patterned tragedy and even the third time Jim repeated the opening line she did not react in any way I could perceive but the same wasn't true of Kurt who up until this point through all our humming had continued to stare into the filing cabinet and to give out thumps at his usual regular intervals and didn't seem to have heard or noticed anything Jim or I were up to but the third time Jim got through She Loves You Jim continued with the descending three-note tune and to our total shock Kurt thumped three times in rhythm for Yeah Yeah Yeah extraordinary miraculous.

Jim and I hummed the line through again and a second time Kurt joined unmistakably in with Thump Thump Thump.

Only think of that as Sister Mary Margaret might have said had she heard.

Miraculous and extraordinary as it was it turned out to be a complete one-off and though we spent much of the rest of the morning trying to get Kurt to respond to any other Beatles song he just kept up his normal regular slow ward-heartbeat thump until we gave up and went back to She Loves You at which point Kurt loyally joined in with the Yeahs for as long as we kept them up Kurt even I think moved his head down the side of the filing cabinet with each Yeah to try to mimic the three descending notes of the phrase so there must have been something about that song that appealed to him either that or in my best hopes he had heard and understood the rest of what Jim and I had been up to and he wanted to send us a simple direct message of support Yeah keep going Yeah I'm with you Yeah.

Whatever the truth was I was never to find out for although Jim and I spent the rest of the thirty-fifth morning and much of the afternoon attempting to find another song Kurt would join us in we failed and it was only as the light outside began to become delicate and diaphanous in winter grey that I decided to try again with Baby You Can Drive My and I don't know what had been going on with Jim in the meantime but the very first time I bum-wiggled on Car and made the choke-crow sound Jim jiggled the wheelchair and hummed louder on the note for Car.

We were there we were not a wheelchair but a Car and straight away I did Yes from Hello Goodbye and Happy from Happy Birthday then back to Drive My Car wiggle and in reply came jiggle and oh how many white and light blue Submarine years had I been waiting for this? I became overexcited and began to repeat quite manically the crow caw-choke sound and this along with Jim's response which was panicked running around soon brought Sister Cécile from the Sisters' Office to rescue me from a choking that was really the purest joy but rescue me she did wheeling me back into my Dorm Dorm 1 and for me that was the end of that day but honestly I don't think my poor mortal frame could have taken much more happiness for the wheelchair was now understood as Beep Beep and the horse of a boy was closer than he had ever been before to galloping.

Sister Cécile although concerned for me as always did not associate my choking and fainting as she saw it with my closeness to Jim and so she did nothing the next morning the thirty-sixth to prevent that closeness thus allowing Jim and I to continue our language-learning in the presence of Kurt but the absence of Lise who I hoped was not reacting to the absurd suggestion that She Loved Me Yeah Yeah Yeah and in the bright light of a pale-sky morning with high fast clouds over the opposite windows and with Jim's big hands I was sure shining on the handles behind me everything seemed set for more vocabulary but Jim and I had only just got Kurt to thump along to the three Yeahs a couple of times when I heard many feet coming down the long corridor towards us so many feet in fact that I couldn't tell anything about them except that they weren't Sisters' shod feet but children's bare ones and that they perhaps included Charlie's feet ready again to score gift goals but no.

The National Anthem started in Finn's dum-dum-dah dum dah-dum version and suddenly I saw the pinkish tones of the Princesses in my peripheral vision a little sparkliness here and there and then felt the magical touch of three pairs of delicate hands not doing anything necessary for me just adjusting my shirt collar brushing back my mouse-brown hair stroking my cheek and all to let me know that the Princesses Beauty Lovely and Pretty had deigned to answer my call and were there to help me if they could with their kindness and their good sense and their magic.

It was too sudden and too wonderful what Finn had finally done even though I had given up asking him to do it because from one moment to the next I went from Jim's companionship to an eager crowd who if only I could have spoken to them would not only have flipped the brake of my wheelchair but also have lifted it from the pale lino to make it and me fly a foot in the air carefully up and down the long corridor making the tinkling noises that magic made when it happened in the ward but I could not but I could not speak but I was not capable of speech.

I did my best I tried to get Jim to jiggle the wheelchair by humming Drive My Car and wiggling myself and at the same time angling my eyes down towards the brake but he Jim was now becoming the object and centre of the Princesses' attention and their light slightly tacky touches were transferring across from me to him as lightly and easily as midnight moths from eyelid to eyelid for he was the newest boy and was already making everyone laugh with his ticklish delight which was contagious and most of this of course was happening behind me so I could see only edges of bright pale hints of it in reflection but I was already downcast in dismay because I had wasted the luck of having succeeded in asking Finn to bring the Princesses and now was surrounded by pink flowery wallpaper mirth redecorating the white wall and when I hummed the National Anthem in an attempt to halt things and change them no-one heard.

Sometimes I wonder how it it meaning my life would have been different if I had been able to get the Princesses or Finn to understand the word Brake and to place Jim's right hand down upon it and show him how the round shiny black plastic knob which to him would have been a smooth ball on a stick how it moved out with a small click and then downwards until it was at the bottom of its parabola where it gave another click as it locked into place meanwhile sliding restraints aside beneath my seat the wheelchair's seat after which the wheels were free to roll forwards or backwards or in guided arcs that left behind them four parallel lines two thick two thin on the pale blue lino sometimes visible on wet or dirty lino but usually invisible.

If this had happened my small white dismay would have ended sooner but I am not sure if my greater green joy would ever have come to pass for such a laughing twittering congregation was always going to draw Sisterly attention and whatever the Sisters saw starting was usually stopped and whatever the Sisters perceived of energy was immediately damped and so if a great public fuss had been made of Jim pushing me up the long corridor for the first time they might Sister Britta especially might have invented an instant rule banning it completely and that would have rendered quite a lot of what happened afterwards an absolute impossibility.

Sister Mary Margaret came and tried to work out what the delight was about so she could join in and show that the Lord's servants were not all about punishments and saying No even though we knew they mainly were but the source of the delight was just Jim being there and being Jim and being happy to be there and so Sister Mary Margaret just saw and heard a lot of children being silly about nothing in particular so she gently began to send them on their way which way was up the long corridor towards the Craft Room and which them also included Jim at the centre of the crowd and he went accompanied by the Princesses and Finn the fetcher without a touch or a hum for me because I am sure he had for that moment forgotten I existed.

Thump was the timpani and muted birdsong was the first and second violins of the Symphony in C minor of my abandonment and disenchantment and betrayal that day and I wished for Lise to come back and be the tragic mezzo soprano but she too had abandoned me so I danced in my chair in dangerous agitation with my breathing rasping up and up closer and closer to hyperventilation and my eyes and lopsided head jiggling the sight of the wych elm as if a volcano were beneath it about to destroy it until someone noticed and said a distant word with two s'es in that I knew was Distressed and then Sister Cécile was beside me trying to find out why I was beside myself but even had I magically been un-tongue-tied and able to speak I could not have explained the agony for a soul of never being able to speak even though you know many of the words because you have never allowed yourself to forget a single one you ever heard because each is more wonderfully radiant with grace than their everyday speakers and users ever know plangent quiescent rambunctious

Sisyphean because an embodied soul needs a throat and teeth and an agile tongue and a broad palate to make itself known or hands that can hold a keen-nibbed pen or lithe pencil to make legible letters not a dumpling paintbrush only capable of splodging red yellow blue.

I cried like a baby and let Sister Cécile baby me by singing to me as a surrogate angel and she must have heard more of what had been passing between Jim and me than I knew for the song she chose to sing was Lennon and McCartney's Let It Be and so by trying to make it better she made it worse and worse with the word Mother until I had no choice but to choke because at least a pretend medical emergency meant an end to music and the idea of mother.

The thing with me and choking however is that the distinction between pretend choking and real choking hardly exists and I can think I am doing one when I am doing the other and sometimes I have found that even thinking about pretend choking can hospitalize me with real constriction whereas at other times I can be halfway through a really horrible duffing up of a cough and I can think Elliott you don't need to do this and at that point I can just simply stop.

On this afternoon I did not want to stop until I had been properly looked after and treated like the spastic imbecile I wasn't but most of the Sisters except Sister Cécile thought I was because although most of the time I wanted to try my hardest to shine brighter and be better and stronger than I truly was there were times from time to time when it when life was too much got too painful so painful that I was unable to keep up my best efforts and at those times it was a blesséd relief to be able to relax back into incapacity even if no-one outside me noticed the difference between an alert observing recording me and a time-passing being-babied me.

If I wanted I could watch my life happen in front of me like television and ignore the part of it that happened below and behind and above me for a bib would always clasp itself around my neck like a flannelette Princess and custard except during Lent would appear in spoons and fly up towards my mouth and my chin would become wet and then be dried and then my jumper would fly off over my head darkening my world briefly and then might or might not return to me in a week's time and all of this when this was automatically happening was when I thought of the Sisters really as sisters who treated me as a feeble brother who needed everything doing for him apart perhaps from breathing.

Looking back I am ashamed of my weakness at giving in to my weakness and allowing weakness to be thought of me.

It is true that I had part-concealed my capacity for language and my knowledge of music but it is also true that no-one before Jim not even Sister Cécile had managed to establish contact with me so rapidly and profoundly yes Sister Cécile understood some signals of mine but they were mainly eye movements in response to her well-timed questions and after I had calmed down enough to stop the real choking that followed the pretend choking she understood from me closing my eyes and letting my jaw go slightly slack that I was exhausted and could do with going to bed with some mashed banana shoved inside me and forget the teeth brushing for once in a while can't we?

Sleep was not so obliging as Sister Cécile sleep was darkly hidden somewhere deep within one of the folds or creases of the white sheets directly in front of my eyes that I wanted over my eyes to cover my whole head like a suffocation risk like a cloud cloaking the moon and making many millions of unlit rooms beneath it darken like this one I was in Dorm 1 but instead I saw a pattern of kinks and shadows that showed a twist that became a vortex into which my left eye went in search of day-closing sleep but out from which my right eye was constantly pushed by unstoppable interest in the surrounding white and dark-blue and light-grey shapes that somehow related to my misery at Jim's abandonment of me.

If I had pencil and paper and better motor skills than I currently have even after the unlocking by Dr Masters I think I could in fact I am sure I could draw a completely clear and accurate picture of how those folds fell that night in front of my prodigal eyes sheet-folds like those that when I was younger and more inventive I had sometimes sleeplessly just as I converted Finn's snores into the sea I had sometimes transubstantiated lovely word transubstantiated into snow on high satisfying hills or moonlight shattering on peaked seas or paint on the legs of Ted's trousers and I would fly over those hills like a vulture from the poster of Wild Animals of the African Savanna or sail upon them like an Admiral of the Fleet of Finn's nose or wonder how it felt to pull them on in the morning crusty over my legs and feet that would spend the day walking back and forth between wall and paint-tin wall and paint-tin all to make a wet cylinder of white into a dry plain of white apart from the dream-drips dripping past the vulture and the nose onto the moon-mottled sheets of Elliott watching Elliott waking.

This head-confusion of failure that overtook me that night did I suppose in the end become something like dreaming even if it fell short of and failed to be sleeping so I had a choice over breakfast as the spoon approached and every unsugared grey mouthful of texture above pink hippo told me I was useless and might as well enjoy being useless and take advantage of being a pointless being still I knew I had to swallow them all every distinct one actively and with full attention to the details of tickly dry flake and slightly scrapey lump as they made their way over my tongue down the back of my throat and into my perilous oesophagus until they reached the relative safety of my self-regulating stomach where if they were rejected it was none of my doing even if it would be considered my fault if they bounced back onto Sister Cécile's clean grey-blue morning habit.

As it so often has trying to eat well made me realize that I had to try and live well as well at least for the rest of the thirty-seventh morning until the next occurrence of the mouth-visiting spoon that once upon a time had been a train choo-choo then chew-chew and although the world in the form first of my mother and then the One Holy Catholic and Apostolic Church had always so far taken care of the milky and spoony choo-choo part of the equation of sustenance through nutrition the chew-chew part was still my sole responsibility and if I did it sloppily could end in intubation and hospital or suffocation and death.

Thank you Sisters Clare and Cécile for being patient with me when I tried to starve myself into higher quality visions of Jesus Christ and thank you for being sensitive enough to let me drink only sugared milk when my swallowing technique degenerated due to failures of moral character for you helped keep me alive until that thirty-seventh morning when I decided to be pitiless with myself for the sake of the wooden gate and what it would mean for all of us on the ward for Jim and I to pass through and beyond it without permission and what it would mean for my eyes to behold the world of green freedom outside the ward.

Either wall or window I did not care and window was where I ended up ready for the hours of test of faith that were indeed horribly to befall after the sheet-night three days of hours of test because Princesses once they have crowned a new king tend to abduct him towards joy and make his days a field of worship and giggles especially when their most favourite thing of all he is a blind king and so every moment is a game of Blind Man's Buff.

I might have weakened but I strengthened I might have gone the inconsolable way of Lise but instead I went the resolute way of Micky determined above all to wait with forgiveness and tenderness for the meatier return of the hopeful one and I could not help but think of Jesus not least because in this part of the liturgical calendar everything that happened and was said in Chapel was an anticipation of Easter and His glorious resurrection after the fearful passion of His crucifixion. But I realized that I was being blasphemous and although of the Trinity I had always for obvious reasons fancied myself as akin to the holiness of the Holy Ghost particularly when I was looking at the whiteness of the white wall I knew that I should avoid this danger of Jesus-thinking for even during my most fervent moments of identification I knew I was just a lonely boy who had fallen away from being the Holy Ghost and was now just a boy sitting still in a wheelchair on a long corridor where time was measured by echoey thumps awaiting the return of a more popular boy from the Craft Room where that boy Jim had possibly been happier than at any time since he arrived on the ward.

On the third day after his abduction the thirty-ninth Jim did not return but on the fourth day the fortieth he did and I afterwards learnt from Finn's re-enactment that he Jim had been sitting in a chair in the Craft Room on the afternoon of the third day with Princess Lovely trying to plait his brown hair when all of a sudden he became wrathful and began pushing her wedge-fingered hands away from his head as if they were a bothersome bee as I had seen Sister Mary Margaret do once running from the Refectory shouting Beast and after a lot of sulking and Princess Beauty and Princess Pretty going back and forth between the wrathful King and the rejected servant everyone was reconciled in time for supper but Jim the next morning the fortieth did not return to his court but instead let his big feet ring out as they approached the wheelchair of his exile and the wooden gate of his destiny.

And here was one of those moments I still struggle to understand even with years of quiet having passed in which to recall and ponder it whilst facing fleur-de-lys wallpaper behind the empty shelves of a dark and dusty cupboard with a dry mop for company before the rescue by shocked young Brother Benedict and the unlocking by Dr Masters and Lioresal for Jim did not wait for Drive My Car or for Vroo and he did not even hum hello he just found with his hands my head in the air which was soon truly to be a head in the air and then after roughing up the brown hair he patted down in handy flollops my shoulders arms and the wheelchair's arms until he came on the left side to nothing and the right side to the black shiny plastic knob which I felt his fingers take and push forwards and my world shifted.

Perhaps Jim had been thinking over what I might mean by my frantic bone-humming of You Can Drive or perhaps in a previous ward he had formed a similarly symbiotic relationship with another floppy or spasmy one but his hands went back to the handles and I could feel myself moving slightly forwards and then slightly backwards as he breathed and as his stomach muscles went in and out and so overjoyed was I after the three days of being ignored that I almost couldn't react my tears were too close and my collapse too imminent with the example of Lise right there to my right but after a moment I managed a bone-hum of Drive My Car Drive My Car and then Vroo Vroo and even if he had not been thinking of it in the king-interim Jim must have understood because he made his throat growl like combustion and his arms tremble like an engine.

We were at the T-junction we were on the starting line but we had not yet moved off because I had not yet given Jim the green light like I had seen from the coach just before the schoolboy threw his green gherkin the day of the second Arndale Centre shopping trip and at this moment realizing the danger and potential after all my years of fantasy I allowed myself an ice-cream vanilla coolness and sweetness of mouth-melt with golden syrup deliciousness on top to think about what it suddenly seemed after Jim's return and the pushing of the black knob we could achieve together.

Carefully for if a Sister saw us and thought I was in danger a new rule might instantly be made so everything must be slow-motion like a lioness catching an antelope everything must be slow-motion until it wasn't and could be amazingly fast carefully carefully I began with Get Back Get Back in the firm knowledge that Jim would understand Back to mean backwards which he did and with the glide of and slide of a Heavenly new ride of pride I felt myself being moved back away from the heat of the radiator and the light of the window until I bone-hummed the words I Say Stop from Hello Goodbye and miracle of miracles because Jim was so profoundly intelligent and sympathetic it worked and after a moment for him to sing the song for himself in his head he and we stopped.

Lise was right there to my right her head down in the soft flowery damp fabric of her obscure trauma and tragedy but she must have heard the slight rubbery crimple of the wheels of my wheelchair reversing because she looked up in mild surprise at not having heard a Sister approach me to be moving me and then gazed in wonder at Jim in excelsis all powerful behind me and because of her position and mine I could see down to her knees which the moment before she lifted her sad head had been as I had seen coppery green with tinges of bile yellow but which blanched to palest blue with silver streaks as soon as she saw the vision of us and then gradually warmed to the gold of Queen Elizabeth II's drawing room at Buckingham Palace at Christmas.

Lise yelped and put her hands over her mouth but could not immediately find anything in what she saw to distress her so she could not stop herself smiling which I knew was disastrous for a smile meant she would soon know her happiness could not last like all happiness could not last and that thought would make her weep anew but for a little while I was able to meet her amazed smile with mine snarly as it was and I could shiver bodily delight towards her beautiful sore pink face.

I was now listening out for footfalls in case a Sister saw me so very far from my usual place and further from the wych elm too although that was a private distance-sensation for me and I realized that we Jim and I had no word yet for Slow or for Carefully so all I could hum was Go Go Go and Jim must have been excited too for a little overenthusiastically he pushed me forwards towards the radiator which approached at such astonishing speed that I didn't have time to hum Stop You Say Stop before the left footplate of my wheelchair hit the radiator with a mezzoforte Tonk that was so very different from Kurt's Thump that surely a Sister would hear and come running.

None did thank the Lord or that Tonk bringing a running nun could have marked the end of all our fun right then and there but as it was the long corridor remained empty but for the fab four and I devoted myself to bone-humming Stop Stop to make sure Jim kept me exactly where I was then Happy to let him know he'd done the right thing and all the while I was trying to think of a way of conveying to Jim the words Slowly and Carefully or Slow Down And Be Careful but I simply couldn't and so Jim became bored and began reversing me away from where I usually was.

Stop I hummed Stop but he continued pulling me awaywards and then curving around 90 degrees to the right as if he was going deliberately to run over Lise but then he jerked and started us forwards again at quite a good pace straight towards the hated wooden gate and I remember for an instant being totally terrified that my body was going to be destroyed by Jim rhino-ramming my wheelchair and my poor legs into the bars just as he had rhino-rammed Charlie into them.

We accelerated and accelerated only to slow to a sudden halt just as Jim had done on the thirteenth and the fifteenth and the seventeenth days halt an inch away from the vertical wooden bars one of which I noticed even in my flutter was a lighter and less orange colour than the others because Ludvik the Caretaker had newly inserted it in place of the one smashed by Jim's first violent attack on the injustice of our confinement.

I was trembling like I sometimes do when I have suddenly and unexpectedly puked but even in this fragile state I managed not to let out a loud noise of anger or fear instead I bone-hummed Get Back Get Back and had another lesser panic when I thought Jim's plan all along in undoing the brake had simply been to wheel me and leave me here as a mysterious protest to puzzle and annoy the Sisters and this despite whatever punishment they might decide on for me.

I don't know how long we sat and stood there while Jim failed to understand me and my humming of Once Belong Once Belong but it must have been twelve or thirteen thumps from Kurt before anything changed in the stillness. It needed an innovation from me so I bone-hummed Back and then immediately Submarine.

Jim took several more moments to take this in but he was fast learner and a beautiful driver because backwards we eventually went quite as if the wheels of my wheelchair were in grooves backwards up the long corridor of a submarine close to but not on top of Lise and then after I bone-hummed Get Back 90 degrees to the right finishing up as far as I could tell exactly to the inch where we'd started off in front of the window and this time to make his point of being in control and knowing what he was doing Jim reached down and grabbed the black plastic ball of the brake and flipped it on.

If I could have applauded I would have applauded and if I could have said Please Jim you great numpty don't ever scare me like that again that's exactly what I would have said but as it was the applause was left to the wings of a pigeon outside that took off from the roof opposite and I could only imagine the noise I knew it was making and the words were left forever unspoken. Instead as if they had been waiting for the performance to be over Sisters Muriel and Mary Margaret came a few moments later out of the Sisters' Office and through the wooden gate leaving behind a loud Cluck that Jim and I both imitated and afterwards laughed at as Sister Muriel said behind us to Sister Mary Margaret Well I never expected those two and Sister Mary Margaret replied just before they both got too quiet to hear You know I'm glad for the pair of them.

Jim jiggled the handles joyfully and I wondered then if he was celebrating because he thought he had shown me his hearing was so superlative that he had been able to tell both that we were safe to pay a quick wheeled visited to the wooden gate because the Sisters were sitting chatting and that we needed at a certain moment to move away because the Sisters were rising from their chairs stretching their spines making noises of mild distress and mild relief no I was never entirely sure if Jim's blind hearing was this good or not for if it was it might explain how he could know so precisely where the wooden gates were and if it wasn't it might explain other things that I don't want to think about just yet not while I can think about my relief at our deliverance from the punishment we would have received had the Sisters arrived ten seconds earlier.

I wanted to say Phew so I said Phew but my Phew sounded almost exactly like my Vroo and this time Jim responded by shaking the handles of the wheelchair in an engine-like way and it was this that made me realize I had been being too clever and wordy with the bone-hums which anyway took too long to get out i.e. You Say Stop instead of just Stop so instead I made Vroo Vroo revving sounds like those I had heard from impatient cars right behind the coach Vroo Vroo I went and Jim understood because he shook the handles with greater force and horsepower although probably he certainly didn't know it was called horsepower but then I Vrooed quieter and quieter and Jim's energy levels decreased until I came to a stop with a click and he immediately lifted his hands away.

I waited making the radiator-like ticking sounds I had heard from the engine of the coach whilst I was waiting alongside it in the rain waiting to be wheeled back in through reception to the lift waiting looking up at the spangly coach window behind which only a few minutes earlier I had been sitting looking at streetlights trapped in backwards-racing raindrops and I had felt happy then just as I felt happy now because my time was not routine my time was an adventure into time that could not be exactly predicted for instance I did not know when the engine would tick again and I did not know when the next juicy raindrop would land on my brown head and I absolutely didn't know when a tick and a drop would happen together as if the one had caused the other like I now caused Jim to tremble again by making a key-click ignition sound and then fiercely Vrooing.

The long corridor was empty but for Kurt and Lise. Jim was ready and I was ready so I bone-hummed Go Go Go and Jim released the brake freeing the giddy wheels and now was the time to be very careful very careful indeed so I made my Vroo gruffer and more chuntery then hummed Back from Get Back and immediately returned to gruff chuntering which Jim understood because once more I started to move away from the window and as soon as I was sure that gruntering meant reverse I made a high wheel squeak sound like braking and perhaps out of shock at my high-pitchedness Jim braked perfectly almost as perfectly as our new driving language was working before Sister Cécile spotted us from the far end of the long corridor and started to walk tippy-tap towards us.

Jim heard I heard and in my peripheral vision Lise heard too for she started wailing more frantically and I knew Sister Cécile would be hurrying in her tippy-tappy shoes to rescue me so she thought from danger so I hummed Go Go Go and then Submarine and was full of Phew when Jim began to push me tremblingly forwards but not fast in a panic and forwards I went until I wheel-squeaked just at the same instant Jim who knew how far away the radiator was from the footplate of my wheelchair drew to a halt and Sister Cécile's breathy arrival in turn was timed perfectly to coincide with me making the ignition sound to get Jim to put the brake back on and with Jim indeed smoothly putting on the brake.

Sister Cécile was worried for my safety how could she not be worried for my safety but as her Virgin Mary face came into view in front of me with her smooth forehead and a few pale blonde hairs sticking out she was smiling in her grey-green eyes and when she saw the look on my snarly face and the look in my eyes she knew I was not scared or being bullied but was having fun so much fun that in what might have been a foolishly trusting move I made my throat full of revving and Jim's hands did their tremulous best on the handles and Sister Cécile smiled even more broadly because as a musician and a beautiful one she understood harmony and how closely harmony is related to beauty.

The harmony continued because before she said what she said next I knew what Sister Cécile was going to say which was All right then you two but be careful and I hummed along to her phrasing of be careful because she had said it to me so many times when I was eating too fast that I knew the exact pitch of it and the exact three notes of it two Gs followed by an E in the octave above middle C so I hummed along to harmonize employing the notes E and A and then resolved on C which made Sister Cécile giggle she was still young enough to giggle as the Princesses and their tickling fingers knew.

Sometimes said Sister Cécile with her face right up close to mine and her gentle grey-green eyes reflecting mine back to me Sometimes I think you're the brightest of all our little stars and I felt my tears come from wherever they waited because in that moment little stars sounded so much like little horse and Sister Cécile looked so much like the mother I wanted to remember looking like that but couldn't only the face close up and the hair-curtains on either side and the small cubic face-space full of protecting breath breath that came again now from Sister Cécile in whispered words that were Be Careful but with a completely different meaning and also tone and tune.

I knew somehow from the tone of her tune that her meaning was specific and not general and that what she meant was Be Careful Of rather than Be Careful About and that the only person I ever needed to be truly careful of apart from made-up watching Jesus and Charlie the puncher was Sister Britta so Be Careful meant Be Careful Of her Of deep deep waters Of Sister Britta finding out and finding a reason to stop this little game which is bringing you delight.

O Sister Cécile how trapped you must have felt all those smouldering years of your youth among the nuns before you left to go as Sister Mary Margaret said Almost indubitably to Hell but at the gates of which I am entirely certain the Devil would have rejected you not only for generally being too good but also for specific acts of goodness towards an impatient obstinate ungrateful immature boy in a wheelchair a horse on a ward not the least of which being that at this particular moment you walked away bless you.

Sister Cécile rang the gong for lunch after the eating of which the long corridor became instantly fashionable with the Princesses and almost all of the other children because Charlie was still confined to the penance of the Craft Room and everybody was able to get away from him but also the Princesses who had even wheeled in Grace Maria and Shirley the Princesses who clearly wanted their blind King back with them and if they could not have Jim maybe they could once again make do with Micky who suddenly as he periodically did became fascinated by my window and by the possibility that he might be able to find some way of opening it and so flying away from it flying all the way to wherever he wanted to fly I am not sure he ever knew not beyond wanting to fly up rather than fall down and with all the time I'd had to puzzle it I had sometimes imagined a fantastic voyage where Micky took off and flew and landed in Kurt's land there to become a valiant warrior and be the people's brave saviour.

Jim was with me hands on the wheelchair's handles but we both knew it was not the time for more driving of the car for we could both sense the building mania the electric giddiness the gigantic giggle dynamo charging up the hysteria machine of that sunny Spring afternoon when we should all have been allowed outside on flat grass or soft sand not confined to such a small space as the long corridor and everyone but Charlie was there in the slanted yellow-grey sunshine even children I hardly ever saw except at mealtimes such as Grace Maria and Shirley such as Jeremy and even black Toby who did nothing but count his fingers perhaps because he found the number 10 comforting or true or perhaps to reassure himself his fingers were all still present and correct or perhaps because he was as Sister Mary

Margaret sometimes used to say of the more troubled and troubling and troublesome of us mad as a bag of sticks.

Everyone filled up my and Kurt's and Lise's and Jim's place the Here near the gate for like the Israelites the children sought escape from the bondage of Pharaoh on this occasion meaning Charlie although often it was Sister Britta who was Pharaoh just as she was deep waters but of all four of us regulars Lise suffered most from the exodus because her area of weep-floor was not held sacred by the Israelites as was my wheelchair which children said sorry if they ever touched as if touching it pained me.

Poor Lise was leaned across and tripped over and run into until she screamed hit out shouted blasphemies and ran to her bed in far-off Dorm 7 where given the circumstances the Sisters wisely let her remain for most of the rest of the fortieth day.

Never had I felt such love for the others even though so often they had been a source of jealousy to me with their working bodies which they did not always use and their sometimes clumsy souls which they did not know how to make elegant but after the first drive with Jim I saw them beatifically a little like their Creator if they had had one would have seen them that is as perfectly achieved examples of unique things that only they and they alone could ever be and for an hour it was as if I understood creation in its What but also in its Why so when I saw Micky at the window it seemed as if he was both himself and the bright shadow of an eternal version of himself and when I looked carefully Micky seemed outlined by a thin bright line of absolute confirmation and so were all the children surrounded like biscuits in baking class with the shape-cutter still around them always just about to be lifted off but never lifting.

And although it decreased waned in intensity and definiteness I continued to feel something similar all through supper-time of pureed vegetables followed by milk posset which looked like the substance all other substances had been spooned from and on into the first pepperminty sleep of the night where I began by being not just fast asleep but asleep and fast dreaming of being fast and then accelerating not being driven or driving or even galloping but simply allowing everything to travel fast past me left and right above and below so quickly it wasn't even a sight to see just an incredibly satisfying and reassuring mum-hum.

On the forty-first day after Jim's arrival the long corridor after breakfast was once again unfashionable and quiet and inhabited by the usual foursome and what followed was to be something like a usual day.

And so the forty-first day since Jim's arrival does not remain with me as livingly as those around it although it is still quite clear because they the other days were punctuated with events whereas the forty-first was the beginning of a new routine or so I we thought and that routine involved a slowly growing sophistication of notes and tunes of hums and squeaks that meant different things some of which began to work on the forty-first and some didn't for example the biggest challenge after winning the brake-battle was getting Jim to steer me Left and Right for if we could crack this then with Vroo and Squeak we could Go Go Go anywhere within the ward but I couldn't think of a way to convey Left through the lyrics of the red and blue cassettes nor any other way and the noises a car makes when it turns left are no different to those it makes turning right.

What I do most remember of our efforts on this in-between day is the being watched by Lise who although tearful to the brim did not begin to overspill until after lunch of Cardinal Newman and mulligatawny soup with for me the bits strained out. Lise palely gazed at us in something like a trance of calm if not of contentment and her knees when Jim's reversing of me brought them into sight were a warm freckling of blue and white just like Sister Mary Margaret's blue and white teacup and saucer had been before Micky broke them both by barging into the Craft Room table they were on and Sister Mary Margaret although able to glue them back together so I later heard her tell Sister Muriel resolved never again to bring them out of the Sisters' Office yes Lise's knees were fine bone china warmed from the inside by an exotic lapsang souchong of wonder at something which could not be me even mobile me because I was too much of a feature of what was always in front of her so I realized it the wonder must be him Jim.

Thump although the forty-first was the day I began to see the changing of Lise it took another couple of mornings of driving for me to understand it as the enchantment of love taking hold perhaps because although not worried about anything her brother Kurt might do she was still restrained by his presence and we all knew that external changes in Kurt's surroundings did sometimes manifest as changes in the violence of his land for example when Sister Clare was given her cake the invasions for a while ceased and it seemed to me the folk of the land were peacefully mourning the death of a goddess or enduring a winter so icy no warlord however rapacious would set out by sea.

By the afternoon of the forty-third day Lise's knees were all the colours of the party balloons that appeared and disappeared from the Refectory sometimes fully inflated and sometimes if the gap between celebrations was long a little dusty and saggy yes Lise's knees had become an easy to understand red yellow and blue and steering left and right had slowly been achieved by me changing the pitch of my Vroo whenever Jim turned to left or right the language being that when he went left I hummed lower and when right higher.

Although it was hard fought for I was never entirely happy with this solution because the going-higher sound sounded like it should mean go faster and the lowering-sound slow down but we instead used volume changes for that so that loud and high Vrooing meant turn left quickly and a quieter and quieter Vroo-Vroo in the middle range meant go forwards slowly slowing before Squeak and Crunch said Stop.

Strangely in our driving language loud did not actually have to be loud for if it had been we would have had the Sisters especially Sisters Britta and Eliza down upon us in wrath and in worry so for loud I think what I really mean is intense because my Vroo could if need be suggest vast volume without carrying as far as the far end of the long corridor which was one of the places we went on the forty-fourth and forty-fifth days of refining Go Left Right Fast Slow Stop when we knew everyone except Kurt and Lise and once or twice Micky was elsewhere weaving dreaded baskets we were weaving parallel wheel tracks into and out of dorms I had only ever visited in utter fantasy. For example the Princesses' until then legendary Dorm 7 that unlike all the others off the long corridor was further down at the end of the short corridor past the Refectory beyond even the Boy's and Girl's Bathrooms and left at some fire doors a place I'd never had cause to go and which did not disappoint with its pink and its fairytale sparkle and its amazing six wardrobes instead of three because of all the dressing up a Princess needs to do if she is to be as beautiful and fashionable as a Princess needs to be.

Lise's bed by contrast alone in Dorm 6 was beautifully unadorned.

This and all the other dorms I had often glimpsed in passing when Sister Cécile wheeled me along to and from supper and lunch and some dorms such as Dorm 2 I had had a longer look at because in the case of Dorm 2 an emergency once happened to do with Patricia and

Sister Cécile just had to let go of me on the way to Mass and sprint away and I happened to roll slightly forwards until my knee was against the doorway of Dorm 2 which at that time had only Charlie and Kurt sleeping in it and Kurt's bed had nothing unusual around or upon it apart from two extra grey blankets but Charlie's had a red Liverpool F.C. duvet and pillow case and a poster on the wall above it of a footballer with a harsh moustache whose name I never wanted to learn because Charlie liked him.

Revisiting Dorm 2 with Jim and under our own magnificent power on the afternoon of the forty-fourth day I saw Charlie's red and white duvet cover was still there but severely faded and that the football poster had come down to be replaced by one of an ugly female pop singer with eye make-up and short white hair and black fingernails holding a microphone but having a face with an angry sour expression and then suddenly I realized it was a man singer with all the things you would expect of a female singer including eye make-up and black fingernails and I was so shocked I hummed to Jim Back Back Back and we backed out of Dorm 2 and I hummed Submarine Submarine and Jim without much more steering took us round quiet Lise thumping Kurt and up snug to the radiator but not quite touching genius Jim genius.

The man–woman poster had upset me and I did not want to think about it so I looked at the familiar sight of birds whose flight and rhythms I knew so well I had been able to tell each one of them apart apart from the twin crows since just after they were fledged and then when this didn't seem to be calming enough I bone-hummed I Wanna Hold Your Hand and then held Jim's hand for a while and then turned on the ignition and had him drive me backwards and to the right and then straight forwards until I was safely parked in front of the whiteness of the white wall neglected for days but awaiting me always as a resource of thankfully not infinite calming power for we had quite enough elsewhere on the ward of the infinite but of more than more than adequate calming power and as I saw and looked at white's whiteness Jim went and climbed up and sat on the window ledge above the radiator his new favourite place I think because it was so toasty warm.

I did my best to keep the blue of the graffiti in the Arndale Centre toilets out of my mind but that was what the poster in Dorm 2 for some reason which I did not then understand reminded me of and I knew the Sisters especially Sister Muriel would have told me this was something to do with how evil pervaded the world outside the ward from which perversion we were mainly protected yet this made me very much very anxiously wonder and worry why such a poster had been allowed by the Sisters into Charlie's eyes and mind and soul and onto his wall when he was clearly already the worst of all the evils on the ward.

I knew there were things I did not know about the world outside the ward and its evils particularly the evils of meaty adulthood but there were also basic facts such as something I once heard Charlie telling Finn which was that Jesus wasn't on the moon because men had visited the moon and hadn't been able to take a film or take a photograph of Jesus there even though at his parents' church Charlie had met a man called James who was one of the men who had been to the moon and had tried with his camera and who still now believed in Jesus and at first I thought this was just one of Charlie's nonsense arguments to upset Finn who believed in Jesus in a beautiful way I envied after I stopped believing myself because life inside me would have been easier and also easier to understand but the idea that a man could be back on earth who had been on the moon was a very disturbing one to me not because I believed in moon-men meaning aliens but because on very bad nights when the spine-pain was bad and the Sisters failed to turn me I would think to myself this sentence these words At least there is the moon At least there is the moon.

How and when I first invented this comfort that wasn't prayer I cannot remember because my sense of dates is worse when it's of dream-events but I think it was around the time of the non-arrival of my eighth birthday card an era when I was much in need of consolation and starting to fail to find it in the figure of the crucified Christ or His suffering mother whose compassion was always especially available to children in bodily discomfort or in mortal agony so Sister Muriel the pink theologian always said although when I made my nocturnal appeal to her to the Virgin Mary she seemed to answer it at the very most with the distraction of changes in the bright blue or harsh grey light of moon-mottle falling within my visual field and I knew I suppose though not in a scientific way that whereas the light upon and alongside me irregularly changed the moon itself only changed in the regular wax and wane from fingernail to orange and back.

At least there is always the moon was what I said to myself in moments of desperation when I knew for certain that I could not survive another single moment of bedbound desperation but that alone in my body and unassisted in my exposed and bewildered mind I somehow had to allow myself to allow time to pass which it never failed to do but which my pain nearer to me than I am to myself always made it seem to threaten not to do to pass that pain not only in my bones or of my bones but before my bones and behind my bones and I can't think it hard enough bone of bones behind my bones to an infinite depth as if my body were the projected shadow of another body whose only purpose like Lucifer's was to suffer and to cause suffering and of course I began as on some other nights to believe that there could be no explanation for why I deserved so much almost-Jeremy pain apart from the fact I must be one of Lucifer's disobedient angels crippled by the landing of its fall and that although everyone said I was in the ward and the ward was in the world that I was actually and could be nowhere else but in Hell.

The moon was proof to me I was in the world because I had never heard the Priest or the Sisters mention a moon in Hell and they talked about Hell often enough and in some detail but if men a single man had been to the moon and then returned to the earth and met Charlie then that for me in my pain made the moon a great deal more part of the world than it had been before which in turn made it more likely the world wasn't the world but was muscle-Hell skeleton-Hell and it was only one birthday card ago that I heard Sister Cécile confirmingly say on the evening of a full-moon-night when the Sisters always had two instead of one Sisters awake because of children running and screaming etcetera that it would soon be ten years since man had first landed on the moon and I wanted to ask what was that man called was it James and did he go to Charlie's parents' church but because I heard the truth from Sister Cécile it made it seem less hellish.

With whiteness in front of me and Dorm 2 behind me and off to my left I said to myself There is always the moon and distracted myself with thoughts like these of how those words first came to me and this helped me recover from the man–woman poster enough to hear what was happening around me which was that Lise's sobbing was muffled and Jim was not a dark shape on the window sill above the radiator and putting these facts together with a closer listen to Lise's exact tone I began to suspect that Jim's body was close up in front of Lise's mouth and causing the muffle to what usually had a crisp edge before it went off to echo down the long corridor.

Oh no I thought not because I didn't want Jim to be kind and loving to others just as he was loving and kind to me but because unfailingly if boys and girls began to hug or kiss or seek out one another's Dorms and beds in the night then the Sisters were without mercy and the boy's meatiness only needed to be lamb cutlets and not beef goulash for him to be moved up the road to the Brothers unfairly I thought always it was the kissing boy moved never the kissing or being-kissed girl and to save Jim from this I tried to end the snuffling muffling danger by humming I Wanna Hold Your Hand before a Sister came along and saw a hug and discovered a sin.

Well I told Jim something three times these being the opening words of the song and louder each time then stopped and listened for his big feet which did come but after I had got him to reverse me and repark me so I could sit very unusually for me with my back to the whiteness and look all the way along the long corridor after this Jim touched my shoulders and my mouse-brown head and then returned to Lise whose crying had noticeably intensified with his departure and put not just his arms but his whole body around her as if she was a tulip bulb in earth and he was a terracotta pot like the one that sat on the window sill of the Craft Room yes Jim's arms and legs and back were bent inwards all around Lise and if this continued everything we had gained Jim and I would be lost but the Supper gong was banged before Sister Britta came past or Sister Cécile came back.

Be careful I wanted to say to Jim and Lise Be careful but also Stop also just simply and absolutely Stop!

There was so much more Jim needed to learn before we could make our way to freedom out of the ward meaning through the wooden gate past the Sisters' Office into the lift down to the ground floor across the reception area through the double glass doors and out into the car park and the green beyond.

At the very least Jim needed to know how to find the zero button in the lift and during supper of cream of chicken I was despairing of my ability to teach him this quickly enough if he was going to get caught getting cuddlesome with Lise and at the same time beneath this I was I must admit jealous of his ability to cuddle beautiful Lise and of her ability if she so wanted to cuddle him back and so I wanted them to Stop but also I didn't because I had so often wanted to comfort Lise and now Jim was doing it for me From Me To You.

Micky would not sit down to his bowl because his mania was now manifesting in him which meant he ran and bumped into the nearby wall of the Refectory just as a heavy buzzer bluebottle dunders up against the windowpane and sometimes does this until it lands stunned on its back then spins fizzes twitches and dies to remain there in my field of vision for two or three weeks.

Micky like a fly would die if he could not fly and I heard Sister Mary Margaret taking him off to calm him with a sweet red drink from a small plastic cup but it was not until I was in bed attempting sleep that I realized I did not have to train Jim how to press the zero button of the lift if I could get someone else to do it for us and I knew Micky knew how for not only had he pressed Sister Penelope's nipples saying Call lift for the left one and Floor four for the right one he had also several times made it gloriously through the wooden gate into the lift and up to the top floor which was the fourth although that was the roof rather than an actual floor for from the window I could see there was only one real floor above our second floor and I knew that was for the adults who were dying in the arms of the church as Micky if he could not fly would very soon die.

Micky could press the zero button for us I darkly thought but then I knew and realized Micky would only ever press press press for the fourth floor because he wouldn't understand why anyone would ever want to go down rather than up and if he got into the lift he would be so excited that he would probably knock himself out by running impatiently into the metal doors to try to pass through the not-open-enough orphan-slit so someone else it had to be someone else. I tried to think of anyone who had ever shown they could use the lift buttons and then when I couldn't think of anyone who had mastered that basic skill anyone who had shown they could read and understand the cardinal numbers from zero to four and who was capable of pressing a single button without going mad with delight and pressing all the buttons.

I thought of a number of others including Finn Gavin and the Princesses but all were far too scared of the Sisters to dare go beyond the wooden gate and in the end I was left with Charlie and Lise because Charlie could do anything mental or physical and didn't really need to be on the ward apart from being evil and Lise could do anything too especially mischievous disappearing things if she could just be persuaded to move from the fabric-heap area and maybe Jim could make her do that by making her believe her life would be slightly better temporarily if she came with us for a ride down in the lift rather than stay secure forever in misery and in close proximity to her brother's misery.

After realizing it was utterly hopeless and then discovering new hope about half a dozen times I closed my eyes on sheet-peaks and opened them to and Shine from Sister Britta and then the usual routine only distinguished by me looking hopefully across the Refectory through the toasty air for possible button-pushers I might not have thought of the night before but no there were none not unless Sister Cécile could be persuaded to do it for us just as compassionately as she spooned Ready Break into my mouth and not up my nose or onto my cheeks and chin as others other Sisters so often had when my head as it sometimes did gave up the ghost and lolled or surges of life-excitement took me and I stiffened until I was nothing but spasm.

The spoon was in my mouth on the forty-sixth day and I was swallowing when I had the thought of closing my lips and teeth on the spoon and keeping it there because with a spoon in my mouth and the right angle of attack I might perhaps press the zero button myself and I immediately wanted to try practising this but Sister Cécile was furrow-browed and harried that day by something perhaps something spiritual before Easter because it was Lenten in my mouth at that moment with no sugar on my Ready Brek and Sister Cécile was as she straight away said in no mood for your nonsense Elliott so I opened my mouth and out flew the spoon down away from my eyes and as the handle now I saw it probably wasn't long enough to reach the zero button at any head-angle I could manage what I would need was a much longer spoon a thing I knew to exist because I had seen it sometimes on the far table serving mashed potato to Priests or Bishops or once an Archbishop.

Sister Cécile knew from experience that if I was being so silly as to indulge in mouth-grabbing I needed white wall so that is where she put me in my place and that is whereabouts in the submarine Jim found me on the morning of the forty-sixth day since his blesséd arrival.

Found me and left me almost immediately not to go to Lise on the floor because as I had heard or rather not heard she had not yet arrived with her usual pitter-patter of small dry feet and flump of tragic fabric to sit alongside Kurt's thump which was by this time already establishing the day's usual lento moderato instead Jim waited and waited until he heard her approaching along the long corridor and then went on big feet and quietly joined her in her soft collapse and although I could not see or hear exactly what he did I have imagined since that he either put his arms around her and then sank with her perhaps with some awkwardness of first-time legs or he waited standing upright alongside her as she went down then plant-potted the soil of her grief with the terracotta of his arms just as he had done the day before resulting in the same distinctive and dangerous muffledness of sob.

And even Sockball with Charlie would have been far preferable to this Act II of Wagner's Tristan and Isolde of the submarine with their live concert broadcast of the imminent possibility of meat and kisses that no Sister however hurried not even flu-filled Sister Eliza in a panic could fail to register as a new feature on the lino beside the filing cabinet inside which Kurt's land was no less certainly to-be-destroyed than would be Tristan and Isolde's idyll of weeper and comforter by gentle but absolute intervention by Sisters of the sort that said only Come along now Come along but that meant precisely You will never see one another again You will not even be given five minutes to say goodbye for any further contact between you shameless creatures is further opportunity for sinfulness that is what they the nuns would not surface-say but would deeply-mean although I could not have been more convinced of Lise's innocence.

It was Jim's ignorance had me singing Get Back after only a moment's pause that pause being spent in wondering whether I should wait for the sound of footfalls before I tried to rescue Jim and Lise from discovery or whether I should use up my limited reserve of Jim-visits which I estimated at three or perhaps four before he began to ignore me and their hug became hug perpetua and so to where Jim once belonged Get Back was the sentiment I now sent him meaning Come put your hands back on the handles of my wheelchair and get in position for safe and simple happiness that promises with practice to bring you the even greater joy of justice through escape.

To my relief Jim did immediately come and I was able to keep him attached to me for a while by running through some of our vocabulary including getting Kurt to join in with the treble Yeahs and during this time of half an hour I could feel Lise's sorrow drawing then dragging away Jim's attention for sometimes he only had one hand on the handles as he began to be pulled away towards her he loved and her who loved him or who at least loved the enclosure and embrace he offered although it did not completely silence her plaint and while Jim was close I smelled him intensely and could not tell in my passion whether his meatiness really was as increased as I feared the Sisters would find it to be if they were prompted to give it second sniff.

It distressed me to distress Jim for I could tell his longing was to be in two places at once and it was here in the middle of the forty-sixth morning I had my next idea which was to disguise the two in their Isolde and Tristan love duet by turning them into a quartet which I knew would be nun-noticed but not in a way that suggested blue biro on whitewash or the smell of freshly baked bread rolls or the forgiven sins of Mary Magdalen or whatever else was in the world the Sisters needed to keep out in the world and away from the innocent children of the second-floor ward and so with bone-hum and throat-Vroo I had Jim unbrake the wheelchair and steer me smoothly until for the first time except in passing I was parked with a tyre-squeak between Kurt and Lise forming I hoped a different picture of us that would come across as what Sister Mary Margaret called Their funny little games for who among the Sisters ever really knew why we the children sometimes gathered thus or thus in trinities quartets and congregations of twitchy communion.

Within the hour all five Sisters had at various times walked past us clacking squeaking tippy-tapping fpping and sliding as did Sister

Muriel's brown tartan carpet slippers and all of them except Sister Muriel had stopped to observe and mutely ponder this new arrangement of us four regulars on the long corridor and to wonder no doubt whether they could find anything wrong with it or sinful in it for how would Jesus look upon it if He were standing there beside them on His sandal-slapping way from supervising basket-weaving in the Craft Room to a well-deserved cup of tea and digestive biscuit in the Sisters' Office would He have said Let the little children come together in a group of four or would He have said Get behind the filing cabinet Satan?

Yet finding nothing explicitly meaty in our all-in-a-row disposition especially when I covered with confusion the floor-hug and sob-duet by repeating and reiterating Kurt's thump thus causing Jim to join in de profundis with a comic thump-echo for the benefit of Sister Britta who looked at us with a hard long look of ice blue eyes that I am sure was nothing like the look Jesus our Saviour would have given us in the exact same circumstances His look being full of mildness kindness and forgiveness and hers being full of suspicions of uncleanliness nastiness and sinfulness of all sorts but finding nothing she could file away under any of these categories as things must once have been filed in Kurt's filing cabinet Sister Britta eventually gave a tut that I understood to mean the opposite of Praise Be.

If I had learned one thing on the ward it was that the only true safety from the Sisters came in routine because routine doings and beings weren't noticed by the Sisters nor by the other children and it was for this reason that I had for years followed the routine of white wall or window and of thus becoming as invisible on the stage of the ward as the filing cabinet or maybe that's too prideful so as invisible as Kurt who had only been punched three times by Charlie for getting in his way during Sockball whereas I had been punched twenty seven times by Charlie including twice on the left cheek three times in the right eye and once in the Adam's apple but Charlie had only punched the filing cabinet one single time and that time he had broken two fingers on his right hand which meant for the following three weeks his punches had been delightfully feeble for all of us.

And so I knew that for the forseeable my time at the white wall and the window was over and in order to protect our project the time of my days would from now on be spent halfway between Kurt and the Lise-within-Jim hug-object which I did not mind at all because in facing that way Lise's knees were usually going to be visible even if her lovely face would mostly be hidden behind Jim's shoulders and those knees over the next couple of days were remarkably consistent in colouring those colours being the blue and white already familiar from Sister Mary Margaret's grandmother's broken teacup and saucer but sometimes within this I found variations of yellow and orange as if the teacup and saucer were sitting upright next to a bowl of fruit and reflecting in their shine the planes of a banana or the dimples of a clementine.

I was also able to observe the changing light during the forty-sixth forty-seventh and forty-eighth days and how it fell upon the hug-object striking the shoulders early on and making Jim's brown hair when he was there which he often wasn't look blonde then around 2 p.m. becoming warmer and lighting his right cheek and from there it moved on down until with the false sunset over the building opposite it sometimes reddened the both of them when the both of them were together as if they were on fire but a fire that had been frozen completely still to give an even light that made even more beautiful what was already to me agonizingly beautiful i.e. the two people I loved more than anyone else except my mother and father especially my mother who I knew because I almost remembered had once upon a time held me just as Jim held Lise.

What I saw in their combined lightsome beauty though only a fleeting thing was the object of my affection and at the same time was the cause of my jealousy and although it was a simple object to look at it was a very hard knot-like object to understand.

My jealousy was because of course I wanted to be Jim holding Lise but equally I wanted to be Lise being held by Jim and yet I also still wanted to be myself and not them so like tulip petals within tulip petals within tulip petals I wanted to be myself being held by Lise being held by Jim and equally I wanted to be myself being held by Jim being held by Lise and both holdings happening simultaneously not just held but beheld for I wanted someone perhaps a purged-by-purifying-fire Sister Cécile with no mandate for punishment or compulsion to report or perhaps ideally my mother to see us behold us as a bigger hug-object and within that her son finally welcomed as part of a more complete trinity of comfort and joy comfort and joy.

But most of all I wanted to be myself but with the physical ability to get in position as myself holding Jim and Lise who would be neither one outside the other but just hugged up against and facing one another with his or her right arm under her or his left and right leg over left in a perfect love-knot of intertwining smart and salve ache and analgesic flaw and fix end and ever.

But between us in reality there was a gap of lino and light and a gap of capacity which reduced me from holder to beholder and this beholding I did as best I could for those three days only breaking off and breaking them apart when I was sure the long corridor was safely quiet and I could practise and refine all the Back Left Right Stop Go Go Go Fast Slow Park Happy sounds and Jim could become fluid in gliding us through doorways of every dorm except Dorm 2 with its horrible man–woman poster and turning and coming out facing forwards but also reversing in and out all as preparation for when we would pass beyond the wooden gate together without Lise unless she chose to follow an act of which she was more than capable and which was not impossible if the magnetism of Jim drew her after it metallic and loving.

On the forty-eighth day after a night's thought for planning and rejection of the idea of stealing a long-handled spoon I had Jim take me during basket-weaving on another thorough tour of all the Dorms except Dorm 2 and in Dorm 5 I found or saw exactly what I needed propped up in the corner a wooden walking stick sometimes used by club-footed Rhys who had once been one of the boys of Dorm 5 but who had gone up the road to the Brothers when he revealed his hairiness and his blue biro sticking up down below to Princess Beauty although from what I understood he had been asked by her to do so and I knew as soon as I saw it leaning there that with the walking stick under my arm sticking up at the right angle I would be able to steer Jim into position with me holding the rubber end just in front of the zero button then tell him to Go Go Go and the pressing would be accomplished.

In Dorm 5 slept Jeremy Gavin Toby and no-one else and I knew Jeremy with his pain and Toby with his hand-obsessed torpor would be no use to us but square-headed Gavin might be helpful so I had Jim take us back to our routine positions and waited for basket-weaving to finish and lunch to begin and be Cardinal Newman and scrambled eggs and messy and finish and then for the afternoon when I was sure Gavin sometimes returned to his Dorm for a sleep if he was not forced by fear of Charlie to play Sockball and although this nap did not happen on the forty-eighth afternoon it did on the forty-ninth and as soon as he was through the door of his Dorm which I had made sure I was parked at an angle to see I had Jim Drive My Car up the long corridor and through into Dorm 5 which made Gavin shriek from the mouth in the middle of his square head because he had never seen our driving but he soon recovered from shock and looked at us like we were special the special which I knew we were although with his help we might become even more so.

All I had were my eyes and my sounds and the ability to get Jim to go forwards and backwards in a line pointing directly towards the walking stick which for comprehensibility's sake I'd decided to refer to as Stick but which sounded when I tried to say it like Hnigg and on top of these difficulties the walking stick was leaned up behind the bed on which tucked beneath the sheet with only heads showing were several cuddly toys including one in the form of a pig and for his first misunderstanding Gavin thought understandably that Hnigg meant Pig although why he thought I had come all the way into his Dorm to demand one of his cuddly toys was as beyond me as the walking stick was and so Gavin who I could see was unnerved if not scared picked up the Hnigg and held it out above me like the Priest elevating the host during Mass.

No-one however simple could fail to understand my No because however loudly and chaotically it burst out of me it was clearly nothing like what would have burst if I had meant Yes by wibbling my head. Instead my moaning bellow of Uhhr accompanied I am sure by eyes that did not twinkle with the little stars of understanding and a mouth that was doing the opposite of smiling at Gavin made him quickly replace the Hnigg which was not a Hnigg and show me in turn and with increasing distress a teddy bear a donkey and a strange-looking animal with a long tail small high front legs and an unrealistic pocket sewn into its belly all of which animals I tried to reject as gently as I could for it was clear that Gavin thought I had become in consort with Jim a new kind of Devil's Child and was bullying people to hand over the things they loved most and this thought gave me a moment's wee-warm delight at the idea anyone might ever think Jim and I powerful enough to act together as a bully and then immediately covered me in nappy-rash shame at the idea that dear Gavin believed I would choose to hurt him first.

Yet it was impossible to explain this to him all I could do was insist that Jim who of course couldn't have an exact idea what was going on that Jim keep pushing me back and forth pointing my left index finger towards the walking stick and simultaneously hope that now-scared Gavin might make the effort to do what I required of him to make me make us go away.

Hnigg I repeated and stared at the walking stick so hard and clearly with my widened eyes that I felt like I was close to making it fall over with mind-control power but my intensity was such that Gavin looked at me and not into the corner where his answer rested against the white wall like an elongated question mark.

After five minutes of this I could tell Gavin was about to cry very hard and loud and that there was no apology I could make or explanation give that would stop this so I hummed Back To Where You Once to Jim who I think was glad to get away from the mysterious sounds of snuffling distress and wheel me smoothly backwards out into the long corridor but also as I knew even if Jim didn't backwards away from the walking stick which diminished in size like my diminishing hope.

It was difficult for me to imagine as Jim took us back to the Lise and Kurt area and parked me and went into hug-thing it was very difficult to figure out even with my usual optimism of spirits how a return to Dorm 5 with Gavin there would achieve anything more than the siren wail that soon called forth from the Chapel the swift harsh footsteps of Sister Britta after which for a few minutes I was in fear that Gavin would manage to tell her he'd been bullied by a new two-headed four-wheeled monster but I don't think he got close because the wail soon became inaudible and when Sister Britta came out of Dorm 5 and walked past the filing cabinet and us she did not stop or accuse anyone but carried on towards the Cluck then the hush of a tap and the quiet-click burble roar and loud-click of the kettle.

But when Gavin came in to supper that evening I saw that he was carrying his four soft toys in an enviable hug not unlike the hug Jim had given Lise most of the wasted afternoon and although toys were usually banned at the long dining tables and in fact banned from anywhere but two places one the specific dorm in which they softly or hardly dwelled and two Chapel on a Sunday which all toys tended to start and stop attending in crazes and lapses of hard or soft religious fervour yes despite that general ban on this evening Sister Britta told Sister Eliza that Gavin had special dispensation just this once to keep the toys where he could see them and in the far left of my vision over their flopped heads I could see him and I could see with mortification he wasn't looking at his toys but at me.

Gavin's logic was poor for if I had really wanted his pig bear donkey and strange pocket animal which I later discovered was a kangaroo then I and Jim would and could have taken any or all of them but Gavin's fear was now my obstacle and it was hard to think of a way I could make him feel safe again apart from leaving him alone for a month a month I could hardly afford because who knew how Jim would meatify in that time or what form his attempts to comfort Lise would take because sometimes within the hug I saw hand movements which were not patting or stroking but which I knew were different because they looked like kissing with fingers and which I later learned was caressing and which sometimes I had to prevent the

Sisters spotting by humming I Wanna Hold Your Hand and when this failed to employ my last resort of Help!

In this manner the rest of the forty-ninth day passed with intimacy and anxiety and I was missing watching the early Spring of the wych elm through the window and also watching the things I sometimes saw in the whiteness of the white wall and come the burning light of evening upon burning shoulders I could smell boiled potatoes and at supper their bland tastiness especially with butter seemed when I ate them mashed to be like eating up the remaining time I had with Jim and for this I was not hungry so tried to leave some of my mash but Sister Cécile called me a cheeky boy and wisely insisted I keep eating and all the time was eventually scraped off my plate every last minute of it and allowed to pass down my oesophagus to where that night I found I felt it as a hard illusion in my stomach of time as a reassembled potato without skin that would soon be digested and turned into new flesh of Elliott-without-Jim and one day Elliott-without-Lise which did in fact happen.

The next morning the 50th Sister Cécile against my whimpered protests wheeled me straight from breakfast into the Craft Room where she presented me with the usual choice of paint or clay and luckily without really considering it I chose paint because clay was what I'd chosen the previous time and if I got messy enough quickly enough with dripped and dropped paint perhaps I would escape sooner for a change of trousers and be returned in mild annoyance to the long corridor where Jim and Lise might even at that very moment be getting caught in a Tristan kiss and an Isolde caress of hope-fatal comfort that would see Sister Britta sadly enraged on the phone to the Brothers and Jim gone before lunch.

But once the paper was on the easel in front of me and the non-bristle end of the long brush was in my mouth dripping bright blue powder-paint because Sister Cécile assumed I wanted to paint my usual slapdash sky with paper-left-white clouds once in position I had the idea of painting the walking stick for Gavin who was not there in the Craft Room to see it but might somehow see it later if I could persuade Sister Cécile to let me keep this painting so with all the neck strength I had I placed the brush on the top of the page and immediately saw a drip of blue descend in the vertical line I was hoping to follow because Sister Cécile had mixed the powder with quite a lot of water and hence the blue of the drip was quite pale.

Also the drip was already three quarters of the way down the paper and if it reached the bottom would make it very difficult to make the whole thing look like a walking stick so with as much control as I could muster I let my chin drop and followed the accidental thin pale line with a deliberate thick dark one but my head was not so good at controlled nodding as it was at wibbling and the brush picked up too much momentum and flicked itself down out of my mouth and into my lap which worked for mess-making on grey trousers but left the oblong sheet in front of me looking more like a raindrop running down the window of a parked coach than anything like a walking stick and so when Sister Cécile put the brush back in my mouth with a pianissimo tck sound I straight away zigzagged over the raindrop shape to cancel it out.

How many hundreds of paintings Sister Cécile had helped me with I did not know for I had long ago lost count but however many it was it was enough for her to know the zigzag was the sign of my frustration and it did not take her long to get the cause of the frustration out of my sight and to replace it with a new whiteness very different in meaning and everything else to the whiteness of the white wall although I had often sat looking at the wall-whiteness and imagined putting blue paint on it to make permanent the falling waterfalls leaping lions dancing skeletons and growing forest of trees that I saw there before I got through to the whiteness behind the whiteness always I had imagined blue paint and because the raindrop or vertical line had been so very different to my usual blue skies and white clouds Sister Cécile stood interested to watch as I a second time put my brush on the page in the middle of the top of the rectangle and pivoted its end between my teeth to bring the line down but again the heaviness of the wooden brush with rusty metal clasping the wet bristles pulled the handle out of my mouth and I didn't even need to zigzag this time for Sister Cécile to know I was going to wreck this painting if she didn't whisk it away.

Before the third time like a proper painter I sat looking at the whiteness just as Ted looked for a while in silent assessment at a wall before he started rollering it just so did I reckon what might be a better way and all in a rush I realized I should use my wibbling neck-strength and forget painting a walking stick as it was when being used or when leaning against a wall in a corner of a dorm but should instead make a mark like a walking stick floating impossibly in the air and then later on have someone turn the paper left through 90 degrees to make it look like what it was when it was what it was.

The third time I used my mouth to put my first blue splodge on the top left of the page then with all my strength lolled my head down to the right as if scanning the lopsided horizon of the flat plain for an imaginary brown-haired horse galloping right and further right until despite the hurt of the effort I got most of the way to the right edge where I let my head droop a little more as it was so good at but before it was too far down towards my chin I started the brush back to the left just a little with my lips and a little more before retracting my mouth and neck as far as I could to jump the bristles off the paper and stop the mark-making.

Oh it was perfect my diagonal upside down walking stick certainly good enough for Gavin.

J said Sister Cécile that's very good Elliott letter j but shall we put a dot at the top and in a twinkle the brush was plucked out of my mouth and was heading straight towards the paper to ruin my perfect walking stick and all I could do to rescue it was go furious really instantly and buck and curse and scare Sister Cécile's gentle hand back from the page Oh she said Oh I see You're really the perfectionist today aren't you? and then Well never mind and because she thought I was angry with myself for failing to make a sky or a J or a j she tore the paper straight off from under the clips to get it out of my sight as quickly as she could crumpling the walking stick into a ball as she walked towards the wastepaper basket made of wicker and I was so frustrated I could hardly bring myself to breathe.

Oh God I thought now is when I should pray I should accept that I have been driven to prayer but because I had made myself a promise four Christmases ago after the non-visit of my mother that I would not send prayers to a thing a God that didn't answer prayers for the basic reason that it didn't exist to be a comfort and a blessing that I still powerfully wanted to believe in for the strength and support it would give me at moments like this so I forced myself not to beseech or even speak to God which was very hard because it left me at that moment alone in my echoey body with my frustration at my body echoing up and down me and a passion to draw a walking stick just to do that one simple thing not to paint a masterpiece of hunters in the snow or to conduct Mahler's Second Symphony with a conductor's baton just to draw a walking stick and then having drawn it to be able to say very clearly Look Sister Cécile that is what I wanted to draw grrr.

But if I could have said that I could have said Please Sister Cécile can you give that drawing I just did to Jim the other way up so that he can show it to Gavin for reasons I do not at present wish to disclose to you and all of these despairing thoughts happened fast as Sister Cécile walked to the wastepaper basket scrunching the perfect walking stick painting and I could hear it scrunch tight and then uncrumple with small crimping sounds as soon as it landed on top of the two vertical line paintings similarly scrunched.

And then Sister Cécile came back and stood in front of me and looked at me assessingly in order to work out what my frustration was and my frustration got worse because I couldn't explain to her what my frustration was and this became one of those loops of emotion that had several times hospitalized me when I had had what Charlie called an epi whenever he hit someone and they reacted and he said to them Don't have an epi meaning epi strop meaning epileptic fit and I was trying as hard as I could not to have an epi though it felt very much as if something like life like fate had whacked me a sly one behind everyone's back like Charlie whacked.

Maybe not painting today then said Sister Cécile and I tried to shake my head and made the sound for Again which I knew she knew Again I said a second time and then said it again Again but Sister Cécile was looking at me with brown eyes of doubt Are you sure? she asked and what could I do but again repeat Again as I tried to nod as if I was 100 per cent painter-horse and not 99 per cent frustration and only 1 per cent painter-horse Again I made the sound one more time and Sister Cécile who had sometimes ridden with me in ambulances to hospitals when she had been awake and concerned and I had been unconscious and cyanotic Sister Cécile heard my snorty breathing of fury and made her decision which was for me and also against me meaning for my own good and against my best hopes and two minutes later the whiteness in front of me was not that of a piece of paper awaiting blue but a white wall awaiting the African animals of my anger but they did not swarm up because I did not let them because Jim and Lise when I passed them had been a pure and dangerous Tristan and Isolde hug-thing of caress that had given even Sister Cécile pause so as soon as she was haltingly consideringly gone I bone-hummed On Our Way Back Home to Jim who frustratingly took his time to untangle unpetal himself and arrive but eventually did and effectively ended the 50th day by parking me between brother and sister between metal and fabric between land and knees between horror and despair.

When I dreamed that night I dreamed about being a knot in a piece of string that turned out to be the trunk of an elephant who wanted to die because she could not find a way to untie her trunk and in a children's book Jesus would have helped or perhaps Mary who has a particular fondness for elephants but my dream just continued until it ended with me waking up worrying about what kind of night Jim had had and whether his dreams had been sinful dreams of the soft warm way Lise felt to hold and kiss-touch and whether his sheets were knotted and matted and smelling of freshly baked up the road to the Brothers or whether we were safe for another day of Beep Beep danger.

As the spoon flew to my mouth I could feel Sister Cécile assessing me in preparation for deciding white or window or paint or clay and so I was the most perfect little horse I could ever be swallowing my Lenten Ready Brek as if it were the special treat chocolate-sprinkled Ready Brek of Easter Morning where the chocolate powder was sprinkled in the shape of a cross Look at me Look at me so calm calm Molto tranquillo and it must have worked despite my fears that the lion of anxiety and rage I was covering over with the skin of the timid antelope would give its golden self away with a powerful twitch or magnificent grrr for when the wheeling out and wheeling through happened Sister Cécile whose face I could not see but whose hands lay tender and not rebuking on the handles wheeled me through into the Craft Room she spoke and said I don't suppose you'd like another go at the whatever it was would you? That is what she did and said bless her. And I knew that nonchalance such as the nonchalance of Maurizio Pollini playing a bagatelle by Beethoven at the end of a concert of late Schubert piano sonatas was the only way to stand a 50/50 chance of getting what I wanted for a really raging Yes would have fallen into the trap of passion and Sister Cécile would have whipped me out of the Craft Room and along to the wall quicker than I could say in my imagination as Sister Mary Margaret did when she was speaking posh Please darling Sister Cécile today I feel like having another little dab at that silly old walking stick don't you know.

I did not even incline my head in the direction of the easels rather than the wheelchair trays and for this restraint I was rewarded with a bib a blue-dipped brush in my mouth and a visual field full from side to side of papery white and even if she is no longer a nun Sister Cécile will always to me remain a saint for this and similar acts of kindness and forbearance and concealment and wit.

The painting I immediately produced was not as perfect as that of the 50th day for although the straight bit was good the handle dropped off slightly at its very end making it look like a little like a bishop's crozier but I did not think Gavin would think I had come in to his dorm to demand a crozier belonging to a Bishop when right behind him was an object that looked fairly exactly like the object in the painting still it was a risk so I had two more head-drooping goes with the assistance of Sister Cécile who after each was done hung it on the swooping line of string so it took its place alongside the splodgy houses families sunrises and bloody battles of the other children all of which looked very rough next to black Toby's pencil drawings of his left hand over and over again his left hand.

The next difficulty was to get the painting to where it could be useful and used and although I had the great relief of feeling I had succeeded in calmly creating it I was not sure my frustration wouldn't lion up again if I tried to indicate that I wanted the walking stick painting on my lap just so when I was wheeled out onto the long corridor and so I decided to return later with Jim because the painting hung I thought low enough for me to grab it with my mouth all we needed to be careful of was that no-one thought I was stealing another child's painting because everyone knew mine were only ever of blue slashy skies and white clouds.

With all the difficulties we faced and might have faced at other times this one after lunch of tomato soup with potato chunks of Cardinal Newman again was bafflingly evaporated by the flood of fashionable children into the long corridor even Charlie and though that was a worry for the future it meant I was able with quiet Vroos to guide Jim past Lise through the watching and quietly amazed throng and along into the Craft Room where the three walking stick paintings of the morning still hung with wooden clothes pegs at the top left and top right corners and some neat forwardsing and backwardsing brought my mouth up against the best painting's left edge which meant I was able to bite hold of the paper then let my head drop and successfully tear down the sheet keeping it in my mouth.

Quickly I bone-hummed Jim and I out of the room and back along the long corridor where things immediately began to go wrong and for predictable reasons or reason i.e. Charlie for although the other children had sometimes caught sight of or heard rumours of Jim wheeling me to Charlie it was something new and of course threatening because it was another proven power of Jim and so of course Charlie instinctively wanted instantly to attack it in front of all the others including principally for what followed the Princesses and Gavin.

As Jim pushed us past him Charlie yanked the walking stick painting from my mouth in the process giving me a paper cut to the left edge of my mouth that took several days to heal and made everything that happened during those days taste slightly of blood and nothing tasted bloodier than the fear that Charlie would rip up the painting before we had the chance to use it after all the difficulty and frustration and risk and wit of making and stealing it but Charlie at first was puzzled by the image and what it might mean.

This I could see because I had got Jim to turn me round to face him down the long corridor looking back towards the Chapel to face him the evil one.

Charlie held the painting up upside down so everyone could see it and Charlie laughed so that everyone who feared him would laugh too which most of them did although of course Jim who was acting throughout entirely out of trust in me did not laugh because the most he knew was the remembered feel of a rustle of paper against his stomach as he wheeled me out of the Craft Room which he knew mostly for clay clay which he shaped into the shape of balls cubes pyramids or other more complex objects with many more angles that had at first amazed the Sisters because where in his blind head or his experience were they coming from these perfections?

The laughter at Charlie's laugh was not real and did not last long for the children on the long corridor sensed that perhaps Charlie's power was no longer what it had been and if they sided with Jim they might be safe not to laugh so much or even oh joy not to laugh at all and this weak response and early-ending laughter angered Charlie who liked to tell a crowd to stop laughing when it was he himself who had started them laughing and when it was only fear of him that kept them laughing because the first person to stop would be the person who got hit soonest and hardest and in the most painful place.

What happened next happened fast happened in a very short space of time but even if that space had been vast I don't think it could have happened any other way because as Jim and I faced him Charlie held the walking stick painting away from his body as if it smelled of something disgusting like someone else's vomit and then he turned it so it was the right way up just for a moment before ripping it down the middle quite neatly but with the vertical rip not running exactly along the blue shaft of the straight line part of the stick but to the left of it and I could already feel the angry energy in Jim's hands on the handles and I did not need Charlie to do any more ripping to know he intended to destroy the painting.

All that was left was to choose our angle of attack.

Vroo I growled because the brake was already off Go Go Go and with a slightly higher pitched gruntle growl than straight ahead I had Jim accelerate us toward Charlie as fast as we could so that we didn't hit him straight on which would have meant Charlie our enemy would have been hit first by my footplates and toppled into me quite likely breaking my neck with a hard-headed headbutt on my skull instead I aimed for his left side with volume and intensity of horsepower as the children around us watched in what I later realized was already a state of delight and I knew my left foot was sticking out over the end of the footplate but there was nothing to be done about that and when we made hard contact with Charlie it was my left toe touched first and bent back and by the time the fifty-first day was over I was in hospital with a broken toe.

That was for later because for now we were speeding forwards through shocked Charlie who had only managed to put one more tear in the painting across the first two pieces but now the full fantastic force of the horse and his rider his friend hit him as my knee hit his shin and the left armrest where my arm luckily was not went into his lower left thigh and his face crumpled just like he was going to crumple the painting and his power was ripped up just like he was in a few seconds going to rip the painting up into small pieces as he lay on the floor behind us after we absolutely mashed through him feeling his weight get lifted and hurt and pushed aside and although I think it is wrong to think of violence with pleasure I find it hard not to be satisfied by the memory of Charlie bending forwards into Jim's oncoming left shoulder which hit him like a fall from a wall onto a smaller wall and sent him to the floor with the quarters of the painting still in his defeated hands.

There was laughter and among it giggling just as there had been for the blood of Micky and it was not the doof-sound of the hit that brought Sister Cécile running but the wild rumpus that was just starting up and which would echo throughout the ward for the whole rest of the day because the total dominion of Charlie was already behind us just as Charlie was behind us and Jim and I knew what we should do to save everyone time which was go directly to the Chapel where we would be sent soon anyway to stay there until my broken toe was noticed dangling and looking wrong but not hurting all that much because I was too triumphantly happy and happily triumphant.

However before this I had Jim turn me round to face Charlie on the ground and see Charlie weeping grasping pieces of paper sur-rounded by looking-down others who hated the king of him and the fear of him and then Charlie got smaller and smaller receding diminuendo down the long corridor because I had told Jim to start reversing and to take us away from the crash that Sister Cécile was now running towards as she had run towards so many injured ones of us but it turned out Charlie was only bruised not broken or else he would have shared the ambulance that took me away from the Chapel and the ward where the lift had been inspected again by myself and yes the lift button for zero was at the perfect height for a walking stick poke.

I checked again when late that evening I was brought back from hospital which as always had been an interesting experience of smells and surfaces but is not really worth thinking about when I can think about how our plans to escape were in fact inadvertently assisted by Charlie giving me this chance to assess again the route for the escape in and out of the ward and the main difficulty after pressing the lift button for zero was going to be getting out of reception without being spotted by one of the strange unknown Sisters from the other floors who were sometimes and perhaps even usually there during the day looking out the clear glass doors with the opaque crosses on that opened by themselves when they sensed the approach of a walking person or I supposed a soon-to-be free horse and its rider.

Sister Cécile had fed me custard from a strange spoon at the hospital and so I was not hungry when she put me to bed with the words Think seriously on what you have done and consider whether it is something for which you should repent but the way in which she said it softly and musically close to my ear so still-alive Finn didn't wake and the fact that when she'd run to Charlie she must have seen the already destroyed painting he was starting to rip up more and from this known who had destroyed it and also when she ran she must have remembered how many times she'd had to run to children injured by the Devil's Child Charlie all this made me believe she was a little bit glad there was this challenge to his dominion and this new restraint upon his evil-doing.

After our violence but before I went to hospital Jim and I had spent a short while in the Chapel with the seriousness of what we had done being impressed upon us by Sister Mary Margaret who for some reason was the one out of all the Sisters who had the softest spot for Charlie perhaps because she thought Charlie was partly Irish which he wasn't as far as I ever learned before he left and before I left. Sister Mary Margaret had us think upon the pain and harm that violence had caused throughout human history and asked us would we be like those men who had nailed Christ's hands violently to the cross? Would we be like the Roman soldier who pierced Christ's side violently with his spear? Or wouldn't we rather be peacemakers for didn't Jesus say blesséd are the peacemakers and that the meek should inherit the earth and what are the meek who should inherit the earth and who are the meek Sister Mary Margaret continued but those who turn the other cheek just as Jesus did who should be our model in all things particularly how as a child he was meek and mild like a lamb.

Although even if I could have spoken I would not have spoken up against this I thought that we were more like Moses and Aaron saying to Pharaoh Let my people go and leading all the children out of their horrible bondage in Egypt and across the desert of the long corridor up to the Red Sea where Charlie the Pharaoh's attempted pursuit of us was met with crashing waters meaning on the left side the steadfastness of refusal from Sister Cécile and on the right side the tinkling of laughter from the others so he drowned in iniquity but I looked as penitent as I could while Sister Mary Margaret said her say and Jim nodded as he did whenever someone was speaking in order to reassure them that he wasn't thinking of other things when in fact I am certain that what it his nodding covered were visions of freedom.

I have thought a lot about what Jim saw and knew during this glorious time so for example could he have known what the ripped up painting meant for us as a step towards our escape even though the line and its shape and colour were beyond his comprehension and when Jim gazed into space as he often seemed to do was it a distance of echoes and high symphonic horn effects such as in Mahler's Second

Symphony or was it a delusory circle of What's The Time Mr Wolf where everything was constantly creeping closer and closer to him but didn't really count until it was upon him touching him?

I did not touch or even see Jim on the fifty-second and penultimate day not even at the first breakfast after my return from hospital because Jim had been woken early and fed and taken to Chapel where I expected to join him but instead Sister Cécile wheeled me into the Infirmary beyond the Sisters' Office and parked me facing the blue-green wall with a photograph high up and to the right of the new Pope Pope John Paul II who unless I made the effort to lift my head and lift my eyes was an out-of-focus face above a crisp pink silk robe done up at the neck where the clearest feature was Pope John Paul II's practical hands.

Jim spent the fifty-second morning in the Chapel and the afternoon in his dorm and I did the opposite but I was the one to eat my lunch separately just as he had been the one to eat breakfast alone and in the evening we both went early to meals in our rooms and I listened to his chewing because I missed him so much but I couldn't hear anything else definite of him until his lovely big and slapping footfalls went off down the long corridor with Sister Mary Margaret's ffps as Jim was taken to brush his teeth for even those in disgrace and mortal sin must consider oral hygiene but I did not hear him return for Sister Cécile had fetched a toothbrush and bowl and was loudly brushing my sinfully disgraced teeth of violence until they were zingy.

When Sister Cécile went away to wash out the bowl and put the toothbrush back in its rack I knew Jim would be listening to her tippy tapping too and I decided to test his hearing his miraculous hearing so I bone-hummed Hello from Hello Goodbye quite quietly and there was no reply so I out-hummed Hello mezzo forte and Jim replied with the same two notes but one octave lower and at his communication

I felt a gush of joy like when I once was given orangeade at a ward party by a young Sister who didn't know me and who poured it into me too fast so it fizzed everywhere inside my mouth and throat and then bounced out in an explosion of orange and foam closely followed by yellow cake in custard.

Missing Jim that night made me miss my mother in a way I had not done since Jim arrived because he had been such a big disruption of my emotions such a big event in my life a life I had tried very hard to keep uneventful so that I could concentrate on watching everything in my visual field until my mother returned to where I could see her as I was certain she one day would but now I felt very guilty for having let Jim become so important to me that I had not exactly forgotten her but had allowed myself to be concerned with a new centre of gravity or sweet spot meaning Jim and the effect Jim might have on my emptied life.

I had time this night plenty of time in an imaginary Dorm off the side of the long corridor of my mind time to worry about whether the two remaining walking stick paintings in the Craft Room and whether they were still hung low enough for me to grab them with my mouth and whether Jim and I would ever again be allowed to form a wheeling horse to get from the filing cabinet to the swooping washing line or if that period was already over because it had climaxed in violence and a change of power that could be reversed as soon as Charlie realized Jim and I were no longer capable of charging him and so the Israelites might soon be back in bondage though not bondage as total as before.

Although I did not know it had no way to know I was not far off in time from the climax of this brief acquaintance with freedom and with Jim and although am I able to separate him Jim both from freedom as what everyone wants and from my own particular galloping version of it still when I think of anyone's freedom for example when I think of an orphan adopted away from the ward into a family I feel long-gone Jim pushing close behind me and there is something perfect in that arrangement of our particular unfree bodies because I was in front of him but he could not see me because he was blind and he was behind me and I could not see him because I could not turn my neck. Yet yet yet when we were moving forwards into open space together we were both completely expanding into complete freedom.

Breakfast was nothing if not ordinary on the fifty-third and final morning with Jim in his usual place at the far end of the near table with laughter around him and me taking the spoon in my mouth every time it took off from the white bowl although I suppose Charlie at Jim's end of the table sulking and seeming a different and smaller boy was something out of the ordinary but after I was wheeled back to the window and left by Sister Cécile with the words Now behave won't you and then after the usual morning beginnings of fabric arrival and thump-start that was when events began to become wonderful for the Princesses soon afterwards arrived bringing pink and glamour and behind their giggling proud fronts I could already see my painting of a walking stick was in their square-ended fingers although it did not stay there for long they said This is for you Elliott and it floated round into view transformed glorified glistening with the sticky back plastic with which it had been magically repaired and the diagonal blue line of it sparkling glittery.

Charlie I could see was up the far end of the long corridor watching this manger scene and because of this I knew he knew it meant the children were against him because the Princesses clapped and squealed delightedly after they placed the painting on my lap where I could love it and drool on it and then they ran off taking all the others except Charlie with them to tell everyone what a wonderful thing they had done and let them I thought yes even let them tell Sister Britta for it was a wonderful thing of compassion and noticing and art and wit because with Jim nearby as he almost immediately was and Gavin somewhere to be found on the ward we could make the progress we did make for Gavin was in Dorm 5 doing forward rolls on his bed legs flipping forwards above his head's squareness and once he had finished which took a while I made him look at the painting by lowering my eyes towards it Look I tried to say Look!

At first I thought he Gavin did not understand and that he just thought I was presenting him with a sparkly gift I had made for him because I liked him and was sorry for scaring him although I had of course never before given him or anyone a proper gift but I did like him very much and would have done so if I could have done so but the apparent misunderstanding turned out to be pure true perfect understanding and to be my first real gift for Gavin did take the walking stick painting off my lap looked at it with joy despite the little drool and then without giving me the chance to start backwards and forwards rolling or to make the Hnigg noise he jumped off his bed went straight to the corner and fetched the walking stick as a gift in return as a thing in return for a picture of a thing as brown and woody for blue and white.

Gavin smilingly as if he had always eventually wanted to give it to someone placed the walking stick not on my lap but across between the armrests of my wheelchair which was exactly the wrong place for me to use it as a lift button pusher but exactly the right place for carrying it in celebration back down the long corridor to my bed in Dorm 1 if we were not interrupted by a Sister and as it happened we weren't but we were intercepted by Charlie who was breathing breathing up and down through his nose.

I hate you he said I hate you he said twice and I came to believe afterwards he said it once to Jim and once to me but that both times he meant I hate you two together and what you've done to me.

Charlie could have stolen the walking stick and been mean and hidden it where I couldn't get it like behind a wardrobe but he was now afraid of us and knew the Sisters might any moment arrive on the long corridor so he let us pass after I said Vroo to Jim to go forwards and Jim went forwards but when we passed close he Charlie spat in Jim's face which I thought would mean reaction anger violence and Jim in the Chapel for another three days of approaching meatiness and silencio but Jim just kept pushing me forwards not at all as if nothing had happened because he laughed and lifted my wheelchair up into a wheelie which he had never done before because I had never found the word for it but which I made sure he knew now and knew I loved because I whooped Wee-eee-eee whooped Wee-eee-eee not only at the amazing wheelie but at Jim's amazing capacity to astonish by not doing what you I expected him to do but instead doing something infinitely cleverer and better.

The shaft of the walking stick was against my belly but the curved end of it was heavier than the end with the grey rubber shoe or pad or foot I did not know the correct word and still don't know it and as the front wheels of my wheelchair came down in triumph on the lino the walking stick was jolted meaning that the greater weight of the curved end went down and the grey rubber end went up and as a result the walking stick began to slip rightwards off my lap and although I tried to make my hands keep hold of it they were sadly not specifically useful enough not fortissimo physically and I felt a quick smooth wooden texture slide across my belly that ended with a small biff from the sticking out rubber bit.

When the walking stick clattered behind us as it landed on the floor and skidded a bit towards the gate I expected Charlie to be the person to take advantage and steal it from us because Jim and I had lost it through foolishness overconfidence swank and bravado but as I hummed Stop I heard no footfalls from behind us instead it was the total surprise of Lise who escaped from the trance of her tragedy long enough to get up spring and sprint past us and pick the walking stick two handed from the floor for when I had Jim turn us round I saw her standing with the stick aloft as if it were the host upon the communion bread plate and Lise held it up in front of me in quite a sacramental way before looking me in the eye with greater curiosity than I had ever witnessed in her Lise before as if to ask What do you want with this? or What do you want of me? and I looked back in love and practicality by aiming my eyeballs first straight at her eyes green beautiful and then down and to the right beneath my arm then back to green then back to arm.

Lise understood the practical if not the loving part of my communication for she reacted by trying to place the walking stick rubber end first beneath my arm but although it pained me at such a moment of intimacy I had to halt her by barking my No sound and wibbling my head as best I could which made Lise look in my eyes a second glorious time for further information for elucidation and all I could find to do was look at the walking stick as if looking were holding and then roll my eyes once stop and roll them again both times clockwise meaning Flip it please Turn it please but Lise first responded by rolling her own green eyes in a way I found a revelation of comic depths as if Isolde had done a handstand and shown her frilly knickers and this was not the lovely tragic Lise I knew for our activity had forced her or encouraged her into her mischievous self.

What else she might do or prove suddenly capable of doing I did not know but for now she showed perfect understanding for she removed the walking stick from where she had pushed it into the gap between my right side and my right arm and she turned it around and re-inserted it hook first just where I had envisioned it going when I first made my lift-using plan and because the walking stick was in place and might never be again and the long corridor was quiet Thump I felt as if now was perhaps the time for carrying out the plan and escaping but I could not go anywhere without first looking at Lise my love closer to me now at that instant than ever she had been before and all the more startling a physical presence and an occurrence of human soul because of it.

Orange freckles I had only ever imagined from a distance of six feet or so I now saw separate and joined in all their glory and separated by skin of Sister Mary Margaret's teacup white but they were on a face that was beginning to rise and tilt away from me as her eyes left mine which could see her more intensely than any human being ever would again and rose up her eyes to seek those of Jim which could see not at all not a thing and I was left looking at Lise's slender neck and upon it the curved shadow of her chin shaped like an inverted bell quite I thought like the one rung during Mass and her neck the newly discovered world of her chin was completely without freckles until I saw a line of three beneath her left ear one freckle for each of us.

So confused was I I found it hard to make butterfly-What memories but I think I thought She really likes me which was a thought I had never allowed myself to have before any more than I had thought Kurt was my best friend and I had always assumed that the centre of Lise's world and grief was Kurt's filing cabinet and if that object were somewhere else then so would he be there and so would she his sister but now there was just a chance Lise went constantly where she did because it was close to where she could hear Kurt thump but also to where she could see me sit and look at birds or into whiteness and she could sit and perhaps look at me secretly for secret comfort. Until that is Jim came and became a different kind of comfort as well as a different kind of blind torment for she was looking at him now in hope in expectation of a specific response specific love that I knew wasn't going to come in the way she wanted it to because Lise's hopes were like towers of wooden bricks the higher she built them the more likely it was another child would come along and knock them down that child often being Charlie who behind Jim behind me but retreating towards Dorm 2 was still in my field of hearing but this time Lise's bricks were going to be knocked over by two people by Jim and I because Lise wanted Jim just to herself but when Jim and I had done what we planned to do one of us or perhaps both of us would be gone and it was indeed Jim who went.

With the walking stick perfectly placed I thought and this I can clearly remember thinking Why not now? and this is how so many plans reach their frustration or their bafflement for there may be a plan but there is no plan for carrying out the plan so I knew what I wanted to do but I didn't yet know when the best time to do it would be. Maybe there would never be a better moment or chance than fully equipped with a button-pusher on a Sister-empty long corridor and morning sunlight on the wych elm and sunlight therefore on the waiting world of green morning outside the ward where we would yippee etcetera be free and because I had behind me the energy of so many years of fantasy and wanting wanting to enter the woods and see trees close up I almost made it never happen by not trying immediately to make it happen.

I had not been watching Lise's hands except as they began to change the shadows on Lise's miraculously luminous neck of white perfection except for the Lise-freckle and Jim-freckle and me-freckle below the left ear but now a darkening came across and I noticed those hands were outwardly stretched towards Jim with outwardly stretched fingers with tendons of tenderness also stretching and palms blanched into pink-lined maps of impossible lands of what I later learned was desire desire for comfort but also desire for what Jim and Lise might do privately if they were as alone together in a dorm or a field as I wanted to be alone with Jim and a circle of trees around us.

Lise stood as I had imagined Maria Callas standing when delivering an aria of pleading such as Casta diva from Norma or Ah! non giunge uman pensiero from La Sonnambula or any of three or four arias from La Traviata and Madam Butterfly because Maria Callas's voice was all tendon-tension tenderness and hand-lands but that was not all was not exact enough because today Lise was Maria Callas as Isolde and I knew because I had heard it said on Radio 3 that Callas had never sung Isolde in German because her repertoire did not extend beyond Italian and French to German-language opera and certainly not to Wagner in the original German but a devoted opera-lover like myself knew that at this moment of her emotional and religious life Lise could be no-one but Maria Callas impossibly singing Wagner in German singing Isolde singing from the third act of Tristan and Isolde singing the world towards death so intensely because life never could be lived more intensely than in that direction and so death met its defeat even in its embrace.

To be inside an opera even as the bass-singing servant sidekick of the high-singing hero even as Leporello was an excitement I had never anticipated happening to me on the long echoey corridor with the grey filing cabinet and the crucifixes above doors and the African Animals and maybe the Sisters had occasionally seemed to surround me like the Sisters in Soeur Angelica an opera too sad for me to do anything but hear it as my mother's worst pain of separation from me but just as Sister Britta would often click off the music divinely left behind by Sister Cécile on the radio in the Sisters' Office so now our opera was ended by the sudden arrival of Ludvik the Caretaker who stepped out of the lift after the doors opened and although I could not see him and did not yet know who he was Lise's eyes went to him over Jim's right shoulder and the fingers of her hands immediately wilted like daisies in a dry spell and before Ludvik the Caretaker had reached the gate Lise was already defensively falling in folds of fabric.

Ludvik the Caretaker cut off the high soprano note Lise would have been singing with a comic rumble of Hello spoken to us collectively as he strolled towards us and immediately Cluck went the wooden gate closing so easily just as it would open so easily and the lift was still on our floor and it was rarely there so there would be no waiting for it and there was no-one in it but where were those who might be?

Sister Britta was in her inner Office of that I was sure Sister Muriel was not around that day not that I had seen Sister Mary Margaret was almost certainly doing catechism in the Chapel with Sister Eliza and her handkerchief helping which left Sister Cécile who was not playing piano or conducting singing or as far as I knew dealing with a child hitting another child or crying or fitting.

How terrible if we were to be thwarted in our escape by the Sister most likely to understand and sympathize even if she would not be able to bring herself to condone such a reckless and disobedient act of what she would see as self-gratification and all this time Jim had been waiting like an engine that isn't running because the ignition has not been turned just as he had waited behind me sometimes when I was at the window until he had let go and left to go and knot himself around Lise as I could tell he was about to do now not necessarily because he understood what had just happened with her although he probably did but because it was what he usually did at this time of day if I was not getting him to do something else.

What decided me finally finally was that if we went now no-one would have to take the blame for putting the walking stick under my arm in the correct position for escape whereas if Sister Cécile helped me to do this in a few days' time by which time it would become clear that for some reason I was attached to having the walking stick sticking up in front of me then she would suffer for not understanding that children are all inherently sinful and that even their mildest and most innocent-seeming whims can turn out to have been Devilry when looked upon with the eye of informed judgement.

There was the issue of the Cluck but Sister Britta had not come out to see who it was when Ludvik the Caretaker went through and as she had heard it once for someone going in and must know it was a going-in person because people coming out usually went straight into the Sisters' Office I felt fairly sure Sister Britta would assume the next Cluck was the same person who had just come in going out and that it was Ludvik the Caretaker on just such an errand of fixing or assessing as he was now.

Go Go Go I sang to Jim then added a high-pitched eee to get him to turn right and continue turning right until we were facing the wooden gate and also facing away from Lise at whose pinky blue knees I had so I supposed taken a quick but poignant last glance and I guided Jim forwards until we were right in front of the wooden gate just as he had been on the days of his defiance the thirteenth and fifteenth and seventeenth days.

Yes we were in the Here he had made of a nothing and with his strong senses I knew he would know exactly where we were and I hoped he would know exactly what that meant.

All that remained for me to do was trust in him Jim after I said Cluck and waited.

Jim laughed very loudly and I was instantly full of fear our escape had suffered revelation even before its genesis for wouldn't Sister Britta immediately set out to investigate unwarranted hilarity upon the long corridor but no Jim's instinct was right unexpected laughs were part of the continuo of the ward just as Thump was and Sister Britta's attention would have been drawn more immediately by suspicious silencio than by child-type noises and outbursts as long as they didn't sound violent or like choking or sin.

Cluck said Jim and leaving me in no doubt that he understood what we were about he reached up in one beautifully swift motion high above my head and to the right where I myself could never reach and pushed the wooden catch down and the wooden gate swung away from us opening like a new Christmas card and I didn't even need to say Vroo for Jim to push me through until I was right alongside the door to the Sisters' Office then turn back and get ready to close the wooden gate behind us two with a second Cluck but what I heard instead of Cluck was a new sound was Eek and before I had the chance to understand I saw what had happened which was that Lise had seen what was happening and had mischievously decided to join us join the escape.

When with a Cluck Jim closed the wooden gate it was behind we three rather than two of us.

We three children one of whom was running on rubber wheels and both the other two were in bare feet which altogether sounded more than twice as loud as one adult's feet in shoes.

Lise skipped along the strange end of the forbidden corridor towards the lift and I considered for a moment whether we should abandon the plan because it was now something completely different and at least twice as dangerous for one third more people but Lise had at least as much right to freedom as did Jim and I and there was no time to be cautious now the first and worst rule had been broken for even if we were caught straight away we would be legends on the ward for having made it thus far as only Micky had done before and him noisily and obviously.

I find it hard to believe he meant or timed it but Jim's Cluck of letting the gate shut happened at exactly the same moment as Kurt's next Thump and so was less conspicuous than it might have been and after this Jim's hands were back on the handles of my wheelchair and we were wheeling forwards.

It was a strange and satisfying feeling to know that Sister Britta and all her rage and righteousness of the near future was ignorantly receding behind me behind a plain wooden door within the Sisters' Office and that she could at any moment choose to come out away from the burdens of financial administration about which I had often heard her complain and with a single glance she and her bleached-blue eyes would discover a conspiracy of unprecedented sophistication and magnitude.

Us.

Lise had reached the lift by now and miracle of miracles although I suppose it was an inevitable next thing to do she pushed the call button for the lift and because it was still in position from Ludvik the Caretaker's arrival the doors opened without more than half a second's delay and the lift compartment lay before us as the final commitment to escape and freedom and capture and punishment beyond all previous punishment but despite this just as the lift did not hesitate in opening for us so we did not hesitate in going inside Lise first and then after a quiet Vroo me with Jim right behind me.

Already Lise might have pressed any of the buttons for any of the floors but she hadn't she had waited until I was in there too and it was exactly as if she had said Go on Elliott you do it meaning I understand and have understood for a little while what you wanted with the walking stick and I am not going to interfere with that with the fulfilment of that ambition and I was aghast with joy at this so I had Jim line me up with the buttons running down from 4 to −1 in front of me and the button-pusher angled up and then I gently went Vroo and Jim pushed me perfectly forwards and the grey rubber pad engaged perfectly perfectly but with the −1 button the button for the basement where the kitchen was and where Ludvik the Caretaker had his workshop.

This was an error but I could make it good so I had Jim wheel me back and then forwards again all the while me trying with all my feeble strength to raise the end of the button-pusher upwards two inches but the second time as the lift doors closed upon the long corridor goodbye for a while perhaps forever the grey rubber perfectly pressed encore the −1 button and Lise saw my frustration and Jim must have felt my frustration in the beginning-to-tremble of my hopeless head but whereas Jim could only get me in position for another press Lise could interfere by putting her pale hand beneath the shaft of the walking stick and raising it slightly so that when I went Vroo and Jim pushed forwards she made the grey rubber perfectly perfectly hit the button for zero and so if Lise had not been with us been one of us we would not have been able to escape.

I know this absolutely.

By this time the lift had begun its descent towards the first floor making the electric motor noise it usually made that might on this day at this hour have already been noticed by Sister Britta or might have been just another passing note in the continuo of her working day and over this we could have no control but Lise and I could watch the amber lightbulbs come on behind the translucent numbered discs to the right of the buttons for each floor and we could all wonder whether anyone else had called the lift and would catch us making our escape or if they did catch us whether they would understand we were making an escape which with three of us there and involved seemed slightly less likely especially as one of us was sighted and able-bodied and also not crying but a moment later giggling in an unprecedented way giggling giggling giddily giggling.

But it was as we went grindingly down with small zings from the wires above the false ceiling above our heads wires I had seen when the lift was being repaired it was during this interlude in the lift-of-unknowing that I realized how afraid I had suddenly become of Lise's hair her ginger hair and that ridiculously without realizing it I had been trusting and acting in the little belief that my and Jim's dull brown hair would make us unobtrusive make us a fading-into-the-background presence once we were outside if we made it outside plus we were wearing our usual drab clothes and Lise's green-with-blue-flowers dress was brighter but was at least not the red one containing bright yellow flowers but her brilliant head of ginger hair would be looked at with love and astonishment wherever it went and once her hair was spotted so would we be sighted and that might end our excursion into the green before it had begun.

The first floor went past and the slow lift had never seemed more slow like a lentissimo lioness on the television about to catch a trying-to-be-andante antelope between her claws gracefully and full of terror and as I anticipated soon seeing the lobby the sight of the lobby and who or what might be there I was full of graceful grateful terror because we were amazing we were here beyond the Here we had pushed the zero button all three of us together and I had inspected the inside of the lift on previous trips but now I saw the inside as if it was an echoey cathedral with Christmas evensong going on high within it and I was a person the size of a rolling eyeball an eyeball aware everything it did was especially watched there by the eye of God because even though He is everywhere He is especially there in cathedrals and even more so in St Peter's Rome when the Pope is there and just before the lift doors opened on the lobby I remember I had the vivid thought What if the Pope catches us escaping?

What if John Paul II has suddenly decided to visit the good children of the second-floor ward about whom he has heard so much and for whom he cares so very deeply?

What if the doors open just as they were just beginning to and what Lise and I saw was not shiny blue lino but shiny purple and pink silk and two practical fingers raised in blessing but soon to drop in infallible dismay?

Pope John Paul II was not in the lobby and the blue lino shone without the darkening of leather shoes or sandals either nearby the lift or further off towards the glass doors with the opaque crosses on them that would open by themselves whenever someone approached but through the glass doors and in the car park I could see the shape of someone getting larger as they got closer and I knew we could not risk being found where we were so Vroo I had Jim push me forwards aiming the grey rubber again at −1 and Lise got there first and for some reason with her fingers pressed −1 which meant the lift doors closed upon us hiding us just as the glass doors opened but we were going down to an unknown place the basement.

Down we travelled until the lift bumped as it hit the bottom of its run and then the lift doors opened left and right though they were both to my right and in the extreme periphery of my vision. I did not see a caretaker or a cook but I did hear a radio playing pop music not a song I knew and I smelled water boiling.

Jim's hands were relaxed upon the handles of my wheelchair but I could hear Lise who had suddenly stopped giggling breathing as quietly as she could and could hear the shhh and prickle of her hair on her shoulder as she looked to the right to see if anyone had seen us though a caretaker I thought was more likely to let us go than a Sister just for the fun of it.

Vroo I said for we had no choice but to get out of the lift and wait there for whoever had just arrived in the lobby to go wherever they were going for whatever reason they were going there so I had Jim steer us out so we were just up against the concrete wall where the call button was and there we waited as inconspicuously with mouse-brown and beautiful ginger hair as we could while the doors shut and the lift gave the metallic clank of being called away.

Jim and Lise and I were huddled together in our wild magnificence as if we were zebras all looking down at something interesting in my lap when the lift chunked up to the ground floor stopped opened and paused and then closed its doors and began to rise up zinging but rose for the minimum time because there was a quieter Chunk and the doors opened on the first floor.

Lise did not hesitate she pressed the call button trusting who-ever it was who had gone to the first floor was not coming straight back down.

Within a few long seconds we were back in the lift and for speed's sake Lise's pale fingers and not the grey rubber pressed the zero button and then after a minute during which I did not breathe she and I were looking out again at the now empty lobby and the glass doors behind which this time there were only cars and no human visitor bodies and already because I had got Jim to turn me to face the right direction Go Go Go I hummed and we all went directly across the shiny blue lino in the bright light of morning just as if we did

228

it all the time because we were allowed to because we were trusted valued children and not imprisoned children who had to spend days repenting for standing in front of a wooden gate.

In thinking of my many memories of it I lose sense of how long it took us to change our angle of view on the lobby narrowing it down from the wide view when we entered it to the narrow one of just what was beyond the glass doors when we reached them and they opened for us just as if we were Sister Britta on her way to walk a Labrador or as if we were Pope John Paul II stepping onto the Papal balcony or as if we were Ludvik the Caretaker going home to his daughter Anoushka or as if we were Maria Callas making an entrance onto the stage of La Scala in Milan an entrance like ours now into caressing cool air an entrance of magnificence dignity poignancy and yes wit.

There was a ramp directly in front of the glass doors and ten parking spaces five to either side three of which were occupied by cars and one the nearest taken up by the coach which would have been a useful bulk to hide behind if we had needed but the morning was a quiet one and the black-shoed visitor we had avoided by our lift subterfuge seemed the only person around at that time although I was aware very aware of the four towering floors behind and above us as Jim and I began to drive away from them with Lise barefoot close upon our left side Lise who must have been feeling the air of outside talking to her through her skin saying Welcome to my temperature which today is cool but helpful.

Holding the victorious walking stick as high as I could I bone-hummed Happy to Jim and Happy he hummed back as he barefoot pushed me over the smoothly grinding black surface and towards the road where we would have to choose left or right at the T-junction but it was no choice because my plans for this point in the escape were already old.

Lise began weeping just like long corridor Lise but she did not flump because it seemed that out by the road she was able to do more than the one thing that is to do both weeping and walking and even weeping and watching for cars and because we were behind her and she turned sometimes I could see her tears were coming slowly enough for her right cheek to be dry even though the area beneath the pink rim of her raw eye was still somewhere that glistened in a familiar and entirely lovely and endearing way yes this Lise was still the Lise of the ward she was just happier and like all three of us having a new experience of a better life that was free and opening out like Beethoven or Mahler rather than routine and closing down like Philip Glass or Vivaldi day night day night day night corridor corridor nothing but corridor.

Rightwards we turned as I raised the pitch of my Vroo right and onto a pavement with a low brick wall to the right behind a patch of bright green grass beneath sunlight and ahead on our side of the road in front of the woody horizon were two large buildings with car parks and yellow-at-night streetlights where I was sure cars often came and went bringing workers and visitors and not Sisters and beyond them the pavement of oblong concrete slabs that chucker-chuckered beneath the rubber wheels carried on for about the length of three long corridors before there was a bus stop made of concrete with as I had seen before a concrete post sticking up beside it with a picture of a bus on it and a number 142.

The sky was the same blue as I would have seen if I had seen it above the building opposite above the wych elm through the window but it was all over me overarching and like an umbrella a Sister an inexperienced Sister has left you to hold without knowing you're not able to hold an umbrella so it has slipped down to cover you but brilliantly and not close and in a welcome way the sky because we were now beyond where any child had ever strayed and every movement we made was into new territory that meant exploration of airy freedom.

I had planned for us to make it to the bus shelter and to wait there for a bus to take us to the nearest forest that is for Jim and I to wait as I had only ever imagined two brown heads on the escapade but as I was wheeled and Lise and Jim walked along the grey paving slabs towards the number 142 I heard a car engine behind us that sounded from the gear changes like a small car driven by an angry person in a hurry and at this my shoulders which beneath the sky's blueness had relaxed as much as they ever did went into tight hunches and all my muscles responded unhelpfully by stretching me out within myself and dipping the rubber tip of the walking stick as the engine got louder and the eyes of the driver more likely to fall upon us and especially upon Lise's ginger hair with horror shock amusement glee.

The car that drove fast alongside us was small and shiny green and from my angle I only saw the side of the driver's face flash pinkly past which seemed a good sign for if I had seen eyes then those eyes would have been more likely to have seen me and more likely to have seen Jim and that Jim had no eyes and more likely to have seen that both Jim and Lise had no shoes on but instead of slowing the green car accelerated in the direction we were heading away from the ward and toward green.

After the car's engine could no longer be heard I began to force myself to enjoy what I was seeing and experiencing with all my senses even the bouncing and jouncing of the wheels of my wheelchair over twigs and stones on the path which did I have to admit hurt my spine but was so different to smooth lino and its tiny snickers that I rejoiced.

It was a beautiful day a day as beautiful as Lise who was miraculously with us to experience and double the beauty of the day.

Around me near me I could hear more birds than ever I could remember hearing in one place at one time before and some I knew already like greenfinches and blackbirds but some I was only able to identify later much later after the unlocking by Dr Masters and the miracle drug Lioresal after the fleur-de-lys cupboard years up the road with the Brothers and the mop until the rescue by young Brother Benedict and the embrace of medical science that believed spastic imbeciles who hummed Mozart could have word-hoards and if you just released their muscles from overenthusiasm they could let you know and tell you a story of their lives. I could not before all this wonderfulness of release into society and hand-moving electric wheelchair and questions answered and special typing machine I could not accurately identify the above-me song as that of common wrens because for the moment of that moving morning's moment all I was aware of was a lot too much airborne information that wasn't information but wasn't nonsense because it was beauty and efficiency and bird-business and twittering that in a bird's fast time was heard as a boom saying this saying something I thought about for a long time saying as singing with this meaning I I I am the kind of thing that sings the kind of song that I am singing and because this song of mine can still be sung this means that I am still alive after the silence of the dark and can survive the next few phrases too and if you can hear my song if you are near enough to hear my song and if you too are the kind of thing that sings this kind of song then you will hear my song is a strong song that very strongly sings I I I am the kind of thing that sings the kind of song that I am singing etcetera...

When we reached the bus shelter a little like Snoopy's kennel without a roof and went inside there were two things inside the first thing was an outstanding smell like the toilets of the Arndale Centre combined with communion wine and Sister Mary Margaret's fish pie armpits and the second thing was a pile of clothing in a triangular shape in the dark corner but then lying on top of the middle of this I saw a pile of fingers that were unlike any other fingers on any other hands I had ever seen because these hands with small chunk wounds taken out at the sides of the fingers looked as if they were wearing thick gloves made of hand-skin gloves that did not quite fit but were split a little where the wounds were and the man's hands for I realized then he had to be a man with hands like these made me feel sick and full of pity. And because I was already feeling quite sick from the smell the sight of the hands this made me think I was truly going to be sick but the stench impressed me because I had never in all my born days as Sister Mary Margaret used to say never encountered anything so rankly strong not even Sister Britta's faith in her own righteousness moved so powerfully and directly in the direction of its own intensification and fulfilment like a lioness hunting if a lioness were somehow hunting herself for within the communion wine smell were vinegar and faeces and sweat and something I could only identify as despair distilled and sprinkled upon a human body in dull drops of uncleanliness until it seeped in and became the skeleton whose bones were what was within the smell but what was astonishing was that outside the central spine of the smell was a halo of itself radiating out and out and getting purer even as it got weaker because despair becomes stronger as it becomes weaker and the thought of this made me think of the works of Schubert in his final syphilitic year of 1828.

Once I had thought of Schubert in that slow moment before the roar that was about to come out of the smell-skeleton's body I could not stop thinking of the poor young dying Austrian composer my second favourite behind Mahler and ahead of Beethoven although I knew Beethoven was the greatest of them all but in ranking them for myself I considered only the things my heart and intestines did when I heard them their great works on the radio not the things my head and mind did when they thought about what presenters said about them during This Week's Composer or interval talks and when I thought about what I should think about them if I were trying to be fair and correct and including special categories for Mozart and Bach who were in my opinion beyond category and even in the bus shelter thinking about dying-Schubert-living made me take the lift down inside myself sinking to the basement where my Caretakers stored all my care and took careful care of it for when I needed it like then.

This poor man with the light falling upon the folds of his waxy coat that was the same light that fell upon Lise's flowery folds when they were on the long corridor or that came through the high window into the Chapel sometimes diagonally down onto the altar and if that light brought any blessing to him who had more need because the light and the care needed to travel to him through a miasma of man-reek that would have kept all the wild animals of the African Savanna away from him even warthogs and would keep away all other humans except the Jesus who I believed didn't exist but who the Sisters believed did. That Jesus would have embraced him and even taken off his boots to make the stench worse before washing his feet as a sign of love even for the lowest of the low.

In my plan we stayed hidden in the bus shelter until a bus came but I was afraid of what the sleeping man would do to us if we woke him up from his snoring sleep which snoring at least meant I knew Jim would know we weren't standing there so long in a dank place surrounded by a toilet smell for no reason but even so I could not ask him Jim what we should do and I could only guess Lise's thoughts from her reaction or rather from the reaction of her bare feet because I could not see her darkened-above-me face or her fabric-covered knees.

Lise gave a moan and from the direction her toes were pointing I knew it was a moan in reaction to the man who I later learned in the aftermath of our escape and the investigation of our journey and the departure of Jim and the punishment of Lise and I was a tramp a homeless person and who I felt all along even before the Schubert-thought and the Jesus-thought deserved our compassion and pity but Lise's pity I knew involved flopping to the floor and weeping and I did not want any more of her than her pale feet to touch this moist urine-smelling floor.

Jim began to reverse out of the bus shelter after I quietly hummed Back but the man had already heard something probably Lise's moan and had begun to move in a more-awake-than-asleep way with injured fingers flying to face to rub it and when they came away I saw eyes and at the same time coincidentally heard another motor approaching on the road this one like a child-version of a car and in the time it took to go past and reveal itself to the corner of my eye as the smear of a small motorbike the man had raised himself up on his elbows and said some words to us that the sound of the motor chopped up beyond comprehension.

But when Jim stopped from shock and there was no other sound left but the sound of our four breathings and birdsong and when the sound of the man's next growled words came I still could not understand what they were meant to mean because as far as I was able to tell trying my very hardest to understand him to understand if he needed help the man's words were more grrr than words and perhaps the man's meaning really was more the meaning of grrr.

When I saw the man's face when it climbed into view like a spider out of the hole of its web like I had seen once on the ward before seventeen days later it the spider's web was dusted away by Mrs Bee the Cleaner that face was a wonderfully literally brilliant thing of burnished bronze which was a phrase burnished like finest bronze I had twice heard on Radio 3 used to describe the tone of the horns in music by Johannes Brahms specifically the Deutsches Requiem and the First Symphony but really also applicable to any Brahms piece scored for trumpets French horns trombones flugelhorns etcetera so Brahmsian was the man's face that seeing it was like hearing a sudden fanfare blaring because his skin shone with a colour between red and gold but on a surface of polished wood like the knees of Jesus on the crucifix in the Sisters' Office which still existed even though we were away from it and not thinking of it except as I thought passingly of Jesus as foot-washing Jesus.

Of course of course he the tramp had a beard like Jesus and somewhere in the midst of it the tanglish brown beard as we had already discovered or had confirmed was a human mouth and such a mouth! such a mouthy mouth that when I saw it I felt I'd never seen a mouth before because when the man roared again I saw every one of those teeth of his that were missing and I saw the inside of his toothless almighty mouth like a glistening pink lesion of a cave within the concrete cave of the bus shelter and so indelible was this fanfare of insight that I have never since seen a bus shelter from a coach or a car without imagining that it had inside it a mouth-lesion roaring perpetually in perpetual wrath.

We reversed away quickly from what was for one or two moments the centre of creation and the greatest most adult danger I had ever known although I suspect both Jim and Lise had known far worse though far quieter at least that is what I came to believe in the years of fleur-de-lys quiet and mop watching that followed this roaring terror of human pink chasing us scaring us with noise out of its homeless home his here and out onto the long bending-down-gently-and-slightly-to-the-left corridor-without-walls of the road.

My plan had been to wait for a bus and see if that bus would take us like a coach along the road until we spotted somewhere we wanted to stop i.e. somewhere like a forest or a wood and I knew from our drives to the pantomime and the Arndale Centre which took an hour in this direction meaning turning right out of the home that on the way there were dark green places where the trees grew tall and thick within sight of the road sometimes with houses there too and sometimes exactly what I wanted with no houses just empty squares of grass with sheep or cows or a plant not grass that was yellow like egg yolk that had been the plan and it had not even in long retrospect been a horribly bad plan but the plan was gone with the hiding place and now we were outside and anyone in a car or on a motorbike on the road could see us and steal us as the Sisters said they might away from Holy Mother Church and Jesus' love.

Yes not a horribly bad plan but we were still where we could be spotted from the windows of the second floor of the home and our next triumph must be to get away from that radius of concern and restriction and really out into the wilderness where wild animals lived meaning animals wilder even than the woken sleeping man whose language was not English or whose language was only English wrath so I got Jim to start pushing us on down the slight slope of the turning road where at least to the right there were tall trees mostly branch but dusted with some layers of friendly green Spring leaves rather than buildings with moonface car parks for the storage and everlasting salvation of children who were not normally properly shaped or decently behaved especially when escaping from those human buildings of God.

I was worried for Jim's and even more for Lise's feet that late Lenten morning very close to Easter to Palm Sunday as we pushed along on the grey pavement slabs tickety-clap tickety-clap alongside the much darker grey road the almost-black-if-it-hadn't-been-a-bit-dusty road where chunks of almost-shiny were embedded in a flat of rough-grippy and white paint was on and off stitched down the middle like the stitches on the front pockets of one pair of blue jean trousers that had been mine on and off for several months two Christmases and one birthday before and whose material I had found especially delightfully soft against my legs and I hoped the pavement surface was soft against Jim's big tough feet and even more Lise's soft indoors feet beneath her knees which must surely be floating forwards in delicious arcs of crimson and gold beneath ivory white.

No cars or motorbikes or coaches came past while we travelled to the end of the pavement where it stopped and grass began and here I had a decision for I had always fantasized galloping galloping happily galloping on fast hooves across a flat surface of short soft grass but although green and shaggy this surface looked uneven with tyre track dips across it so I sang Squeak then bone-hummed left-turn then sang Squeak again when I realized we Jim and I had no word for Step or Stair because we had never encountered one and that the drop in front of me over a concrete edge from pavement to road was as high as two of my fists on top of one of Sister Cécile's as she moved my hands to play one potato two potato.

I think Lise thought I was waiting to hear if a car was coming which it wasn't but she didn't say anything to Jim about the drop we were facing and this forced me to Back him up a step then bone-hum him in a circle until we were backs to the road and faces to a patch of grey grass and silver-grey nettles and it was a risk but Back I sang and Slow and Jim took one two steps and then the third had him over the edge with a jolt I felt through the handles and then the handles were free in air with no human control as Jim fell backwards onto the road surface and I waited a small part of a vivid second to see whether I too was over the edge and in danger of falling or whether I was safe on the balanced pavement.

In front of me with my life maybe ending soon I saw the pointed tall shape of every blade of grass carving in front of and curving behind every other blade of grass like a fugue and knew them all it seemed as well as my hands or the view of the wych elm from the window then bump the whole world's horizon tilted up fell away in front of me as if God-in-my-image had powerfully spasmed the wheelchair backwards into a wheelie and then bump and tip I was looking at a cloud in the blue sky that I had time just enough time to think looked like a tree before I tipped back and back and would I die?

I was falling on top of Jim but not exactly on top so one of my handles the left was towards his chest and the other the right one was in the space to the right of his chest which meant that when the first landed on him like a hard poke from a walking stick the fall of me was stopped on the left but on the right with nothing to stop it it continued and I fell further beginning to roll and pivot with sky becoming green then black and I felt with great clarity my right elbow with the walking stick above it shatter at bone level as it met the hard road.

The pain was instantly such that when I later thought in comparison of the other pains of my life I did so with a kind of nostalgia oh those mere aches for some of me was left behind a mouth to gasp and feel cold air and eyes to shut but most of me went for a transparent holiday in the agony and only came back to the road for a brief visit of panic before the road hit my right cheek and fractured my weak skull and the holiday slept.

Then I was awake and hearing another engine.

Over the years I have thought a great great deal about the person the driver the man the woman whoever it was in the small silver car that came during this time and what it was they saw on the road which was not the side of the road they were driving on when they came past the home and the other two buildings what did they see? What did they think of what they saw? And what after seeing that and thinking that made them like the Pharisee drive past on the other side?

They saw a brown-haired child with thin waving arms and bloody head in a capsized wheelchair on the road and they just kept driving thank God bless them bless them for their sinful indifference or callous evil which saved our day the greatest day of my life even greater than the first touch of Jim and perhaps in mitigation they the atrocious silver sinner behind the steering wheel did not just see but they also heard and what they heard was not distressing like what they saw but was unharmed Jim laughing up above my red head laughing as if we were on a fun adventure and falling over in the road was just part of it.

I thought all of our adventures were over as absolutely as my elbow was absolutely painful and as the car's engine drew closer and I did not know yet it was silver but as its tone did not change but continued to drone on as it drove past and on I felt there might be some chance of more day and I was right because after the car had gone Lise came to help Jim get up and the easiest way to do this was to use her wonderful hands to help him raise me off him for the left handle of my wheelchair was still pressing on him and I have often wondered whether by himself Jim would have had the strength of arm to push me up away back into sitting position again which is what after some struggles and more laughter from Jim they managed to do I suppose because I was and am light in body as compensation for being burdensome in soul.

Jim continued to laugh and to Lise's distress continued to lie on the road where a car coming down the dip and up the hill towards the home would have killed him and so a second time Lise shrieked and this made me remember the danger of discovery the tramp's first Schubert scream of a few minutes earlier had put us in and I was about to disgrace myself by becoming frantic when I realized I should be more worried about Jim being driven over by a car than about Sister Britta seeing us from a high window in fact better she did and saved Jim than that he died because he was so happy at being beyond the wooden gate and outside in a fresh space even a treacherous space that made him fall over.

Lise's screech may have been a bad tactic as far as the Sisters hearing us was concerned but it was a great bit of opera for getting Tristan off his bum and back onto his big feet for which manoeuvre he used my handlebars a bit so knew where they were and with a moment for Lise to thump him on the chest and then another for her fabric to rub against his fabric we were off down the curving slope which seemed to me a slope into a blankness neither dark nor light that I later realized was unconsciousness.

When I woke up it was with a cold wind over my face and my right eye not working properly because things in my field of vision were becoming larger and then disappearing both to right and left but right was behind my agony of an elbow with the walking stick put back in place and left was just a normal passing like Dorm 5 Dorm 4 Dorm 3 as when Sister Cécile pushed me to the white wall after breakfast.

The facts as I gradually came to see them were that I was in my wheelchair I was moving forwards and forwards meant down a slope I was wet on the face and the wet was blood and the blood was warm on my forehead and cold on my neck so I was bleeding from above my forehead on the right hand side and the right hand side had a new focus my elbow which was where everything in creation started from and flew towards because of all facts the pain of it was the greatest.

We three were moving we three because I could feel Jim's control on the handles and I could see flashes of Lise's ankles and bare feet to my left we were moving down the curving slope away from the ward whose gradient and slow turn to the left I can still feel throughout me if I close my eyes for it was the most memorable part of our journey on the road.

And as we were on the road with no more steps or drops in view and as I wasn't dead even if dying from a broken head I was able to revel in the sights my field of vision encompassed of road ahead and hedgerow to left and right the left being the most exquisite because down towards the bottom of the dip a wave of tiny white flowers on a tree I later learned to call the hawthorn were crashing almost onto the road like one of the waves Sister Cécile sometimes let me make with my legs in the white bath when she was in a particularly good mood.

It was not difficult to remember that the ward and its corridor and rooms still existed but at the same time it was hard to believe in it for it seemed with its rules and routines so much less vivid and valid than the happening world spreading around us and revealing more and more of itself the further and further we went into it and away from the ward where maybe even that moment our absence was being noticed and our escape being discovered that is our specific absence from the long corridor drawing attention to our general absence from Dorms Chapel Craft Room Refectory and Infirmary and the only explanation being direct physical assumption into Heaven or escape through the wooden gate but how?

Only we knew.

I still had and was very aware of the walking stick beneath my right arm for it went ahead of the three of us as the furthest point of our escape and exploration of fresh space and I was very grateful to it not only for what it had already accomplished but also for its sensible prosthesis and its shield-like aspect because as much of a delusion as it might have been I believed that its presence ahead of us made us appear more purposeful and intended so that as we forged forwards a car was less likely to stop and a person roll down their window to ask us what in hell's name we thought we were doing in which case Jim couldn't answer I shouldn't answer and Lise wouldn't answer.

I whooped Wee-eee-eee as we moved and Jim responded as I had hoped he would by putting the wheelchair into the kind of wild wheelie that usually made me whoop only in dreams front wheels off the road and my hands rearing like hooves of a galloping horse towards the future of good air and further galloping.

Abruptly I lowered my Vroo and steered Jim left across the road in a sharp diagonal to get us closer to the flowers or if possible into the flowers which abrupt turn might have been orange button-swallowing suicidal behaviour for although I could not hear a car approaching my ears might not be working quite so well as usual and it is true that although my sight came back in my right eye my left ear was ever afterwards deaf.

As we got closer I saw that at this point the road widened for the length of half a long corridor and there was a sign with a large white P on it against a square blue background inside a soft-edged white square mostly hidden by the lower boughs of a tree and a little dulled with spotty green growth that was what I later learned was lichen.

It was a layby and over the years it was to become the immortal layby of blessèd memory in which the position of every empty disposed of and faded blue packet of Salt and Vinegar crisps and every urine-coloured cigarette butt and especially the ripped white carrier bag caught in the thorns of the hawthorn about the height of my knees that billowed like the sail of Finn's nose-galleon in the wind that I had hardly noticed before the cold of the blood made it colder yes every bit of litter was to become for me immortal beneath and within the hawthorn blossom that was to grow forever but never to yellow wrinkle fall and decay in my homed head.

Ever afterwards for as long as I was on the ward another three Christmases it turned out before my meatiness arrived and I went up the road to the Brothers and their neglect I was always able to turn the whiteness of the white wall at will into the whiteness with green centres and circles of pink dots on yellow sticks later stalks stamens that made up this absolute close vision of the harmony of the beauty of nature and this vision was enough to justify not just our escape but my entire life of seeing rather than doing.

My stiff red head was on my right shoulder but there was no horizon to the hawthorn blossom it went deep into dark green as I could from that angle see.

I looked I saw I looked and saw it all. It was going into me blooming and was coming out of me flowering at the same time even before it had gone into me and I looked at myself from the eye of every bloom and even as this was happening to thousand-me and we knew it would soon end and we also knew it would could never end because it had always been happening and would always be happening like being in the mother-cave of hair and like dying my curled up death whenever in the future.

I did not have to wait for anything any longer because it had all already happened even the wonders just about to happen.

My vision by which I mean my sight but also my vision was bloody on the right hand side and though I knew it was wrong to think of Christ as myself or myself as Christ still I knew from imagination in Chapel that his final visions from up on the cross with the crown of thorns upon his brow at the time of the year that became Easter because He made it Easter by dying and resurrecting I knew I knew Christ's final visions were of gathered-beneath-Him looking-up-at-Him-curious mankind seen through and seen through by His own blood.

I did not see mankind but I did see things among the nettles among the green that were not leaves that were not green for example the empty blue faded cellophane crisp packets and many cigarette butts of various oranges yellows and off-whites some straight and some crumpled into Vs and Zs.

At first these remains of human presences dismayed and distressed me because all I wanted was blossom and more blossom like tulip petals within tulip petals within tulip petals until there was nothing but blossom spreading throughout the vastness of the whole darkening space within my shattered windy head like I could feel it feel them feel it doing like swans flying and I knew this spreading was not usual because I had never seen such beauty because after the road-bang fall my skull was all awry. But gradually over the long long course of a few seconds I became reconciled to the little bits of litter I could see throughout the hedgerow some old some very new to the right of my left eye's field of vision a packet of cigarettes emptied quite new mostly white uncrumpled with a rippling stripe of beautiful papal purple down the front and this along with all the other thrown human things became something I was eventually glad to see because I realized it made the place a human place and not just one for plants and animals and for bees like the first bee I now saw visiting a white flower coming into my field of vision buzzingly from above and to the left and that was where the bee should be and when it moved to a new bloom that too was where the bee should be for nothing here or anywhere could be where it should not be. Even me.

And when it seemed there was no more to see I had patient Jim push me forwards until the wheelchair was tipping on Tarmac edge and thorns were touching my forehead.

For a moment I was worried to the point of terror that by doing what I wanted to do I would get Jim into more trouble than he was already in but the fact I was already so smashed up meant Jim would already soon be getting into the maximum trouble because no-one none of the Sisters Sister Britta especially would ever find or work out that I had twice been tipped out of my wheelchair to get the injuries I had and so within our danger we were strangely warmly safe because although the worst had not yet begun it was guaranteed to begin.

If we were already damned then why not sin the more?

But we were not damned because in such a world as the immortal layby and in all the human world there was no such thing as damnation.

So I sang Go Go Go and Jim kept pushing me into the hawthorn until I tipped and flopped forward with rips upon my brow and nothing but pain in my elbow as I went down to the ground but spasming in a twist with a left hand not gripping anything but a right hand grabbing with all its sudden power the walking stick to flick me sideways in a turn upon my back to land on my back looking where?

Where I settled in nettles where I fell into a view not of expected white on green with pink prinks and grace notes of yellow but of mottled grey from the left eye the non-Christ eye and as I focussed with new scratches distracting me through my clothes and awkward-nesses and lumps of ground I focussed on me being in a new impossible instant room with angles of lion-less walls and ceiling and lino-less floor but mottled like concrete window sill growth and I mourned above all the white flowers above me that had been taken away from me by my angle of vision because I soon figured out I had fallen into the area of undergrowth within which had been thrown the purple cigarette packet that now when bashed by body-thorn-wobble and rearrangement of bending stem had fallen upon my edgy face.

No real room before me then but an illusory outdoors-indoors showing me a glimpse in miniature of the warded limits of my future and imprisoning my vision by placing angled cardboard between me and what I did not realize I had already seen enough of i.e. the hawthorn blossom seen enough of because already immortalized whereas my ears my ear one ear had not been listening well enough as now with blood veil over the right eye and mottled cell in the left and skull grating like coconut shells in Sister Cécile's music lessons as it now my one good ear was compelled to do to listen.

I listened.

I was listening practically for more dangerous engines arriving to end our idyll but it was something else I heard first and blessedly a blackbird singing a blackbird that had a high and non-repeating alto soprano song of piano notes Debussy-dripping but with trill and thrill beyond technique of fingers blackbird a bird I had heard before but never from beneath and through flowers as a follower of sound as well as of bright right sight.

As I bedded further and further down in the undergrowth I realized that the smell there was quite similar to the smell of the man in the bus shelter and that this was not due to the presence as there of a stinky human body but of course of course due to men having stood and used where I lay as a toilet whilst their cars waited with the engines ticking and I was glad at the time that I did not smell human faeces too in that place but I was glad later and just as much glad that my body had lain within a urine-scented cradle of green as glad that white hawthorn blossom had twirled down upon me because the urine made it definitely real and mixed rather than too purely pure during the while that soon was to become more than a while.

Lise came close before the time began to extend into afternoon and evening and night and put her hands on me in concern and not without affection but I didn't want her physical interference I just wanted to give her and Jim to one another I just wanted to be left where I was which was exactly where I wanted to be not restored to the wheelchair in my broken body and with my usual horizon instead I wanted the up-close peripherally seen outside the cell where leaves were umbrellas and stalks were tree trunks and so I was glad when Jim somehow got her away perhaps by reaching out and gently pulling her arm or hair.

Beyond my feet I heard the wheels of my wheelchair snicking as they took weight and I suspected though there was no way I could know definitely that Lise had sat herself down in the warm-from-me seat which would fit her as we were about the same size and weight not big like Jim and then I heard her say Vroo.

The wheels began to roll away Please I thought roll away taking the wheelchair as a gift Roll away not back Keep going down the road Away from the home not back to the ward.

And yes they were further and further to my left not my right those rolling-without-me wheels so going up the other side of the dip towards further fields where I hoped Jim and Lise could hide and be invisible until they were caught and meanwhile do whatever mischief they wanted in that thumpless time as Tristan and Isolde as my hands and my knees.

I listened through the blackbird until they were completely gone. One gone from me forever and one not for I was to see Lise again on the long corridor but I was not to see Jim because he went the next day up the road to the Brothers and when I reached the Brothers he was already elsewhere.

I listened.

And then I heard things made from met from thoughts before of several times year on year of mother and of giddily giddily happily happily because beyond the flowering hawthorn tree were suddenly hooves not like my hand-hooves hooves like my fantasy hooves and I was able to look above my head around the edge of the cardboard at a thin slice of brown flanks shining and passing chestnut-close with nostril snort like Finn and whinny like Valerie dead but the clatter of clods was like nothing I'd ever heard through my skull.

Three horses at the edge of a field running for the sake of running. And I did not need to be with them to be with them.

But I was with them now because I had imagined myself with them before and wasn't it too much to believe a family a stallion a mare a foal but I heard their hooves and the first to run past was heaviest and the last was lightest and the one in between was different to both meaning not as terrifying or as ticklish not like the nettlestings that were happening along with aching and bleeding and becoming aware of the presence of fainting.

Three horses shining behind a hawthorn head behind a hawthorn hedge behind which with all their power life speed wit they sensed me a boy and a horse of a boy.

Three horses were lucky enough although they did not know what luck was except as continuing to be horses-running-lucky that I had happened upon them to honour them with my best perception of what they and we were.

I wished Sister Cécile could have been there she and I near the edge of a field beneath white blossom in a urine-smelling layby just that with fainting darkening and rain inside my head just that not anything more just that, just everything as it is.

GALLEY BEGGAR PRESS

We hope that you've enjoyed *Patience*. If you'd like to find out more about Toby, along with some of his fellow authors, head to www.galleybeggar.co.uk.

There, you will also find information about our subscription scheme, 'Galley Buddies', which is there to ensure we can continue to put out ambitious and unusual books like *Patience*.

Subscribers to Galley Beggar Press:

- Receive limited black-cover editions (printed in a one-time run of 500) of each of our four next titles.
- Have their names included in a special acknowledgements section at the back of our books.
- Are sent regular invitations to our book launches, talks, and other events.
- Enjoy a 20% discount code for the purchase of any of our backlist (as well as for general use throughout our online shop).

WHY BE A GALLEY BUDDY?

At Galley Beggar Press we don't want to compromise on the excellence of the writing we put out, or the physical quality of our books. We've also enjoyed numerous successes and prize nominations since we set up, in 2012. Almost all of our authors have gone on to be longlisted, shortlisted, or the winners of over twenty of the world's most prestigious literary awards.

But publishing for the sake of art and for love is a risky commercial strategy. In order to keep putting out the very best books that we can, and to continue to support talented writers, we need your help. The money we receive from our Galley Buddy subscription scheme is an essential part of keeping us going.

By becoming a Galley Buddy, you help us to launch and foster a new generation of writers.

To join today, head to:
https://www.galleybeggar.co.uk/subscribe

Jane Johnson
Alice Jolly
Jupiter Jones
Diana Jordison
Benjamin Judge
Dani Kaye
Laura Kaye
Andrew Kelly
Michael Ketchum
Vijay Khurana
Jeffrey Kichen
Jacqueline Knott
Brian Kirk
Philip Lane
Jackie Law
Noel Lawn
Gage LaFleur
Thomas Legendre
Joanne Leonard
Mark Lewis
Joyce Lillie-Robinson
Nick Lord Lancaster
Jerome Love
Sean Lusk
Simona Lyons
Anne Maguire
Philip Makatrewicz
Anil Malhotra
Emily Marchant
Chiara Margiotta
Robert Mason
Sara McCallum
Ella McCrystle
Kieran McGrath
Victor Meadowcraft
C.S. Mee
Tina Meyer
Ian Mond
Clive Morrison
David Musgrave
Polly Nash

Linda Nathan
Anna Nsubuga
Georgina Nugent-Folan
Seb Ohsan-Berthelsen
John O'Donnell
Alec Olsen
Laura Oosterbeek
Sheila O'Reilly
Liz O'Sullivan
Eliza O'Toole
Nicola Paterson
Scarlett Parker
Stephen Pearsall
Alexa Pearson
Tom Perrin
Nicholas Petty
Jennifer Pink
Jonathan Pool
Giacomo Pope
Ailsa Power
Trine Prescott
Richard Price
Alan Pulverness
Sarah Pybus
Alex Pykett
Polly Randall
Euan Reed
Dawn Rees
Barbara Renel
Pete Renton
Ian Rimell
Brian Ronan
Angela Rose
Kalina Rose
Clive Rixson
Libby Ruffle
Amanda Saint
Alison Sakai
Robert Sanderson
Valentina Santolini
Ros Schwartz

Richard Sheehan
Yvonne Singh
Hazel Smith
Daniel Staniforth
John Steciuk
Cathryn Steele
Gillian Stern
Justina Stonyte
Jochen Stremmel
Juliet Sutcliffe
Helen Swain
Justine Taylor
Cennin Thomas
Sam Thorp
James Torrence
Steve Tuffnell
Nick Turner
Harriet Tyce
Edward Valiente
David Varley
Essi Viding
Stephen Wademan
Stephen Walker
Steve Walsh
Guy Ware
Emma Warnock
Ellie Warren
Stephanie Wasek
Tom Whatmore
Wendy Whidden
Robert White
Claire Willerton
Lucie Winter
Simon Winter
Emma Woolerton
Ben Yeoh
Ian Young
Rupert Ziziros
Carsten Zwaaneveld